PSYCHOTOPIA

PSYCHOTOPIA

R. N. Morris

This first world edition published 2018
in Great Britain and 2019 in the USA by
SEVERN HOUSE PUBLISHERS LTD of
Eardley House, 4 Uxbridge Street, London W8 7SY.
Trade paperback edition first published
in Great Britain and the USA 2019 by
SEVERN HOUSE PUBLISHERS LTD.

British Library Cataloguing in Publication Data
A CIP catalogue record for this title is available from the British Library.

ISBN-13: 978-0-7278-8839-6 (cased)
ISBN-13: 978-1-84751-964-1 (trade paper)
ISBN-13: 978-1-4483-0174-4 (e-book)

All Severn House titles are printed on acid-free paper.

Severn House Publishers support the Forest Stewardship Council™ [FSC™],
the leading international forest certification organisation.
All our titles that are printed on FSC certified paper carry the FSC logo.

Typeset by Palimpsest Book Production Ltd.,
Falkirk, Stirlingshire, Scotland.
Printed and bound in Great Britain by
TJ International, Padstow, Cornwall.

LEVEL ONE

I t starts in a blank, fairly nondescript room. Slightly rundown. An air of neglect, bordering on despair. It's despairing to look at. Ever so slightly. All very subtle. Nothing too heavy-handed. Just maybe a tad sinister. If you can imagine a sinister edge to it. That would all come from the colours. All very monochrome. Cold. Yes. Everything has to have this definite cast of coldness to it. (Very important.)

Bare boards on the floor. Maybe the walls are papered but the paper's peeling away in one or two places. No, just one place. Keep it understated. Subtle. No furniture. Not at the beginning. That's for the player to decide as the game progresses.

This is where he lives, you see.

There's one small square window. No curtains. The room must be high up, in a tower block, because we can't see any buildings or trees from the window. Just blank sky, which changes in real time from day to night, and also changes to reflect the weather. Can we make it that it actually shows the real-time weather for wherever the player is? That would be cool. And freaky.

Maybe there's a crack in the pane. A fine hairline crack. You can't see it, not to begin with. But a draft comes through it. How do we make the player feel this? The sound. When the wind strikes the window in a certain way (determined by exterior real-time conditions?) it sets up a weird vibration. It makes the sound of a baby crying. And the room rocks. Ever so slightly.

The door to the room is in the wall facing the window. As to the size of the room, this is subtly unstable. It should somehow reflect the mood of the player at any given time. It always feels like the same room but it manifests its dimensions differently now and then. When the player is feeling persecuted and anxious, the walls close in. This is done slowly, very gradually, so that the player doesn't notice it happening. Other times, when the player is in a more positive frame of mind, the room expands, even infinitely on occasion, to reflect the limitless sense of power that the player feels.

When I say player, I mean the character that the player is inhabiting. Obviously.

The door is locked. (Is the player held in some kind of secure unit?)

The player does not have a key. So the player's first challenge is to open the door and find a way out.

Development notes for PSYCHOTOPIA VR game.
Internal Alpha Games document. Not for release. For approved circulation only.

ONE

To begin with, we pulled them in. Then there got to be so many of them we couldn't keep up.

There were a number of theories as to what was causing it. Some people blamed it on the new breed of VR computer games that were coming out. But when you looked at the facts, that just didn't hold up. No, games like Psychotopia and its ilk were one of the symptoms of whatever it was that was going on. Not the cause. The bad shit was already happening, way before that game got released.

Some said it was a disease. An epidemic. *Psychodemic*, the tabloids called it.

Some people blamed the MindNet. Said it had gone mad. And that the madness was affecting us all. But my view was the MindNet had always been mad.

Then Dr Arbus came forward with his theory and we realized it wasn't computer games and it wasn't an epidemic and it wasn't the MindNet. It was something bigger. You might say worse. Much worse.

Once Arbus's theory took hold, everyone started to panic big time.

Some of them were very young. That was what scared people the most, I think. It was almost as if the whole next generation was turning out that way. I didn't give too much thought to it myself. What will be will be. That's my motto. You have to be a fatalist in life. Otherwise you worry too much. Worrying never changed a thing. Me, I'm more someone who gets things done. If you want something done, you ask me. That's what everybody says.

I heard it first, that thing about the next generation, from some random guy in a coffee shop. I have to have my coffee. It's my greatest vice. Numerically speaking.

So there I was waiting for the barista to make my fifth flat white of the day when this guy next to me started going off on one. I don't even know who he thought he was talking to. The girl behind the counter? She was one of those retardistas that make you all nostalgic for the cheap, over-educated foreigners we used to have to do the shit jobs. Bring on the robots is what I say. Anyhow, she didn't have a clue what he was banging on about.

I knew, though.

He was talking about the Ardagh case. You remember. It was all over the NewsNet. Every time you switched on a screen, you'd see her sweet angelic face staring back at you. She was a little cutie, curly blonde hair, blue eyes, the big gap in her smile where she was waiting for her front teeth to grow. The first time you saw that picture you probably thought it was another missing child case. At the time, we were seeing a spike in child abductions, rapes and murders. Of course, the number of these cases was still small compared to the overall population. And over the preceding decades, rates for violent crimes of this nature had declined. So even with this spike, we were not up to the levels we had seen before. All the same, it was the kind of statistic that journalists have a field day with. It was bad enough with them just reporting all the cases that were happening. People were beginning to pick up on it. Things were starting to get a bit edgy.

The riots people could handle.

It was the involvement of children that freaked them out.

So, as far as we knew at the time, it was just a blip – the rise in child abductions, I'm talking about. Maybe even the kind of thing you could put down to one prolific offender. A one-man crime wave. Except the cases were geographically widespread, with some of them happening simultaneously. If it was one man, how did he manage to lift a four-year-old boy from his bedroom in Doncaster the same night he anally raped and left for dead a two-year-old girl in Exeter? It certainly was a conundrum.

So I guess I was kind of attuned to pictures of children popping up in the media. That kind of thing makes everyone jumpy. The top brass come down heavy on us foot soldiers. Like it's our fault. We have to be seen to be doing something. Knocking on doors. Combing wasteland. Tracking down known sex offenders and all the other usual suspects. Hours and hours of watching deathly dull CCTV footage.

It's always a pain in the arse when the job starts hitting the headlines. You feel like the whole fucking country is breathing down your neck. I don't like it.

From that point of view, it was not a good time to be a cop. On the other hand, you had the feeling that there was something happening out there. Something exciting. Something momentous, even. I mean, everyone likes a good serial killer case, so the thought that there might be several of them active at the same time, it was enough to get you hard. Certainly it was something to get up for in the morning.

But no, this was not another child abduction case. I knew it because she was one of the cases that crossed my desk. But it wasn't long before everyone pricked up their ears and knew it.

She was like the canary down the mine. Or her little brother was. The Ardaghs were a nice, well-to-do family, classic white, middle-class, educated elite. Wishy washy liberal ideas with a lifetime of privilege and comfort ahead of them. Until this hit them.

Father was something in IT. Mother was an architect. Worked for a fancy-arse firm in Islington. They had a live-in nanny. Swedish, I think she was. Or Danish. One of the Scandis.

So there was this guy in the coffee shop mouthing off about the Ardagh case. 'We're raising a whole generation of psychopaths,' he shouted. He was pretty agitated.

'You've got to be very careful who you label a psychopath,' I told him. 'Especially at such a young age.'

'Did you see what she did?'

'She was only a child. You know, kids . . . Who knows what's going through their little fucking brains?'

'She showed no emotion at all. She didn't give a literal shit.'

'You seem to know a lot about it.'

'I'm a psychologist. I study these things. And I'm telling you, it's on the rise. Children. Psychopathic children.'

'You're talking bullshit, pal. Violent crime is down. These freak cases get a lot of attention. But it's all out of proportion. I know what I'm talking about. I'm a cop, a plain-clothes detective. So you'd better watch what you say.'

'What? There's no law against talking about something that's in the news. It's a free country, the last I heard.'

'There's such a thing as a public order offence.'

'Bullshit.'

'Section Five of the 1986 Public Order Act. Causing harassment, alarm or distress. If I, or anyone here is alarmed or distressed by what you're saying, you could be guilty under the act. Certainly I'd have grounds for arresting you.'

'No one's distressed. Who's distressed?'

'Maybe I am.'

'You don't look distressed. You look fucking complacent. Let me tell you, I don't think you have anything to be complacent about. I don't think we've seen anything yet. This is the tip of the iceberg.'

It was then that one of the baristas shouted his name. You know how they write your name on the side of the paper cup? I had to laugh. This one couldn't read the writing so well, and what with her not being the brightest spoon in the cutlery drawer it came out wrong before she realized. 'Fuck?'

'Rick! The name is Rick. How do you get Fuck out of Rick, for fuck's sake?'

The male barista who wrote it in the first place came over to have a look. 'I'm sorry. It's the pen. It doesn't write so well.'

'I hope you've got my name right,' I warned him. 'Otherwise I *will* kill you.'

He looked at me like he didn't know whether I was joking or not.

When I looked round, the random guy was gone.

CHARACTER DESIGN

As is usual in games with a strong role-playing element, the player is free to design or modify the appearance of their game persona. A wide range of pre-set physical types will be offered, representing the full range of ethnic groups, as well as a spectrum of gender identity possibilities. Facial and bodily modifications, such as piercings and enhancements (e.g. sharpened teeth, horns, artificial tails and reshaped ears) will also be available, allowing the pre-sets to be modified, so that entirely new and original characters can be created. Players will even be able use their own photographic or video files, of themselves or others, to create fully animated, 3D-modelled characters capable of integrating into the game. These may either play the part of the protagonist, or alternatively may provide potential targets for the protagonist within the first-person shooter aspects of the game. (NB the methods of dispatching targets are not limited to firepower, so we should perhaps talk of 'killer' rather than 'shooter' aspects.) The facility to incorporate real people into the game in this way will add an extra level of frisson and excitement which will help the game to stand out from its competitors. In other crime-based or warfare shooter games, the victims are invariably anonymous or fictional.

Further character visual refinement is available by means of clothing choices, including the 'uniforms' of various youth subcultures and tribes, such as goths, metalheads, punks and Juggalos (or Juggalo-esque characters). Note for Legal: look into copyright implications of incorporating styles reminiscent of well-known horror protagonists, such as Freddy Krueger, Ghostface, Michael Myers, Jason Voorhees and *Clockwork Orange* gangs. This possible feature is not core to the game and should never be advertised as an attraction – we should not acknowledge it as a feature at all. (It would be preferable to create an iconic character of our own.) However, given the limitless flexibility of character creation within the game, there is nothing to stop players from exploring and discovering these possibilities themselves. If we include a hockey mask in the character wardrobe, are we infringing the copyright of the Friday the 13th franchise? Perhaps it can be included secretly – the player discovers it by means of a hack or cheat leaked through chat groups. I can imagine the inclusion of a pig mask and a straggly wig as separate items. When the player combines them, and perhaps elongates the snout of the pre-set pig mask, they create a mask that is reminiscent of that featured in the *Saw* movies. It is up to the imagination and skills of our horror-fan players.

One fun refinement would be to allow the protagonist the ability to remove the faces of victims so that they can wear them as the game progresses. Indeed, this could be a key either for moving up a level or unlocking rewards. The player has to work out that it is necessary to remove a victim's face and wear it. If they fail to do so initially, they will have to go back to retrieve the face, which will inevitably be more difficult once the forces of law and order have discovered the body. This aspect perhaps needs more thought to work it through fully, however it could add an interesting dimension. One of the issues to be resolved is how core it is to overall success in the game. Is it essential or merely helpful? I think we should allow for a range of MO among players. Some will be victim face-wearers, some won't. This brings us on to the next feature of character design, which is possibly the game's USP.

Development notes for PSYCHOTOPIA VR game.
Internal Alpha Games document. Not for release. For approved circulation only.

TWO

S he saw him as soon as he came into the room. There was something about him that drew the eye. At first, she wasn't sure whether it was a good something or a bad something. But there was definitely something.

She felt it in the pit of her stomach. The fluttering play of attraction. Or maybe of fate. Sometimes it comes to the same thing.

Who is he?

She asked the question with a layering-in of irony, as if she was trying to detach herself from any suggestion that she was interested in the answer. *Who* is *he?* As in *Who the fuck does he think he is?* With an almost distasteful wrinkling of her nose. But her eyes told a different story. Her eyes couldn't stop looking at him. Drinking him in.

It was fascination. It was admiration. It was astonishment.

And it was instant, powerful and dangerous.

No one she asked seemed to know. And yet he spoke to everyone as if – well, almost as if – he was their best friend.

'I love your hair.'

'That looks great on you.'

'Have you just come back from holiday? You look so *well*!'

He didn't seem to have any of the awkwardness that you would have expected from a guy on his own at a party meeting new people. *Someone* must have invited him. But nobody challenged him about it, because the truth was he seemed to belong there.

The assumption was he was a friend of Rick's or Dave's or Si's or Ash's. And because he had to be someone's friend, everyone treated him as if he was theirs. And there was no doubt the party picked up after he arrived.

The first thing he did was change the playlist on MindMusic. Without asking anyone, naturally. But no one objected because everyone agreed he had great taste in music. Somehow he seemed to read the mood perfectly.

'I do a bit of DJing,' he explained. 'On the side. And producing.

I'm actually doing a PhD in psychology. But I have my own website and sell my beats. To bands. I sold a whole set of beats to DeeZay Fontaine. It's basically how I funded myself through college.'

Someone asked him for the name of his website. But he didn't hear them and moved on without giving it.

You didn't doubt him when he spoke. Or, certainly, Aimée didn't. At the same time, somehow, you didn't really listen to what he was actually saying. You didn't care. You just wanted to believe him. So you did. He could have told you he was the Pope's son and you would have believed it.

Maybe he was.

He certainly could throw some slick moves. And that smile. It would have been hard for any ordinary human to resist that smile.

Another thing. He looked you in the eye. She noticed that immediately. He met your gaze directly. And held it. Which had to mean something. For one thing, it meant you could gaze a lifetime long into the bluest blue eyes you've ever seen. For another, it meant he had nothing to hide. Manifestly. No guilty secrets. You got the impression he was a stranger to the very concept of shame. He must have lived a blameless life. You even got the feeling he could wipe away your own sins.

Here was walking absolution. Just to be close to him was to feel yourself a better person, or at least believe in your potential to be one.

He moved confidently around the room, latching on to huddles and chipping in without inhibition, so that pretty soon he was dominating the conversation wherever he was. He didn't seem to be getting drunk. Didn't need to. He was naturally at ease. He made all the other guys there, the guys she knew, look like teenagers at a school disco. They glowered at him half in resentment, half in admiration. But before too long, even they were smiling at the sheer undeniable charisma of the stranger in their midst.

He seemed to have the knack of tuning into whatever conversation was going on. 'That exact same thing happened to me,' slipped from his lips more than once. His anecdotes were lively and amusing. Or you felt that they were, without really taking in what they were about. Whenever he moved on, he left everyone laughing and feeling better about themselves.

People were drawn to him. Guys as well as girls. But mostly girls. He shook hands with the guys – the high, give-me-some-skin handshake favoured by footballers and rappers – and winked at the girls. Yeah, maybe the winking was a bit corny but he could get away with it. Because of the eyes. And that smile.

The simple fact was he was the best-looking guy at the party. Maybe even the most physically attractive person of any gender identity there. You liked everything about him that you saw. His bluer than blue eyes, his sin-washing smile, his baby blond curls, his gym-primed torso, his perfect skin, his old-school movie-star features.

'Hi, I'm Charlie. You have the loveliest smile I've ever seen. Just that.'

As soon as he said it, he moved off. And immediately Aimée wanted him back. She ached for him to come back. The truth was, *he* had the loveliest smile *she* had ever seen. And she was bereft without it.

She found herself following him around. Abandoning the friends she had come with, even Callum, who she knew was a little bit in love with her, and who maybe saw tonight as his chance to take it to the next level. And maybe that would have happened if this guy, this Charlie, hadn't shown up.

She caught a glimpse of Callum's confused, uncomprehending face and hated him for it. How dare he take her for granted. How dare he assume. Just because he had been manoeuvring towards a situation, it didn't mean she had wanted it. Though the truth was, she had. And when the part of her mind that controlled these things allowed that truth to intrude, then she hated him even more.

He'd get over it. He was a big boy. They didn't owe each other anything. No promises had been made. They were mates, that was all. And if he was really her mate, he'd want her to be happy. He'd want this for her as much as she did.

So she did it. She made a play for the Charlie guy.

'Hi, I'm Aimée.'

Of course, the music was loud. So she had to get right up close to him to shout in his ear. No problem with that. It gave her the chance to press herself against him.

'Amy?'

'No. Aimée. It's spelled the French way. A-I-M-E-E. With an accent on the first e.'

'The loved one.'

'That's right.'

'And are you? Loved by anyone?'

She gave a bashful, happy shrug. Then dared everything on a look into the impossible blueness of his eyes. It was a look in which she invested every emotion that she was feeling at that moment, and every half-flickering beginning of emotion. Shyness, surrender, desire, supplication, invitation, courage, fear, happiness and hope.

He saw it all and read it all and understood it all.

Her lips went out towards him. He stooped to meet them.

She took him home with her that night. It was not the sort of thing she did. But she did it.

In fact, she practically pulled him into the U-car after her.

Her three flatmates sharing the ride could hardly keep their eyes from popping out.

'Who's this?' said Aryan. Was there an edge of hostility in his voice? It was possible. Aryan was Callum's best mate.

'Hi, I'm Charlie?' The hand came out and was reluctantly accepted. The open rising interrogative in his voice was an invitation for Aryan to reciprocate. He didn't.

It didn't matter. He already knew who Aryan was. 'You must be Aryan. Aimée has told me all about you.'

She had?

She must have. It was possible. It felt like she'd told him everything. Her whole life. Somehow he'd drawn it all out of her.

They'd gone outside to smoke. She didn't smoke, but she wasn't going to let him out of her sight. He offered her a cigarette and she took it without thinking. So now she smoked. She guessed.

He seemed to have a way of getting her to do things she didn't know she wanted to do. Dangerous, maybe. But exciting. Liberating, somehow. To be ever so slightly surrendered. She felt that was what was happening and didn't run from it, as she would have done if it had been anyone else. Callum, for instance.

'And you're Sal and you're Edith?'

'Other way round,' said Edith. The pointless lie provoked a snigger from Sal. Rude. Why were they being so rude and horrible? Sal was Aryan's girlfriend. She could be expected to side with Callum. But Edith? She had a right to expect Edith to understand. To get it. To be happy for her.

Fuck them. Fuck them all. What did she care?

But Charlie wasn't fazed at all. 'No. You *must* be Edith. I can see the resemblance.'

He kissed away the frown burgeoning on Aimée's brow. And their mouths locked together for more or less the rest of the journey. Whenever she came up for air, she purred and giggled and snuggled into him contentedly. She felt like she had never been kissed before. She could hardly wait for what was to come.

Her heart was a bird fluttering in its cage. Its beating was feather-light and joyously fearful. It was only right that there should be fear at such moments. The elated fear that presages some momentous transformation, such as flight or freedom. This was what he was bringing her, she felt.

She did not do one-night stands. Not any more. Watching some of her friends in action, she'd come to the conclusion that it was more about low self-esteem than sexual adventurism. And there had been that one disastrous occasion with some guy called Simon. God, it made her blush just to think of it. He had given her money for a U-car, so eager was he to get her out of his flat. Somehow the handing over of money made the whole thing feel even more sordid than it already had. More like a transaction. She had virtually suppressed all memory of the encounter. The only conscious evidence of it was her rule: *no more one-night stands*.

Somehow she knew this was not a one-night stand. This was the start of something. Not some closed-off aberration.

For one thing, he had said it before she had: 'I don't normally do this kind of thing.'

'Me neither.'

'I'm really nervous.'

'Me too.'

He knew exactly how she felt, because he felt it too.

And so she found herself cast in the role of reassuring him, encouraging him, drawing him out. She was the one who took the lead.

It wasn't exactly that he was passive. It was just that he waited for her to initiate before responding. He had perfect bedroom etiquette. More than that, he created a space into which she could expand. She found herself wanting to do things she didn't know she wanted to do. That knack of his again? No, she couldn't put it down to that. He wasn't doing anything. She was doing it all. She was shaking off the vestiges of her Catholic upbringing all on her own. She was growing up. And it felt good.

It was not her first time. But it felt like all the others had counted for nothing.

And yes, it's true, she didn't make him wear a condom. The question never came up. It's true he didn't volunteer. But then again she didn't insist. Because she didn't want anything to come between them? Maybe it was that, or maybe she just knew it would be all right. Everything would be all right. Nothing could spoil the magic of their bodies coming together.

In the morning, as the brutal sunshine crashed in beneath the half-open blinds, the fug of last night's couplings still thick in the room, she groaned.

'What's the matter?' He pulled her to him, his chest a pillow for her head.

'I need to get to a chemist's. Morning-after pill. We didn't . . . you know . . .'

'It's OK.'

She sat up and looked at him quizzically.

'A couple of years ago, I had testicular cancer.'

'Baby!'

'Well, that's the point. No babies. I can't. Sorry. I should have said. Maybe. I mean. If that's what you're looking for. In a man. I can never.' He started to cry. She saw actual tears brim and break from his eyes.

She consoled him with a kiss. Which he quickly and deftly directed to his bobbing cock.

They didn't leave her room for four days. Except to go to the bathroom and answer the door to pizza deliveries, taking turns to wear her shimmering silky dressing gown. (Naturally, she paid for all the pizzas. It was her place, after all. So it sort of made sense.)

She MindMessaged in sick to work. She felt a little guilty about that, it's true. It was a crucial time for her. She was in her second year of a professional placement with one of the best architectural practices in the country. Her final year of training after five long years at uni. She was getting close to the end, close to the point where it all became worthwhile. It would have been crazy to throw all that away. But a part of her began to wonder if she'd ever really wanted to be an architect. Was she doing it for herself or her parents?

It was just one of the ways he liberated her. And yes, it was a little bit scary. She felt herself on the edge of a precipice. Freedom is a scary prospect.

But then again, it was kind of true, the excuse. She *was* sick – lovesick. *It's a thing!* And besides, she was owed a little bit of slack. She'd been a conscientious student until now. And it wasn't as if a couple of days of depravity would undo all the years of good work. She could make it up, she was sure of that. It didn't mean she was turning her back on everything that had meant so much to her until now. On her life as it had been.

She was just taking a holiday from it.

Charlie didn't seem in a hurry to go anywhere. Presumably his beats-for-sale business pretty much looked after itself. And as for his doctoral thesis, he never gave it a second thought.

On the fifth morning, he said, 'This works, doesn't it? You and me. It feels right?'

'Yes.'

'You and me against the world.'

'Well . . .' She hadn't quite seen it like that, but yes, it was like that, when you thought about it.

'If only we could make the world go away.'

'About that . . .' She really ought to go back to work.

'I love being here with you.'

'I love having you here.'

'I don't ever want to be anywhere else.'

'I don't want you to be anywhere else.'

'Really? You mean it? I can move in?'

'Yes?' It was what she had said. She could hardly go back on it now. Though really she ought to clear it with the others first.

'That's great. It's going to be so cool. Look, I need to get some things. You know, my clothes and shit. You'd better give me a key.'

'I only have one key.'

'You'd better get me another one cut then. I could do it if you like?'

'I really need to get back to work.'

'Oh yeah, that's right.'

'I expect you do too? Your PhD won't research itself, will it?'

'My . . .? Oh, right, no. I guess it won't. So can I have your key? Just till I get another one cut?'

'Y–yes, sure.'

'You don't sound so sure.'

'I'm sure.'

'Don't you trust me?'

'Yes, of course.'

'You have to trust me, Aimée. If we don't have trust, we don't have anything.'

'I know.'

And so she let him have her key.

'Oh, you're still alive then?' It was exactly the kind of sarcastic greeting she might have expected from Edith.

'Yes.'

'And where's lover boy?'

'He's gone to get some things.'

'What?'

'I said he could move in.'

'You did what?'

'He'll be in my room.'

'Well, not all the time. Presumably he'll be using the kitchen and the bathroom. And generally everywhere. This is not a five-person house. I can't believe you did it without talking to us. You'll have to tell him no.'

'I can't do that! I've already said yes.'

'Why does he even want to? Doesn't he have a place of his own?'

'Of course he does. He wants to because he wants to be with me. And I want him to be with me.'

'I can tell you one thing for certain – Aryan's not going to like it.'

'Well, Aryan'll just have to . . .'

And of course, it was at that precise moment that Aryan came into the kitchen. 'Aryan'll just have to what?'

'She's only asked him to move in.'

'Who?'

'Yes, exactly. Who is he?'

'Charlie. His name's Charlie. You know that.'

Aryan shook his head. 'No way.'

'Why are you so against him?'

'Because he's a wanker?'

Edith was a tad more conciliatory. 'We've no idea who he is. He could be anybody.'

'*I* know who he is. He's not a stranger to me.'

Aryan was not impressed. 'He's someone you've fucked. That's all.'

'No. It's more than that.'

'Well, he's not moving in. It's as simple as that.'

'This is because of Callum, isn't it?'

'You think I'm that petty? You think I give a shit who you fuck? I don't care. It's not about that. It's about someone we don't know moving into our house.'

'Who's moving in?' Sal had joined them, drawn by the raised voices.

Aryan closed the discussion down with a final, 'No one is.'

Edith did her best to reconcile Aimée to the situation. 'It *is* very quick, Aims. I mean, you've only just met him. Maybe if we had a chance to get to know him better? In the normal way? I mean, don't you think it's a bit . . . odd?'

'Fine. I'll talk to him. It won't be a problem. We just got a bit carried away. I guess. He'll understand.'

Of course, Aryan had to have the last word. 'I don't give a shit whether he understands or not. He's not moving in.'

Lying to work came shockingly easily. 'I think it was food poisoning. One of my housemates decided to cook mussels for everyone this weekend. I must have eaten a dodgy one. Never again, I can tell you!' That didn't mean she escaped the Catholic guilt thing, of course. She was convinced everyone could see right through her, especially Sandeep Josh, the partner she was working under. Not only that, they knew exactly what she'd been up to with Charlie. But fortunately there was an urgent tender document to get out, which offered her some kind of expiation.

She checked her MindPhone pretty much every ten minutes. Nothing. Maybe he had taken down her number wrong. So she

MindMessaged him on the number he'd entered into her phone. To say she was surprised by the reply would have been an understatement: *Who r u?*

She called the number on her lunch break. A girl's voice answered. 'Yeah?'

'Is Charlie there?'

'Charlie who?'

It was the first time she realized she didn't know his surname. 'Charlie whose phone you've got.'

'This is my phone.'

'It can't be.'

'This has happened before and I'm getting sick of it.'

'What has happened before?'

'Some random guy giving out my number as his. One week he's Greg, the next he's Carl. I guess he's Charlie now.'

'No, it can't be!'

'It is. Get used to it.'

The line went dead.

She was shaking and numb as she made her way outside for some fresh air and a sandwich. She opened her purse to discover she was out of cash. It didn't surprise her after the long weekend she'd had. All those pizzas, she supposed. Except those had been paid for by card. She riffled frantically through her purse. There was no sign of her bank card either, or her credit card. She must have left them at home. She had a mental picture of the Santander Visa lying on the bed from when she had used it to book the last delivery.

She suddenly felt very cold. It was the icy, empty coldness of a desert at night. A fatal, lost coldness. It had got inside her and taken hold of her. The utter indifference of a godless universe.

She tried to get hold of Edith. Needing to hear her sister's voice.

Edith didn't pick up.

The rest of the day went by in a blur. Until she got the MindMessage from Edith at five.

We need to talk.

She answered: *What is it?*

And waited frantically for a reply. None came.

The strange, mute discourse of MindMessaging, with its interrupted dialogue and unanswered questions, was a kind of anti-communication. It created a soundless vacuum which she filled with all her fears. Nothing was resolved. The only thing that was communicated was an ominous sense of disaster.

It was Sal who broke the news. Aimée had hardly made it through the door. 'We've been burgled. They've taken my MindPad.'

Aryan was incandescent. 'And *my* MindBook.'

'I've got jewellery missing,' said Edith flatly. Aimée picked up some extra layer of unhappiness in her demeanour. The others were almost excited by the outrage that had been committed, Aryan fired with rage, Sal nervily hyper. Edith's voice was glum and affectless. She hung her head and avoided looking at Aimée.

Aryan was incandescent. 'They've nicked my clothes! I mean, for fuck's sake! They've been through my wardrobe and nicked some of my fucking clothes! My Timberland boots are gone. I got those when I was in New York last year.'

'The sandwich maker's gone!' announced Sal gleefully.

'They've even been through my vinyl collection. The fuckers.'

'We don't know how they got in. There's no sign of a break-in.'

'Aims? Are you all right?'

She was weeping. She was more than weeping. She was convulsed by sobs. It was Edith who saw it. Between the sobs Aimée managed to get out: 'I gave him my key.'

'Oh, for fuck's sake! You're fucking joking, aren't you?' Aryan drew back a fist as if he was going to punch the wall. But thought better of it. And just shook his head at Aimée, fixing her with a look that was close to hatred.

She lay down on the bed, the bed that still smelled of him and their time together. There should have been no comfort in it. It should have sickened her. And yet she buried her face in that scent, indulging herself with one last return to him. Clinging on to the last faint vestige of what there had once been between them.

She knew now that it had been a lie. That it had meant nothing to him. And so it ought to mean nothing to her too. She owed it to herself to hate him.

And yet, for now at least, she could not quite bring herself to surrender all that she had felt in that small room over the last few days. She had been transformed. He had transformed her. He had taken her to a place she had never known before. He had expanded her universe.

It was not just the sex. He understood her. They were on the same wavelength. Within hours of meeting each other, they were finishing each other's sentences, like an old married couple. And bursting into laughter about it at exactly the same moment.

There had been a connection between them. Something spiritual. She had felt it. It was real. They were soulmates.

With him, she had felt her soul unburden. Her heart had opened, like a newly hatched chick emerging from its shell.

He had promised her love, not in so many words. But by every gesture, look, kiss and touch. By every token of his consideration for her. He had given her hope.

She couldn't believe it was all a lie. There had to be some small particle of truth in the things he had said to her. One atom of love.

She heard the door open and felt Edith slip under the duvet behind her.

They lay together for a long time, saying nothing.

She felt a small, slight lifting of the stone of misery that lay on her. A kind of awe entered her. An understanding, of something momentous and true. This wordless presence of her little sister in her bed beside her. This was love. And this was strength. Quiet, undemonstrative, but real. This was what would take her forward.

It would be enough. Because it *was* real.

Then Aimée remembered the signs of unhappiness that she had picked up from her sister earlier.

'You MindMessaged me.'

Edith said nothing. Aimée wondered if she had fallen asleep. She lifted herself up and turned to face her. Edith was staring blankly into nothing.

'Was it about the burglary?'

Edith shook her head but said nothing.

'What was it?'

'It's nothing. It doesn't matter.'

'Ede?'

'Honestly. It doesn't matter.'

'What did he do?'

'Nothing. You don't want to hear it.'

'I need to hear it.'

'He came into my room.'

'Oh, God.'

'I was getting ready. Brushing my hair. He came over and asked if he could do it. I said, *No.* I mean, it was so weird. So he started massaging my shoulders. I said, *What do you think you're doing?* He said, *Oh, come on, I saw you looking at me. I know you want it.* He put his hand on my tit. I told him to get out. He said, *You don't know what you're missing.* Then he said it's a way to get back at you. *Wasn't she always Mummy and Daddy's favourite? Did better at school. The perfect child. Never got into trouble. This is a great way of getting one over on her. Think about it.* I told him to fuck off, Aims. Maybe it was my fault he did this? Because I made him angry?'

She pulled her sister to her and squeezed. It was more than a hug. It was a desperate cleaving to.

'No.' She said the word quietly, simply, factually. In gentle reassurance and stern refusal. There was more she could have said. But for now she left it at that.

PSYCHOLOGICAL ATTRIBUTES

As well as being able to design or modify the physical appearance of the character they inhabit, players can select from a range of psychiatric conditions and personality disorders, to dial up a unique pattern of behaviour. Counter to reality perhaps (this is a game, after all, and our emphasis should be on providing an enjoyable and entertaining player experience, rather than adhering to the rigours of academic or clinical psychiatry), players may combine elements from different disorders. Narcissistic traits can be combined with auditory hallucinations. In fact, when you think about it, is this so counter to reality after all? No two psychopaths are alike. Even copycat killers can't be said to be the same as the originals that they copy – far from it. They are imitative whereas the original killer is innovative. Psychopathy itself may be considered as a spectrum, much like the autistic spectrum. The same is true of every personality disorder we can imagine. And so the game should offer a kind of mixing desk control panel, much like the mixing desks in a recording studio. Each row of knobs on the control panel will represent some attribute of a recognized disorder. (But why limit ourselves to recognized disorders? Could we invent new ones? Can we allow players to do so?) The player may turn up or turn down each attribute, or mute entirely whole rows of attributes.

It is certainly possible that this approach will create personality types that do not exist in reality, or have not yet been recorded within the psychiatric or judicial record. I don't see that as a problem. In fact, it will make the game more interesting. The psychiatric profession can never truly understand what goes on in the mind of a psychopath, because ultimately they can never trust what psychopaths tell them. And so, despite the best efforts of psychological profilers, it is possible to imagine, and indeed create, a species of killer that is entirely novel and without precedent. Let's hope so! Again, this is a game, people. Let's not tie ourselves in knots over what is or isn't possible in reality.

Where the game comes alive, and gets really interesting, will be in the interplay between the behavioural outcomes of the dialled-up disorders and the player's own choices in the game. The player's control is circumscribed by the condition from which their character suffers. For example, they may actively seek to control their character into a given action, and the character will either refuse to execute it, or will execute it in such a way that frustrates the conscious aims of the player. Let us say that certain rewards will accrue if the player manages to refrain from killing for a period. The game will put the player in a position where the opportunity for killing arises. The player will try to control the protagonist in such a way that the rewards are accessed. However, depending on the disorders or conditions that have been dialled up at the start of the game, the protagonist may still go ahead and kill. Perhaps there will need to be a dual system of rewards: Dark Rewards and Light Rewards. The former given in return for twisted behaviour. The latter for socially acceptable behavior – i.e. for passing as non-psychopathic.

Development notes for PSYCHOTOPIA VR game.
Internal Alpha Games document. Not for release. For approved circulation only.

THREE

What you have to remember about these people – I'm talking about the cases that were coming across my desk almost daily at the time – is that most of them were not slick psychopaths like you see depicted in the movies. If that had been the case I could have respected them.

No, most of them were a complete joke. Ridiculous. Honestly. These people, they were a mess, I'm telling you.

They're easy enough to spot, by the way. Just look for the trail of chaos and mayhem they leave in their wake. You would not believe it.

The string of pregnant, abandoned women. Most of them beaten up or bullied to some degree or other. All of them bewildered.

The larceny and shoplifting.

The confused pensioners frogmarched to the cashpoint to withdraw the last of their savings. For solar panels that never arrive. Or a new 'security system'.

The 'borrowed' cars smashed into walls or turned over in ditches. Glove compartments stuffed full of parking tickets. It's amazing how quickly your average psycho can accumulate parking tickets.

The brawls in pubs that flare up for no reason.

Arson and vandalism. Some of it minor. Some of it postal. All of it pointless.

Random acts of senseless destruction.

Like the guy who broke into a primary school at night only to defecate on some climbing equipment they had there in the playground. He had no connection with the school. No beef with it at all. Hadn't been there as a kid, didn't know anyone who had. No children of his own there. He was just walking past, saw the playground equipment and, in his words, 'Thought it would be funny to take a shit there.' He was even caught on CCTV. That's how stupid he was. A lot of them are. It's how we catch most of them. It doesn't even occur to them to hide what they're doing. They don't give a literal shit. And now, of course, it's getting to the point where they can more or less get away with it. There's just too many of them for us to keep up with. We've reached the tipping point is what Dr Arbus reckons.

What I was dealing with in the beginning, most of it was pretty petty. The worst you might see was a rape or an assault. Sometimes the assaults could be quite serious. We had this guy once, a young guy in his early twenties. Name of Julius. I remember it because it's not a name you come across that often. Julius de Silva. Came from quite a good family, if you can ignore the foreign name. Dressed a bit like a street hoodlum, like a black kid, but really he came from this nice middle-class, even if a bit off-white, family. Not smart, though. I mean, you might think he was smart to hear him speak. But only if you didn't listen to what he was actually saying. I mean, he sounded like he ought to have been intelligent, but what was coming out of his mouth was literal garbage. He had a very plausible manner, but no substance to it. And when you looked at what he actually did – his deeds – well, it just didn't make any sense. You know what they say, actions speak louder than words. What his actions said to me was that he was a total tool.

So what he did was swing a crowbar at this homeless guy's head. Victim went by the name of Eddie Daniels. A harmless old hebephrenic who was living in cardboard box city beneath the underpass. Young Julius smashed in his skull and left him brain-damaged. Left him for dead, in fact. But somehow the tramp managed to pull through. Would have been better off dead, I reckon.

Our boy Julius made no attempt to conceal the crime or evade arrest. He didn't even throw away the crowbar. Just carried on walking down the street with it all bloody in his hands. It happened in broad daylight. There were witnesses. One of them called the emergency services and Julius was picked up by a patrol car just moments after the attack. The blood was still wet on the crowbar.

When the arresting officers got to him, Julius was perfectly polite and reasonable. Even affable, you might say. If it had been rage that had made him do it, it was all spent now. He just smiled and chatted and joked. He didn't deny the assault. When asked why he did it, he said, 'He stank.'

I was the one who interviewed him, back at the station. 'Let me get this right, you hit him because he smelled?'

'Not smelled, man. It was worse than that. He was rank. I mean, really honking. It made me feel sick.'

'So why didn't you just move away from him?'

'Why should I? I had a right to be there. He should have moved away from me.'

'Did you ask him to?'

'I told him to get the fuck out of my face and take his disgusting honk with him.'

'I see. And he failed to comply with your request?'

He seemed to approve of my way of putting it. He pointed his finger at me and nodded once, like some big-shot rapper or something. 'That's right.' All the time, as usual with this category of offender, he kept his gaze steady and fixed on me. One thing you have to give them is they are not your shifty types.

You can take it for granted that I gave as good as I got. That kind of shit doesn't faze me. 'So you hit him with the crowbar?'

'He had it coming, man. I mean, he smelled so bad. In a way, I was doing him a favour.'

'I expect he will thank you for it, if he ever recovers his powers of speech.'

He liked that too. 'He should. Damn right, he should.'

'Can I ask you one thing, Julius? Why did you have the crowbar on you in the first place?'

'I found it.'

'You found it? Where did you find it?'

'It was just there on the pavement. I thought, hey, that could come in handy, so I picked it up. Lucky I did. Otherwise . . .' He gave a shrug and left it for me to fill in the gap.

'Otherwise you wouldn't have been able to beat the crap out of Mr Daniels?'

'That's right.'

'So where exactly was it? You said it was on the pavement? What street was this?'

'It was in a car park. You know the Four Feathers Pub in Elmer Road? This guy had flipped out and was waving it at these little children . . . you know, like he was going to kill them. They were all screaming. So I ran up to him and . . . I'm a Hapkido black belt, you know? So I could see these little kids . . . What am I going to do? I went to the rescue. That's the kind of guy I am.'

'A true have-a-go hero.'

'That's right.'

'How many children?'

'Two. Maybe three.'

'How old?'

'I don't know. What does it matter? They were shit-scared. He was swinging this pickaxe at them.'

'A pickaxe now, is it? I thought it was a crowbar?'

'No, at this time he had the pickaxe.'

'So where does the crowbar come into it?'

'Well, his mate had the crowbar.'

'He had a mate?'

'Actually there were four of them.'

'Four men? Terrorizing three small children?'

'They were terrorizing everyone in the car park.'

'Why?'

'I don't know. I guess they flipped out.'

'All four of them flipped out?'

'That's right.'

'So there was one with a pickaxe, one with a crowbar . . . Did the other two have any weapons?'

'One had a knife.'

'I see.'

'And the other had a sword.'

'A sword?'

'That's right.'

'You can say this shit, Julius, but it doesn't make it true.'

He laughed at that. I have to admit, I kind of liked him. Even though he was the dumbest idiot I'd ever met. He had a sense of humour. That counts for a lot with me. 'OK, it was a baseball bat.'

Like you could negotiate the truth.

'The fact is we have no reports of an incident of this kind happening in the Feathers' car park.'

'Did I say the Feathers? It wasn't there. It was outside MegaSave. In the MegaSave car park.'

'Nothing from there either.'

'Yeah, I was going to report it but I didn't have time. Then I forgot.'

'You forgot?'

'Yeah, I had other things on my mind.'

'Like what? Beating the crap out of Mr Daniels?'

'Well, there was that, yes.' He laughed, as if that was the funniest thing. I swear to God he even winked at me, like he knew it was all bullshit. And he knew I knew. And he knew I didn't give a damn. Because I really didn't.

I won't bore you with the rest of the interview. You can take it from me, it was a tissue of lies from beginning to end. And it kept changing. Sometimes because I caught him out in a detail. Other times, just because a different idea occurred to him that he liked better. Honestly, I think that's all it was. He was making up this story to amuse himself. And maybe he hoped he would get off if he made it interesting enough. None of it made any sense. It was as if he couldn't be bothered to make up convincing lies. He basically didn't care whether I believed him or not.

Of course, after he'd been in the cells for a few hours, he did what a lot of them do. He claimed he was suffering from some kind of schizoid psychosis. Said the voices told him to do it. It was all bullshit. Like everything else. But they all use it, the diminished responsibility plea. It's their get-out-of-jail-free card. Thing is, it works. And who wouldn't rather be in a hospital than a jail? It's easier to get out of a hospital. Unless you end up in a secure unit, and even then there are ways if you know how to play the game.

But he was no more insane than I am. Than any of them are.

The thing is, they have no control, these people. Whatever comes into their head, they do it. *Why* it comes into their head, no one can tell you. Believe me, I've spoken to a lot of so-called experts – psychiatrists, neurologists, criminologists, sociologists. They've all got their pet theories. All different, of course.

Nobody has ever asked my opinion. I'm just a cop. However, if you're interested, I do have a theory.

My theory is everyone has these thoughts or impulses or whatever you call them. It's just that most people don't act on them. That's what I mean about them having no control. It's like Tourette's. Like a Tourette's of action. A physical Tourette's. You know how with Tourette's, people can't stop themselves shouting out all kinds of shit that comes into their heads? We all have those thoughts. But we have a filter that snags them before they come to light. People like Julius act out any weird random impulse that occurs to them. The same weird random impulses that we

all get, but which most of us do nothing about. Because, basically, we have been conditioned by society not to do them.

My theory is that these people are just more free than other
people. Given half a chance, everybody would like to do this
shit. And it's not letting themselves do it that makes people so
unhappy. But it's also what keeps society together. It's for
society's good. Not for the good of the individual.

That's my theory, anyhow.

Whatever else you say about psychopaths, they are for the
most part – if left to their own devices – fairly happy people.
It's only when you cross them that they start to get pissed.

They say there are other differences between psychopaths and
so-called normal people. The main one being that psychopaths
feel no remorse. So it's not just that they do this shit, but they
don't give a shit about who gets hurt along the way.

I guess that means they don't feel love either. That either
makes them the loneliest people in the world or the happiest.

I haven't quite worked out where I stand on the whole love
and remorse thing yet. Some days I believe I know exactly where
they're coming from, our psychopathic friends. I don't give a
shit about anyone or anything. I don't even think I give a shit
about myself. I don't know what that makes me. A free spirit?

I used to try. I pretended so hard I almost convinced myself.
Had my mum and dad fooled. And a few other people along the
way. I think about some of the scrapes I got into when I was a
kid. Somehow I always managed to get away with it. Never got
caught. So people ended up thinking I was a much nicer person
than I actually was. I'm talking about shoplifting. Driving under
the influence. The usual teenage high jinks. One guy got messed
up pretty bad because of me. I didn't do it, but you might say I
caused it, if you wanted to be harsh. OK, he got beat up on my
say-so. I tipped off this gang. I can't even say why I did it.
Anyhow, I guess he recovered. He must have, I don't know. I
would have heard if he'd died, anyhow. I can honestly say I've
never given it a second thought till now. I can't even remember
his name. Does that make me a psychopath, or just a shit?

Weird thing is, I once had this dream where we were best
mates. Him and me. I was trying to tell him I was sorry and he
said, 'Forget about it. It's OK. We're good.' So is that remorse?
If it is, it's not so bad.

And as for the love thing, I have a theory about that. So many songs have been written about love. 'I love you baby'. 'She loves me yeah yeah yeah'. It's all bullshit, in my book. There's no such thing as love. It's just the sex drive, dressed up. Or the gene's self-interest. A reproductive strategy. That's a term I learned from Arbus. He was talking about something else, of course. But it's just as true here. Marriage is a form of legalized prostitution. You look after me and I'll let you fuck me. Nobody ever loved anyone. They pretend they do. They even pretend to themselves that they do. The whole thing couldn't get off the ground without a big old helping of self-delusion.

I even tried pretending I was in love myself once. But then she ran off with this sergeant in the Flying Squad. I wasn't even upset. She was already getting on my nerves, if you want to know the truth, so I was glad to see the back of her. Wounded pride, that's all it was. Not a broken heart. So I don't even pretend any more. I'm happier that way. And everyone knows where they stand.

But you know, when it comes down to it, who gives a shit anyway? About why anyone does anything, I mean. You've just got to deal with the crap people do. That's the job. Ours not to reason why and all that.

These people I was dealing with were all basically borderline idiots. Incapable of thinking things through, like Julius or the playground dump-artist. Buffoons, you might call them. A waste of everyone's time, mine especially.

The interesting psychopaths are the clever psychopaths. The brilliant psychopaths. They are the ones who fool people. They are the ones who know how to get away with shit.

They are the ones who wreak the most havoc. Because they are able to do it on a massive scale. Without anyone realizing they are doing it.

They are the ones who are hard to spot.

Mind you, I can spot them.

Damn right. You could even say it's my speciality.

My partner Rashid has this thing he likes to say. 'It takes one to know one.'

MEDICATION/INCARCERATION

The object of the game, from the player's point of view, is to fulfil the dictates of their given psychiatric condition/personality disorder. To do so, they must remain outside the attention of the medical and judicial authorities. They must remain free, in other words. Should they come to the notice of the authorities this will inevitably lead to their natural behaviour being curtailed. If they fall into the care of health professionals they may receive a number of treatments, or combination of treatments, including talking therapies and medication. The aim will be to repress the antisocial behaviours they are programmed to exhibit. If they fall into the hands of the police, they will inevitably be incarcerated, or placed in long-term secure psychiatric units, where the medical interventions mentioned above will come into play. The game requires that if they are curtailed in this way, they must escape by one means or another.

Ideally, they will perpetrate their 'crimes' in a way that does not get them arrested. They must develop strategies to facilitate this, much in the same way that a real-life psychopath will do all he can to evade capture.

One of the most noted attributes of psychopaths is manipulation. Through rewards and reinforcement, the game will teach the players to become highly manipulative. The more manipulative they are, the more successful they will be at both evading capture in the first place and in escaping from custody once arrested. For example, they will be able to persuade psychologists that they are 'cured', or they will persuade journalists and civil rights campaigners of their innocence. They will not hesitate to frame other innocent parties for the crimes they commit. This is all part of the game. If they are successful in getting another character locked up for their crimes, they will receive bonus points. The longer the sentence, the more points. We should look into the possibility of offering a number of country options in the game, for example, to play it under the American judicial system, where the death penalty is of course a possibility. (That should be the default setting?)

If the player is prescribed medication, they must of course find ways to avoid taking it, as they will see their meds as a form of chemical incarceration, taking away their freedom to behave in a manner consistent with their nature.

The game eschews simplistic body count targets. However, it is true that if the protagonist's nature is to be a prolific serial killer, then the more victims they notch up, the more successful they will be.

At the same time, we should consider the option that the game may be played in a counter form. That is to say that the player may select the opposite goal: not to express their nature, but to suppress it. In other words, to control their psychopathic behaviour so that they can function in society for as long as possible. In this version of the game, the player is in effect playing against themselves, or against the behavioural traits produced by the disorder/condition they have dialled up. They will seek out help, so that they can receive the treatment required to prevent them from fulfilling their nature. However, the psychopath that they are programmed to be will subvert their best efforts to receive treatment. They will find themselves giving in to their true natures when they least expect it, or when it is most inconvenient to their consciously acknowledged goals.

Development notes for PSYCHOTOPIA VR game.
Internal Alpha Games document. Not for release. For approved circulation only.

FOUR

The first thing he thought when he saw her was that he wanted to fuck her. Really fuck her. In that deep, devastating way that would totally unravel her. (He knew that he could do this. It was a gift he had.)

It seemed to be precisely what she was asking for. And his sense was that he would have no peace until he had done it. He sensed that she felt that too.

She was sitting outside his office. They were recruiting at the time. She was one of the candidates for Assistant Experiential Architect. He could tell she would be perfect for the job. It's not that she radiated confidence. Quite the opposite. She looked nervous as hell. Classic Impostor Syndrome. (It was not a condition he suffered from.)

Perfect.

He always tried to look for something in all his employees that he would be able to use against them. Everyone has an Achilles heel. It was another of his gifts that he seemed to have a radar that unerringly detected it. He knew she would make a more than competent Assistant Experiential Architect. He'd already read her CV and looked at her online portfolio. It was all very impressive. All the requisite boxes ticked. She was eminently qualified for the job. But what clinched it was that he also sensed her fundamental lack of self-belief. She craved reassurance. That made her vulnerable. He liked his women vulnerable.

He thought how easy it would be for him to build her up and tear her down.

How easy it would be to play havoc with her emotions. To destroy her.

What struck him most about her, as he spied on her through the platinum white blinds of his glass-walled office, was her evident fragility. Here was a thing that could be broken. That demanded to be.

He made a point of not looking up as she came into his office, busying himself over something on his MindPhone. He considered himself to be a pretty good judge of how long it is possible to ignore someone before it becomes uncomfortable for them (it was never uncomfortable for him). And yes, he always carried on for just that little bit longer.

He knew exactly what was going through her mind. *Should I say something? Perhaps make a noise to signify my presence? Should I sit down? Or wait to be asked? Should I cough? Clear my throat? Or be more decisive and boldly say hello?* (Obviously she would never go for this last option.) In the end, she made a little noise which sounded like she was choking on a fly. He ignored it, of course.

He was aware of her taking out her own phone to check for MindMessages, as a way of subconsciously normalizing his rudeness. It was precisely then that he looked across and said, 'Am I interrupting you?'

She was as jumpy as a sackful of kittens on the way to the canal. 'Sorry, I . . . I was just . . . Sorry . . . sorry.' She hurriedly pushed the phone back into her bag.

She had naturally pale colouring, Nordic blonde hair and translucent skin. And so her face flushed with a squid-like rapidity, the red ink of embarrassment shooting into the fine capillaries of her cheeks. He found it unexpectedly touching. It was strange the things that moved him. And erotic. It made him think of the heat of her body, the blood pulsing beneath her fine, colourless skin. It made him think of her as a creature of flesh and blood. It made him want her. It made him want to know her secret places, to plumb the source of that blush. He thought of her heart steeped in blood, pulsing and pumping and straining to do its work. For some reason, he imagined it doing all this with a kind of Girl Guide earnestness.

He looked at her for a long time without speaking. Taking her in. He took it way past uncomfortable this time. Just to the point where her embarrassment was beginning to tip into anger. Then he hit her with: 'It's not easy, is it?'

'Sorry?'

'Don't apologize. Why are you apologizing? You've got nothing to apologize for.'

'I . . . OK?' Naturally, she spoke with that rising interrogative intonation that is found among Australians and the incurably unconfident. 'I only meant . . . I wasn't sure what you were referring to?'

'Then *I* should be the one apologizing. But I've made it a rule never to apologize.'

She didn't groan, exactly. But her face flinched in the direction of a groan. It was quick. Almost subliminal. But he caught it. He always did. 'I know. It's a cliché. You've heard it all before.'

'It's not that so much. It's just, well, maybe there are occasions when, you know, a person should apologize?'

'Everyone makes mistakes? Is that what you're saying?'

'I guess so? Something like that.'

'But we learn from our mistakes, so . . . that's good, isn't it?'

'Not if other people get hurt?'

'They learn from our mistakes too. In a sense, we're doing them a favour.'

She wrinkled her nose in distaste. 'Sorry?'

'There you go again, apologizing!'

'I wasn't apologizing. I was expressing . . . scepticism. I was using the word . . . *ironically*?'

'Ah, yes. Irony. I don't do irony. I find it only confuses things. If you mean something, you should say it? That's what I believe.'

'Well, maybe it's OK for you. I mean, you're the boss. You don't need irony. But we mere mortals . . . I kind of think it's sort of a defence mechanism? Maybe?'

He pretended to think about what she said. He thought it would be useful if he gave the impression that what she said mattered to him. 'You may be on to something there.' He counted it as one of his talents: to be able to carry on a conversation with someone while only half listening to them. He found he didn't need to listen to people all that attentively anyhow. He usually got what they are about within the first half second of meeting them. Everything that happened after that only ever confirmed that first impression. 'And I guess, being a woman in a man's world, it's useful to have these defensive techniques. That's what I was talking about when I said it can't be easy. I was talking about being a woman in a man's world.'

A quick little frown danced across her brow. Rather charmingly, he thought.

'What's the culture like at . . .' He made a point of looking down at her CV. 'Imagineers? I've heard it can be a little laddy there?' He had started to adopt the rising intonation himself. To mirror herself back at her. We all have enough of the narcissist in us to respond to that.

'It's fine.'

He let her know he understood, and appreciated, the meaning of that 'fine' with his best *simpatico* smile. 'You never experienced any harassment or anything?'

'A few of the guys could be wankers now and then. I didn't take it personally. They didn't know any better.'

'Did you report it?'

'What?'

'The harassment?'

'It wasn't really . . . I didn't . . .'

'Perhaps you did report it, and they've made your position untenable. They're forcing you out?'

'No. Nothing like that has happened.'

'You must work for Darren Travis?'

'Yes, that's right.'

'I know Darren.'

'It's a small world?'

'Would you say he's one of the wankers?'

'I . . . no. Of course not. Darren's great.'

'He's not one of the ones who hassled you?'

'Nobody . . . I don't think I said anybody hassled me? Did I? I'm sorry if I gave that impression. I didn't mean to?'

'What would Darren say about you if I rang him up now?'

'Well, I've put him as a reference. So I hope you will ring him up if you decide to offer me the job? Not before, I hope. He doesn't know I'm here? Obviously.'

He pretended to make a note of something. 'What would you say are your strengths and weaknesses?'

'My strengths? I'm a good team player?'

'Everybody says that. I mean, nobody says *I'm a lone wolf. I can't stand other people.*'

'No. But. I think I am. Genuinely. I think collaboration is at the heart of what we do? You tend to get more surprising, more creative results when you bring lots of people into the process.'

'You can't create something by committee. You need a strong creative individual driving things. Someone with vision.'

'Yes, I agree. But I think that leader also needs to share their vision with their team. And allow everyone else the opportunity to contribute.'

'Why?'

'Why? Well, I think you get better results. Other people take your idea in directions you couldn't foresee?'

'Don't they just compromise your original vision? Don't you just end up with mediocrity? Design by committee. There's nothing worse. The creative process is not a democracy. It's a dictatorship. Isn't it?'

'I—' She broke off and looked around. 'Isn't there going to be anyone else here? I mean, in the interview?'

'Who else would you like here?'

'Isn't it usual for someone from HR to be present?'

He let her see that he was disappointed. 'I didn't see you as a stickler for the rules.'

'I'm not, it's just . . .'

'Look, I'm Head of Game Development and Virtual Architecturing. Two of the most important departments in Alpha Games. Two. Got that? Not one. Two. Answering to me. The experience that we offer our gamers is what makes our games unique. Basically, I have the most important job in the company. It's me you'll be reporting to. And I don't report to anyone else, except the board. And the board basically does whatever I tell them because they don't understand what it is I do. How I make the magic. So it's my decision. Whether we hire you or not? It's got nothing to do with HR. It's me you have to impress.'

'I see.'

'So how're you going to impress me?'

'I think I sent you a link to my online portfolio? I like to let my work speak for itself?'

'OK. I get that. I looked at your work. It's OK. I think it could go to the next level.'

'Yes, yes. Of course. What I'm looking for is the opportunity to do that? To take it to the next level?'

'What about your weaknesses? Or don't you have any?'

'Well, I, err, yes . . . of course, I . . . I think I could be more *assertive*? Sometimes?'

'You lack confidence. I can see that. I bet you suffer from Impostor Syndrome?'

'How could you tell?'

'I'm a good reader of people. It's the way you say sorry all the time. It's a woman thing, do you think? Whatever it is, it's a bad habit?' He was really laying on the rising intonation. He decided to pull back just in case she thought he was taking the piss. 'We need to break it. Inside you're a strong, confident woman. I can see that. That's who I want working for me. Every morning when you get up, I want you to look in the mirror and say *I'm a strong, confident woman.* Can you do that for me?'

'Uh, OK?'

'Will you do it for me now? I'll be your mirror. Look into me like you're looking into a mirror and say it. Come on!'

'Ummm?'

At first her eyes flinched from looking at him directly. But she knew there was a lot riding on this, so eventually she forced herself to turn her face towards him. It was fascinating to watch the turmoil on her face. At one point, he thought she was going to cry. 'Come on,' he whispered. 'You can do this.' He could tell she was exactly the type to go for that shit. 'We'll say it together. After three.'

He counted her in and they said the words in unison: 'I'm a strong, confident woman.'

A little smile throbbed on her lips then rippled into half-abashed but kind of happy, or at least surprised, laughter.

'Feels good, hey?'

'To be honest, it felt a bit . . . weird?'

'Weird in a good way or weird in a bad way?'

'Is weird ever in a good way?'

'It can be.'

'This is the strangest interview I've ever been in?'

'So, let's talk about your current position?'

'Yes.'

He sensed her relax now that the conversation seemed to be heading in a more conventional interview direction. 'Why do you want to leave Imagineers? They are a very good company?'

'I just feel that the time is right for a new challenge.'

'It's nothing to do with the culture there then? I've heard it can be a little laddy.'

She frowned. 'You said that? Already? Just now?'

He gave a minuscule shake of his head in denial. Keeping his face utterly deadpan. One of the biggest kicks he got in life was making someone believe something was true when they knew it wasn't.

'Sorry, I . . .'

He made an electric buzzing noise. 'I'm going to have to wire you up to a battery and give you an electric shock every time you say it.'

'I don't think you can do that?'

'You're funny. What if I were to say to you that I want you to carry on working for Imagineers but I will pay you the same salary on top of what they're paying you – into a numbered offshore account, so tax-free, of course – for you to report back to me about whatever projects they have in the pipeline?'

'I would say no.'

'Why?'

'Because it's unethical?'

'You don't sound too sure.'

'Because it's unethical.' This time she left out the rising intonation. 'Probably even criminal.'

'You're frightened you might get caught?'

'It's not that. It's just wrong.'

'If a tree falls in a forest and there's no one there to hear it, does the tree make a sound?'

'I'm sorry?'

'Don't apologize! It wasn't your fault the tree fell over.'

'No, I'm sorry, I don't understand the point of the question?'

'If you don't get caught, you haven't done anything wrong?'

'I have to live with myself.'

'So it's a question of money? You'd need more money to make you comfortable with the situation?'

'You're not seriously suggesting this, are you? It's some kind of test?'

'Is it?'

'I've heard you can be . . .'

'What have you heard? Who from? From Darren?'

'Nothing . . . I mean . . . You have a reputation for . . .'

'For what?'

'This kind of thing.'

'What kind of thing? Exactly?'

'Playing games?' She pulled a squirming, apologetic face.

'I'm not playing games, Miss . . .' Another deliberate look down at her CV, though of course, he knew full well who she was. 'Mann. That's right, Sally Mann. Are you a man's Mann, Sally?' He was quite pleased with that.

She started to get up. 'Look, I don't know what's going on here but I'm not interested. I'm not interested in you, your games, your job . . .'

'You got the job, by the way.'

'What?'

'You're right. I was testing you. You passed.'

'I don't know what to say.'

'Thank you?'

'No. I mean . . . it's outrageous. Your behaviour has been . . . outrageous. I ought to . . .'

'Complain?'

'Yes.'

'To HR? Is that why you wanted them here?'

She didn't answer. Was closing down on him.

'Sally, let me explain something to you. This is a high-pressure environment. You know that. Plus I have some people working for me who are . . . how can I put it?'

She didn't help him out.

'They are *men*, let's say. You know what I'm talking about. And they are a special kind of men. Men who are brilliant at programming but not so brilliant at . . .'

'Women?' The fact that she answered told him that she was coming round. His chipping away was beginning to pay off.

'Exactly. So I had to make sure . . . you could handle it.'

'Oh, that's it, is it?'

'Of course it is. What else could it be?'

'I don't know. Anyhow, who says I *want* to handle it?'

'Because you're the best candidate I've seen, the best there is. And Alpha Games is the best there is too. The market leader. You have to work here. There's nowhere else for you to go after Imagineers. Whatever else you do in your life, you have to come here. And you have to make it work here. Before you say no, Sally, hear me out. Listen to what the job is. We haven't even talked about the job yet. This is the brief, my brief to you. I don't want you to come here and design game environments, Sally. I want you to come here and architect the very environment we work in. To transform Alpha Games so that it becomes in turn a transformative place. So that those men I was telling you about become transformed. And through them . . . well, this is where we're going to start it, Sally.'

'Start what?'

'Our greatest project yet.'

'Which is?'

'To change the world.'

She shook her head incredulously and laughed. 'You're mad.' But he knew. He knew he had cracked her.

'The next generation of human beings will be formed through the games they play. Games created here. In an environment created by you. You'll be in on the ground floor of the future. In a sense, you will be the mother of a whole generation. That's what I'm offering you, Sally.'

'I . . . Y . . . Wh . . . You make it sound almost possible.'

'It is possible. With you on my team, anything's possible.'

'That's just ridiculous.'

'Believe in yourself, Sally. If you don't believe in yourself, how do you expect anyone else to?'

'How do you know I can do all this? Whatever it is you're talking about. Which I'm not sure I know what it is.'

'I believe in you. You passed my test, remember?'

'It doesn't make any sense.'

'It doesn't have to make sense. It just has to feel right.'

She shook her head and gave a disbelieving laugh. 'I don't know? It wasn't what I was expecting?' He felt her disbelief turn into astonishment.

The truth is he hadn't expected it either. When she walked through his door he had no idea he would say any of that. But sometimes you just have to wing it. 'I'm serious, Sally. The games industry needs reforming. And the only way to reform it is from within. And by stealth. And the only person who can do that is a woman. And you are the only woman who can do it. You are the woman for the job. Cometh the hour, cometh the Sally Mann.'

She was still shaking her head. But though her head said no, her eyes, he knew, said yes.

LEVEL ONE, CONTINUED

S o, to go back to the actual gameplay. It begins, as has been noted, in a blank, nondescript room.

Question to be explored/resolved: is the room a real room or does it represent the protagonist's psyche? The player is trapped within himself. (I am using the male pronoun for convenience. Statistically, most psychopaths are male – but the player may just as easily have designed a female protagonist, or a character that is of indeterminate, non-binary gender. Anything is possible in the game, as in life.)

The player feels himself to be alone. Utterly alone.

The player's first instinct will be to test the limits of his environment. To find a way out. The player cannot manifest his nature in isolation.

If the player has selected some degree of auditory or visual hallucination in the dial-up of psychological attributes, these may start to be manifested. And so the player may begin to believe that he is not alone. He may even imagine that he has escaped from the room before he actually has. (Note to developer: perhaps some secret traits, such as hallucinations, occur whether or not the player requests them? Might make it interesting!)

The player is not, in actual fact, alone. There is another creature in the room with him, whose presence gradually becomes apparent. The other creature is a spider. It is the appearance of cobwebs that alerts the player to the existence of the spider. The player has to work out that the spider is the key to escaping from the room.

So the player's first task – which he must work out for himself, there will be no guidance or clues, though we will possibly leak online cheats through the forums – is to hunt down and capture the spider. He then must act in accordance with his nature towards the spider.

At some point it will occur to the player to pull off one of the spider's legs. The spider will be released and it will be noted that there is a change in the shape and patterning of the webs that the spider produces. The spider is trapped again and another leg removed, and so on. Each time a leg is removed the webs that the spider produces subtly change. When (let's say) four legs have been removed, the spider creates a web in which the words HELP ME are spelled out. When this happens, the door to the room automatically opens.

The player now moves on to LEVEL TWO.

Development notes for PSYCHOTOPIA VR game.
Internal Alpha Games document. Not for release. For approved circulation only.

FIVE

The first time I saw Dr Arbus in person was at the Police Federation Conference in Bournemouth. It must have been about ten years ago now.

Time flies when you're having fun, they say.

He was a big guy. Well over six foot. And solidly built too. So physically at least he was not out of place at a conference of coppers, though he was not as paunchy as the average CID detective and lacked the fat-thigh waddle in his walk caused by years of cheap takeaways, lager tops and donut abuse. But what really gave it away that he wasn't a cop was his bird's nest of hair, Orthodox priest beard and the mustard-coloured tweed jacket several sizes too small. I had the suspicion that it was someone else's, it clashed so violently with the purple paisley shirt he was wearing. (With a green tie, believe it or not, which looked knitted to me.) Maybe he'd stolen the jacket or grabbed it hurriedly from some generic egg head's cloakroom, mistaking it for his own. Or maybe he'd bought it years ago, when he was a skinny undergraduate, and was wearing it now because it was his way of hanging on to his youth. Or something.

A pair of thick-framed spectacles gave him a demeanour that managed to be both myopic and focused, like he was staring fixedly at something that was just inches in front of his nose. To me, he didn't seem to suffer from the normal neuroses that dog intellectuals. By which I mean people who think too much about things and who can see every side of an argument. He struck me as a man who knew of what he spoke. He allowed himself a little kink of a smile in the corner of his mouth as if he thought the rest of the world fools but was trying hard to keep it to himself. Certainly he wasn't short of self-confidence. Maybe we all need to know one thing in life that we've worked out for ourselves. His one thing was pretty interesting too.

Anyways, you couldn't miss him.

He gave a speech to conference and took part in a fringe event about social order issues. This was a few years before the

Ardagh case, which turned out to be some kind of watershed in the public awareness of PGD. Some people even called it P-Day, the day that pretty seven-year-old girl hammered her baby brother's head against the wall and left him lifeless on the nursery floor.

PGD. I take it you know what that is? Psychopath-Generated Disorder. Arbus came up with the term and the first time I heard it was at that conference. There were journalists there, naturally. So pretty soon you started to see it crop up everywhere. There was even a thrash metal band who called themselves PGD. They started a whole new genre. Psycho-Thrash. Psycho-trash, if you ask me. I hate that fucking noise. All that growling. I mean, that's not singing, is it? Do they seriously think psychopaths go around growling all the time? No, your true psychopath is more likely to be the one who sings with the voice of an angel. The one who melts everyone's hearts, especially your nan's.

It wasn't mainstream, back then. Psychopathy. A subculture, Arbus called it. But it was starting to take off. Arbus claimed it was becoming a badge of honour. People actively presented themselves as psychopaths. Boasted of their psychopathic tendencies. Some of the more extreme headcases even had P or PSYCHO tattooed on their foreheads.

Not all of them were, of course. Some of them just had Antisocial Personality Disorder. That became a term of abuse among the psychos and wannabe psychos. If you were called an Antisocial, it meant you were inferior.

If you ask me, most of them were just losers.

Dr Arbus billed himself as a Psychoanthropologist. I thought he'd made it up but apparently it's a thing. He was there to talk to the assembled Fed reps about this new test he and his colleague Adam Lubany had developed. It was quicker to administer than the old Hare Psychopathy Checklist and, Arbus claimed, more reliable. This was because you didn't need a clinician to interview the subject and make an interpretative review of their record. Anyone could do it, provided they had an Arbus-Lubany machine. Of course, the cynical among us couldn't help thinking that he was there basically as a salesman. His aim was to get Arbus-Lubany machines into every police station in the country. So that whenever any suspect came in at all, they could be instantly tested for psychopathy.

Coming to speak to the Federation was a way to drive the demand from below, so all the reps would go back to their forces and start asking for the machines from their chief constables, who would in turn go cap in hand to their police commissioners. A kind of grown-up version of pester power.

At the time, my own view was, for me personally, it was a waste of money. I could tell just by looking at someone if they were a psychopath. And, from a policing point of view, what good did it do you to know the suspect you had in front of you was a genuine verifiable psychopath? Contrary to what some people believe, it has never been illegal just to be a psychopath in this country. Not like in some other countries, which have a more hardline approach to these things. The Arab states, for example. (The closest we got was when Gleb Jackson put it in his Peace of Mind manifesto at the last election – the reason he lost, according to some. But I'm getting ahead of myself here.)

Basically, it was just a label. And so what? Ultimately.

The test result, one way or the other, had no evidentiary value in itself. Not at that time, anyhow.

Still, he gave an entertaining address, and he knew how to play his audience. By the end of his talk, the hall was practically gagging for those machines.

I guess not every cop has my special gift, so maybe there was a call for it. Certainly many of my colleagues thought it would be a useful addition to their armoury. It was a handy portable device that you held in front of a suspect's face while you flashed a sequence of images at them. At the same time you put this shower cap type thing on their heads, which was full of electrodes that could read their brainwaves. Or something.

Within seconds you had a simple definitive reading. P for psychopath. NP for non-psychopath. Of course, what you then did with that information was another matter. And maybe the Arbus-Lubany machine raised more questions than it answered, from a legal-judicial point of view. Not to mention the human rights aspect of it.

But in my experience, your average Police Fed rep is little troubled by the human rights aspect of anything. And that's me speaking as one. Or a used-to-be one, anyway.

What I remember most about Arbus's talk that day, the one he gave to the main conference, were the video clips he showed of young psychopaths talking. There was the thirteen-year-old girl who filmed herself committing sexual acts on her six-month-old baby brother so she could sell the clips online to paedophiles. She made 500 MindCoins. When asked why she did it, she said she wanted a new laptop. Classic psychopath thinking. Arbus argued that he didn't believe she herself was a paedophile. It was just that she'd heard about these men who would pay good money for child porn. She thought, hey, I've got a kid brother now, maybe I can make some money! Arbus reckoned there was no sexual aspect to it at all for her, and certainly no moral aspect. When he showed the clip of her talking about it, there was no sign of shame or remorse. She was angry at her mother for calling the police and having her arrested. She cried at that. So you might have thought maybe there was some vestige of human feeling there after all. But then she kind of spoilt it by saying, 'How'm I going to make money like that now?' And laughing. She thought that was a good joke. Then she'd change her tune again and claim she was a good babysitter. 'Everyone says I was a good babysitter!' Yeah, darling, but that was before you filmed yourself with your finger up a baby's anus. That kind of undoes a lot of the good work you put in earlier.

Then there was that twelve-year-old who set fire to a Scout hut when there was a Beaver colony meeting inside. The adults managed to get all the children out safely, despite the fact that the young psychopath had done his best to block the exits. The only fatality was the Beaver Scout leader herself, who died in hospital from burns and lung damage.

I've watched that particular interview a few times now. It's fascinating and frustrating at the same time. You think you're going to find something out, about what goes on in these morons' heads. But you never do. No matter how many times you play it.

'It was her fault,' said the kid. 'She should have got out earlier. Besides, she was a paedophile.'

Needless to say, there was no evidence to back up this claim. And the logical inconsistency of setting a fire which recklessly endangered the lives of a group of small children in order to punish a supposed paedophile somehow escaped him.

Asked why he did it, he said he wanted to see how quickly the hut would go up. He had an idea that the hut would burn 'good'. 'It's made of wood, see. Wood burns good. I reckoned I'd get some nice big flames.'

You hear Arbus off-screen ask: 'And did you?'

'Yes. I was not disappointed.'

'Did it not concern you that people might die in the fire?'

'That did not concern me.'

'Why not? Did you not know there were people inside?'

'I knew there were people inside, yes. I could hear them. It just didn't concern me.'

'Are you saying you didn't think anyone would die? Or you just didn't care whether they died or not?'

'I just didn't care, I guess.'

'Those children were very young.'

The psychopath's brow wrinkled in confusion. 'That did not concern me. I mean, they were fucking annoying little brats. They were like screaming, you know? It was doing my head in.'

'You mean before you set the hut on fire? They were noisy before? Is that why you did it?'

'They were noisy before. They were noisy after. They were just fucking noisy. Somebody had to shut them up.'

'So that *is* why you did it? To shut them up?'

'I guess so.'

'Did it work? Did they quieten down?'

'Hell, no. They were screaming like fuck after I done it. Screaming worse than before.'

'So it didn't work?'

'I guess not.'

But you don't get anywhere trying to fathom what makes these people tick. Half the time *they* don't know why they do shit. He wanted to see the flames. He wanted to shut the children up. He wanted to punish the paedophile who wasn't a paedophile. He had a thousand reasons for doing it, but none of them amounted to a reason for doing anything.

I guess that's the point Arbus was making. Trying to understand them is a waste of time. What you have to do is identify them. And contain them.

'It used to be believed that psychopaths constitute approximately one per cent of the general population, though the ratio of psychopaths in certain populations, such as prison populations, is naturally higher. My contention is that there has been a dramatic increase in PGD-related incidents such as these in recent years. The proportion of psychopaths in our midst is rising. Not only that, as these clips show, we are seeing PGD behaviours emerge in a greater number of young individuals. Psychopaths are psychopaths from birth. So, naturally, the existence of psychopaths of every and any age is to be expected. What has changed, and to a striking degree, is just the sheer number of these juvenile, or even infant, psychopaths. A more systematic screening of offenders using the Arbus-Lubany machine will enable us to have a clearer picture of what we are up against. It is only when we understand the scale of the problem that we will be able to determine what we must do to tackle it. For that reason, I would propose that not only are all those who come into the criminal justice system tested, but that we conduct randomized tests on the general population. These could be done completely anonymously, for the sole purpose of gathering demographic information. However, it stands to reason that if you are able to identify someone as a potentially dangerous psychopath, it might be advisable to, uh, in some way tag them as such. Furthermore, given the issue of increased juvenile psychopathology, the earlier the test is administered the better. I personally would not leave it to secondary school age. I think we should be testing children at infant school entry level, or even in preschool settings.'

We all sat up at that. Including the Home Secretary, who was there on the platform waiting to make her keynote speech.

There was one thing that no one who was present argued with that day. It was palpable, the sense, among a hall full of cops, that the amount of crazy in the world was increasing.

And many of them there also felt that something had to be done about it.

Me, I was sufficiently interested in what he was saying to cut short a semi-boozy lunch at a faux TexMex restaurant on the sea front and hie along to his fringe event in the afternoon. I couldn't help feeling that his theories had some kind of pertinence to me personally. I mean, I was dealing with a lot of the kind of PGD events he was talking about. I was seeing it, if not daily, then certainly once or twice a week.

The event was in a gloomy side room some way from the main hall. I got there early so I managed to get a seat in the front row.

I was glad I did. The seats filled up quickly, and latecomers were crammed in standing at the back and sides.

Arbus took the stage carrying a sleek aluminium briefcase in one hand. An excited buzz went round the room. Were we finally going to get a look at one of his machines? He placed the case on the floor next to his seat and sat back with the smug air of a man who knew he was on to a good thing. Talk about the cat getting the cream.

The session consisted of an interview with this female journalist who was playing devil's advocate to Arbus. You must have seen her on your screens. Krystie Rothwell. Dark hair, great body, a real looker, even if she likes to come across as a bit of an ice maiden. In my experience, the ice maidens and the steely bitches, when you finally crack them, are the best. They come magnificently. It's like the surf crashing over rocks, I'm telling you. You can actually make them sob with gratitude, if you know what you're doing.

I digress.

After the introductions, and a bit of warm-up chat, she went straight to the point: 'I'm not quite sure I understand what the practical benefit of the machine is? And why you would give them to police officers. I mean, being a psychopath isn't in itself illegal, is it?'

'Not yet, no.'

'Are you suggesting it should be?'

'A positive result on the Arbus-Lubany machine is an indication that the individual concerned has a high propensity towards committing illegal acts. That they do not recognize the normal laws and constraints of civil society that the rest of us conform to.'

'But what if they've done nothing wrong? What if they've committed no offence?'

'They will.'

'Would you be in favour of incarcerating them as a preventative measure?'

'I didn't say that. For one thing, I don't think it's practical. Our prisons are already overcrowded. Ideally, we would want to cure them. But, as yet, there is no known cure for psychopathy.'

'So what's the answer?'

'I'm not a policymaker. It's for others to decide how to act on the information I provide them with.'

'That sounds like a cop-out, if I may say so, Dr Arbus. I mean, surely, you must have some opinion. You've spent a long time thinking about this.'

'One possibility is that a positive Arbus-Lubany result could go on their record, so that in the future, if there was a criminal investigation, it would show up in any search and would mark them out as being worthy of consideration.'

'Isn't that a breach of their human right to privacy? What about the Data Protection Act?'

'I'm not sure we can talk about human rights when we're dealing with psychopaths. The only human right they recognize is what they consider their right to destroy other people's lives.'

'You obviously feel very strongly about this.'

'I've spent a lot of time working with them. Looking in their eyes.'

'I sense that you'd like to go even further? That you'd like to find some way to . . . take them out of circulation?'

'The problem with offending psychopaths traditionally is that they are able to avoid jail by pleading insanity. They are therefore admitted to secure psychiatric units, where, in time, they are able to prove themselves to be perfectly sane. They may even be clever enough to convince clinical psychologists that they have been cured by their ministrations. And so they are released. Whereupon they resume their PGD behaviours.'

'So . . . what are you suggesting?'

'We can't cure them. We can't contain them. Logically, the only option left to us is to remove them. From society. Permanently.'

'You mean kill them?'

'I don't think we have to go that far. And I think that would be a difficult policy to get through any parliament. What you have to understand is that psychopathology is a . . . well, I was going to say a genetic condition. However, it's perhaps truer to think of it as a genetic trait. In a sense, it is a reproductive strategy. And actually, quite a successful one. Male psychopaths are highly promiscuous. Their strategy is to impregnate and then move on. They form no bonds with their offspring, or with the multiple mothers of their offspring. That's not important. The important thing is seed propagation. It is contrary to the accepted model of human reproduction, but that in itself is breaking down. The traditional model is the couple as a closely bonded unit, nurturing and bringing up their children together. That's not the only way it can be done. What we may be seeing here, in this rise in juvenile psychopath numbers, is a new generation of psychopaths created by the exponential reproductive success of previous generations of psychopaths. Their evolutionary strategy is paying off. We are evolving into a more psychopathic species. If we do nothing about this, the future of the human race will be psychopathic.'

'What do you mean by that, exactly?'

'I mean there will come a point when there are more psychopaths than there are non-psychopaths.'

'But surely that's not going to happen? This is just scaremongering!'

'Is it?'

'Well, a lot of the behaviour you've depicted is self-destructive. Surely it's not a very efficient reproductive strategy? Won't the inherent risk-taking and impulsiveness of psychopaths be enough to keep their numbers down naturally?'

'It doesn't matter how self-destructive the individual is if they succeed in passing on their genes. Besides, not all psychopaths are self-destructive. Some of them mask their psychopathic traits so successfully that they are able to rise to quite prominent positions in a range of diverse sectors.'

'But society depends on people coming together, working together, for the common good. And we've evolved as social beings. Not antisocial beings. That is surely the stronger force?'

'But there has always been an antisocial element there. What I see is that becoming more dominant. We are seeing psychopaths in positions of corporate and even political power. Of course, that's happened before. In isolated instances. But I think we're seeing a lot more of it now. Not only that, they are celebrated by an ever-growing constituency of fellow psychopaths. It's becoming more open. More shameless. You are getting people in power who openly don't care about the weak and the vulnerable, and who are massively popular because of that. That lack of empathy, I would say, is indicative of psychopathy.'

'Are there some world leaders whom you would like to undergo the Arbus-Lubany test?'

'There are.'

'Are you prepared to name them?'

'I don't think that's either necessary or wise.'

There was laughter from the floor, which Arbus acknowledged with a wry smile.

'We all know who they are. And psychopathic leaders in the past have not responded well to those who would criticize them.'

'You still haven't explained how you would remove psychopaths from society, if you can't incarcerate them.'

'Well, one solution – if we're allowed to put anything on the table . . .?'

'Please do.'

'Well, we could consider sterilization. Admittedly, it would not eradicate the psychopaths that are in our midst already, but it would prevent further proliferation of PGD in the future. It's a long-term strategy, the benefits of which would only be felt by future generations. Unfortunately, politicians tend to shy away from this kind of long-term planning. They are not elected by future generations. But, I'm afraid, the only alternative is we let evolution take its course. And I hate to think where that may lead us.'

'Sterilization? Isn't that a little . . . extreme? And ethically . . . can you do that?'

'You might think it's extreme. But anyone who has had contact with any of these individuals – who are responsible for the majority of the antisocial behaviour and criminal offending in our society – anyone who's had any contact with them will not think it's extreme. I would say it's unethical *not* to do this. But as I say, I don't make policy. I just provide the data for the policymakers.'

'The Home Secretary was in the hall today, listening to your speech.'

'Yes.'

'Would you like a meeting with her?'

'Well, we did have a brief discussion in the hall . . . and . . .'

'You're going to be meeting her?'

'She has asked for a meeting, yes.'

'Will you be conducting the Arbus-Lubany test on her?'

'I don't think it's necessary.'

'You don't think she's a psychopath?'

'Not everyone is. Yet.'

I think he meant it as a joke. It was hard to tell behind those glasses. At any rate, there was an involuntary nervous laughter from the floor, and some uneasy fidgeting.

Krystie Rothwell had a mischievous glint in her eye. Sitting in the front row, I swear to God she winked at me. The ice-maiden mask had slipped. 'Of course, the thing that's always said about the police – I heard the current Chair of the Federation, Charles Woodbridge, make this very point today in his address – it's always said that the police are just a reflection of society. Just as you get good and bad people in society as a whole, in the same way you get good and bad people in the police. Is the same true for psychopaths? Are there psychopaths in the police?'

'Well, yes. Obviously.'

To be honest, I'm not so sure that one was meant as a joke. If it was, he had the best deadpan delivery *ever* – myself excluded, of course. We cops love a good deadpan delivery. So the hall erupted. It was the funniest thing we'd heard for a long time.

Krystie waited for the uproar to die down. 'If I can be serious for a moment, this raises an interesting question. In that case, should there be routine testing with your machine for all police officers?'

There was a great heckle from the floor. 'We wouldn't have any fucking coppers left if we did that!' OK, it was me, I admit it. Krystie saw it and flashed me this delicious, groin-tautening grin. I couldn't help feeling, after that smile, I was in with a chance.

Arbus did his best to ignore my contribution. 'I think there is an argument for that, yes.'

'I suspect, Doctor, from that reaction, that you might have some trouble getting the Police Federation to sign up to it.'

'They may have no choice.'

He was losing his audience. There were some boos at that.

He tried to recover. 'It's not . . . I wouldn't say it was neces-sary, or inevitable. Perhaps the testing could take place if and when a police officer is found to have breached procedure or committed an offence. It does happen. There are corrupt police. Even officers who are effectively sponsored by criminal gangs. The chances are such individuals are psychopathic.'

'Wouldn't it be too late by then, if your machine is intended to be a prophylactic measure?'

There was some guffawing at *prophylactic*. We can be a childish bunch. Especially in the afternoon.

'If my suggestion of testing all children at school-entry age is taken up, then we could identify known psychopaths at an early age and bar them from certain professions, such as the police.'

'Weed them out early, you mean?'

'Yes.'

'Well, Doctor, no one can accuse you of not being prepared to think the unthinkable.'

'There's a lot at stake here.'

'I understand you've brought one of your machines along with you today. I wonder if we could see it.'

There were encouraging cries of 'Get it out!' from the floor. Not me, that time. That said, I was as curious as everyone else. We'd seen photos of it in Arbus's talk earlier, but this was our first opportunity to eyeball an actual machine in the flesh, so to speak.

Arbus picked up the aluminium briefcase and laid it flat on his lap. It almost seemed like, at the last moment, he was reluctant to open it. As if he was afraid of opening Pandora's Box. Maybe he was. I also had the feeling that he was going to make some kind of speech. Something like, *What I am about to show you is so momentous that I must insist you swear on all that you hold sacred never to reveal what you have seen to another living soul. If you break your oath, I shall be obliged to hunt you down and kill you.*

Of course, he didn't say that. Or anything like it. What he actually said was, 'This is just a prototype, you understand. We're still working on the design. But basically, yes, all the elements are here. It is a functioning prototype.'

The bottom of the case contained a bed of grey foam, into which were cut several recesses of different sizes. One of these contained a device that looked somewhat like a traditional MindPhone, though perhaps a little chunkier. Arbus lifted this out and handed it to Krystie to examine. A second recess contained a thing that looked to me like a VR frame – you know, the kind of thing that's used to hold a VR device in front of a viewer's eyes. In a third was a small see-through case containing some kind of white fabric folded up small.

'It's lighter than I expected,' observed Krystie, weighing the device in her hands.

'It's been a priority to keep the weight down to a minimum. We want it to be fully portable.'

Arbus took the machine back off her and connected up the cap.

'That's it?'

'Pretty much. The hand unit connects with a base dock for charging and downloading of data on to the network. But as far as the individual officer is concerned, this is all he or she needs.'

There were a few quiet blips and vibrations as Arbus switched the machine on. The screen glowed and flickered in his hands as some kind of animation played across it.

'So,' said Krystie, 'all we need now is a volunteer.' There was no doubt about it this time. She was looking straight at me.

LEVEL TWO

As soon as the player leaves the security of his room, and the company of the partially dismembered spider, he must learn to interact with the other characters in the game. (Consider the possibility of developing the game in a multi-player online version. In that, there is the chance that every character the player encounters is another psychopath, or another sufferer from some kind of boutique, dialled-up psychiatric condition or personality disorder, which would make things interesting to say the least!)

There are basically two kinds of interaction possible. To kill the character encountered, or to allow them to live.

Within the second category of interaction, there are obviously a whole series of sub-interactions.

The player may choose not to kill a character immediately, with a view to killing them later at some more appropriate, or less risky, time. Given that psychopaths are known for their impulsive behaviours, the protagonist may end up killing the character encountered even though the player deems it too risky. This adds to the tension and excitement of the game and the sense that the protagonist is out of control – they cannot even be controlled by the player.

However, if the player engages in a killing spree immediately upon his release from the room, the chances are he will very soon come to the attention of the authorities. Remember, the ostensible premise is that the room is inside a secure psychiatric unit. The first people he encounters will be psychiatric nurses and doctors. If he is going to kill one of these, it has to be done very carefully, deliberately and purposefully: the purpose being to assume the identity of the victim (an opportunity for a face mask here?).

Counterintuitively, the player makes more progress in the game if the first thing he does on escaping from his room (or cell) is to surrender himself to the first psychiatric professional he encounters. This will result in his being returned to the room, but with the reward of increased privileges. In addition, he will succeed in winning the trust of the staff at the facility.

And so, the interaction takes the form of one kind of manipulation or another. The player must consider what he wants to get out of the interaction (ultimately, the ability to act in a way consistent with his nature) and then work out how best to manipulate the character encountered so that he achieves that aim. The player will come to represent the controlling, rational aspects of the protagonist's nature. The dialled-up psycho settings will determine the unruly, irrational aspects. There will always be some inherent tension. Of course, if a true psychopath were to play the game, then there would be no restraining influence on the in-game traits, which might be interesting.

There is also the possibility that the player may recognize in the character encountered a kindred spirit. This opens the door to two highly disturbed characters working together to further their mutual goal of spreading mayhem and destruction.

Development notes for PSYCHOTOPIA VR game.
Internal Alpha Games document. Not for release. For approved circulation only.

SIX

In the immediate aftermath, there were practical things to deal with. She welcomed them as a distraction from her pain, her grief and her shame. Though she knew that she'd have to deal with those soon enough.

First she had to contact the bank to stop her missing cards. He'd already been on a spending spree with her contactless debit card. Wasted no time there, racking up thousands of pounds of spending on small items. The number of sandwiches and sushi rolls he'd bought in half a day from various branches of over-priced fast food outlets was staggering. He couldn't possibly have eaten them all. What was he doing with them? Selling them on? But who would buy a random lunch off some stranger when you could just go to the shop and buy your own? Or maybe he just gave them away to homeless people. Was he some kind of modern-day Robin Hood? Stealing from the rich to give to the poor? But she would hardly describe herself as the rich. The thought elicited a bitter ironic sob of half-amusement, half-rage. The truth is it didn't take him long to clean out her account completely. Even though she'd just been paid.

As for the sandwiches, or whatever it was he was buying, she had a feeling that the most likely explanation was that he simply bought them and then immediately threw them away. There was no reason to it. Except that he knew she would see the transactions on her statements. Each pointless purchase he made was designed to twist the knife and hurt her even more.

He managed to withdraw some cash as well. He hadn't gone mad. Didn't want to risk having the withdrawal refused. But he got away with five hundred pounds before the card was stopped. How on earth had he worked out her PIN number? But then she remembered. Closed her eyes in a rush of hot private embarrassment and remembered. She'd willingly told him what it was. He'd played this trust game with her. 'I trust you absolutely,' he had said. 'I'd even tell you my PIN number and all my MindNet passwords.' And he had.

How could she not reciprocate?

Of course the PIN number and passwords he'd told her were completely false. Or she assumed they were. Besides, she'd made no effort to remember them. And she couldn't imagine how he had managed to remember hers. After all, it wasn't as if he had rushed for a pen and written them down. But obviously he didn't need to. He even played with her, pretending to get them wrong as he recited them back to her. Enough to reassure her that the numbers and letters were completely jumbled in his head. And then, of course, he'd buried his head under the duvet and found a way to completely take her mind off what she'd just done. There was more hot shame at the memory of that.

He had her credit card too. And was able to buy some high-end objects online with that. More laptops and other gadgets to go with the ones he'd stolen from them. As well as electric guitars, smoothie makers and even a massage chair. Oh and van rental, to go round and pick it all up. Because of course he did it all at MindNet cafes and arranged click and collect, so there was no delivery address logged.

He just melted into the daylight.

She kept herself going. Turning up to work and putting on a brave face. Well, that was the intention. But it was hard to pull it off when she felt that the whole inside of her body had been scooped out and replaced with toxic fumes. From time to time, whenever she remembered, she shaped her mouth into something resembling a smile. Whenever she caught herself doing it, she had the feeling that her face was tensed into an expression of existential horror.

She knew from the number of times people had to tell her things, the number of times someone asked, 'Are you all right?', that it wasn't really working.

It went without saying that she couldn't concentrate. Her mind was trapped in a loop of humiliating and pornographic replays of the days and nights she had spent with him. And when she thought of him now, she imagined him laughing at her. Telling his friends about what he had done to her. Maybe he even ran workshops teaching other men how to do the same.

He was a player. And she had been played. Big time.

He hadn't raped her. She couldn't claim that. She had given her consent willingly to everything that had happened. And yet, he had misrepresented himself. Massively. So the person she had given her consent to was not the person he was. She had been violated. That was not overstating it.

Somehow she managed to get through that first day without making any major cock-ups. She was on autopilot and her training kicked in.

But she couldn't wait to get home.

Where her pain, grief and shame were waiting for her. She rushed towards them as if they were the only friends she had left in the world.

She ran to her room. The last thing she wanted was to face Aryan. Or Sal, for that matter, who admittedly was making consoling noises to her face and telling her that it wasn't her fault and she didn't blame her. But Aimée knew that when someone tells you they don't blame you for something, what they are actually saying is you are the biggest fuckwit ever and of course you're to blame and how could you be so stupid, what were you thinking? It wasn't that she thought Sal was two-faced. She just couldn't see how anyone could not blame her for what she had allowed to happen.

It hurt her to admit it but she couldn't even bear the thought of seeing Edith. It was almost as if she felt she didn't deserve her sister's compassion and sympathy. As if she had to deprive herself of her sister's love as a conscious form of self-punishment.

Edith's goodness – any human goodness at all – was unbearable right now.

The pain was physical. A balled fist inside her throat. The only thing that would ease it was crying. But she couldn't give in to that yet.

First she had to strip the bed. She wanted to burn the bedding. It would always remind her of him. It was permanently sullied by its contact with his naked body. How had she managed to sleep in this bed last night? Breathing in the lingering scent of his hated skin. Of course, she had been exhausted. And Edith had been there with her. She had not wanted to disturb her sister, for fear of losing her. So she had just lain there on top of the duvet, drifting in and out of queasy dreams.

Dreams of him. Dreams in which he came back to her and

explained everything. It had all been a misunderstanding. He hadn't stolen their things. He hadn't ripped out her heart and laughed at her wound. He had been coming back to the flat when an extraordinary series of catastrophes had held him up. His legs had simply ceased working. He had been running back to her, as hard as he could, for hours, days, only to discover that his legs weren't working. He couldn't believe it! He had spent all that time running on the spot. His lungs bursting, his heart aching, tears running down his face.

And at that point he had been attacked by . . . by . . . by . . . Well, he couldn't say by whom he was attacked, he didn't see them, but the thing is they stole the key she had given him. So, yes, while he was stuck there – still running on the spot in his desperation to get back to her – they, the unseen assailants, went to the flat and cleared it out. He had tried to get word to her but they had stolen his MindPhone as well. And they had brain-washed him so that he couldn't remember who he was. No. It was worse than that. Sadder than that. They had killed him. That was why he couldn't get back to her. That was why his legs were no longer working. He was speaking to her from the other side. He was just a ghost now. A ghost condemned to run on the spot forever.

He would never reach her. He would never be able to come back to her.

And though this saddened her immeasurably, it was some comfort. Because it meant that he had not betrayed her. He had died loving her.

But then, of course, she had woken from this beautifully consoling dream to realize that it was a fraud. He was still cheating her now, even in her dreams.

And his scent was still there in her room. Poisoning everything. Even so, was it possible that a part of her wanted to hold on to it, and, in fact, refused to give it up?

The image of him in the height of his passion came back to her. A pang of desire – oh, her treacherous body! She tried to will herself into a feeling of revulsion at what her mind was forcing her to contemplate. But for as long as she could still smell him there in the room, a part of her wanted him back. And, she realized, part of her pain was the ache of missing him.

The tears came as she tore at her bedding in a frenzy. She

was trying to pour the duvet out from its cover as if she were trying to rescue it from the contaminated sheath that contained it. But somehow it resisted her efforts. It overwhelmed her.

She collapsed again on the bed, huddled herself around her pain, and pulled the duvet, half out of its cover, around her.

It still smelled of him. She didn't care. It was all she had left.

But no. When she realized that she had allowed herself to think that, to wallow in that, something fierce and angry took her over. She threw the tainted duvet from her, on to the floor. She stripped the bottom sheet from her mattress and pulled the covers off her pillows. It calmed her to get somewhere with the task. Suddenly she felt it was possible that she could do this. Strip the bed. Get over him.

She was still crying. And quaking from her tears. She wiped them on the heel of her wrist, consciously refusing to use any of the stripped bedding because she didn't want to think of his touch in it coming to her relief.

So she was shaking a little, and shivering, and snot was running from her nose, but at last, on her own, by her own efforts and will, she managed to extricate the duvet from its cover. She bundled the foul bedding together and took it to her window, which she had left open to air the room. She threw her arms away from her. The pieces of bedlinen fell out of the window and caught on a listless breeze, fluttering and folding over themselves as they fell to the ground.

Her room looked out on the back garden. One pillowcase got snagged in the branches of a pear tree. The bottom sheet ended up draped over their neighbours' fence. The duvet cover lay disconsolately on the gravel.

She wasn't sure what she had hoped for. For the wind to bear it all away, she supposed. That would be better even than burning it. Even though that hadn't quite worked, the absurdity of what she had done lifted her. She started to laugh. She was behaving like a psychopath. And it felt good.

Still, being who she was, there was a tug of responsibility pulling at her. She'd have to go down later and deal with it. She'd also have to explain her actions to her flatmates. Or maybe not. Maybe they could work out for themselves what was going on. It was an act of temporary wildness. A release. There would be a price to pay. There's always a price to pay. But in this case, for now, it felt like a price worth paying.

She'd tipped the memory of him out of the window. It felt almost as good as if she had tipped him out.

She realized that she was still laughing. And her laughter sounded unnatural to her own ears. It hardly sounded like laughter at all. And soon it wasn't laughter any more.

She staggered back to the bed, picking up the duvet on the way. She threw herself down on the bare mattress.

At last she felt that she could give in to the crying. And she did. Her tears soaked pillow after pillow. Her sobs shook the bed, as once, not so long ago, their lovemaking had.

The light faded around her. Her cries became hoarse and monotonous. Almost mechanical. The reflex convulsion of her emotional system.

Her mouth was dry, as if all the moisture in her body had leeched out from her eyes.

But she still felt the pain. So she didn't, couldn't, stop crying.

In the event, Edith retrieved her bedding for her and washed it and presented it to her, neatly folded, smelling sweetly of fabric conditioner.

'I don't want it.'

Edith nodded, understanding. She didn't try to reason with her.

Some days had passed. Aimée had somehow managed to get herself to and from the various places she needed to be. She hadn't eaten anything the whole time. And couldn't even remember if she'd drunk anything. But she had stopped crying, though her room still smelled of her tears. But that was better than what it had smelled of before.

It was a miracle she hadn't keeled over.

'You look like shit.' It was the kind of thing only a sister could say.

Aimée didn't know what she was supposed to say to that. She felt maybe that some kind of witty comeback was called for. Or a plucky, brave, laughter-through-tears nugget of wisdom. She had nothing.

'I made some spag bol.'

Aimée could smell it. Her stomach felt like it was gurning

with hunger. She didn't have the strength to resist.

'Oh, one other thing,' said Edith, in that casual-but-not-really way that signalled this was what she had come to tell her all along. 'There's someone come to see you.'

Insanely, absurdly, cruelly, stupidly, her heart leapt at the thought that it might be him. Hating herself, and inconsolable at the realization that it wasn't him, would never be him, she closed her eyes and whimpered.

'It's Callum,' said Edith. And there was perhaps a note of impatient recrimination in her voice. 'Oh, and don't worry. Aryan and Sal are out.'

'Callum?'

The truth was she was amazed to see him.

'Hi Aims.'

'What are you doing here? I mean, Edie said Aryan's gone out?'

'Well, I just, you know . . . I . . .'

'He came to see you. To check that you're OK,' supplied Edith.

Callum bowed his head modestly, half-afraid of how this would be taken.

'Why?'

His face showed that the question wounded him. He didn't offer an answer.

So it was left to Edith to supply one. 'Because he cares!'

Callum winced and flashed a pleading look in Edith's direction. 'Hey, Edie, could I . . . could you . . .?'

'What?'

'Could I talk to Aimée alone for a bit?'

'Fine. I make you spaghetti bolognese and now I'm banished to my own room. I shall take my dinner and fuck off.' But she wasn't really cross. She gave a little encouraging smile to Callum on the way out.

'Yeah . . . I . . .'

'You must hate me.' It wasn't a question.

'No, I . . . I was worried about you.'

'You heard what he did?'

'Yes.'

'I caused that. By my stupidity.'

'Don't. It doesn't do any good blaming yourself.'

'Everybody blames me!'

'Nobody . . .' He was about to say *Nobody blames you* but realized she wouldn't buy it. 'Well, maybe Aryan blames you. But he's a dick.'

'He's your best friend.'

'He's still a dick.'

'How could I have been so stupid?'

'You fell in love. You fell in love with him.'

'But I hardly knew him. I'd only just met him. Actually, I didn't know him at all.'

'That's not how love works. Love hits you. And takes you over. You can't control it. It controls you. Whatever happened, that love that you felt, that was a good thing.'

'No! It was madness! It was stupidity! It was destructive. It was a totally bad thing. A very bad thing.'

'No, it was . . .' Callum tried to think of a different way of phrasing it, but all he could do was come back to: 'It was a good thing. Love can only ever be a good thing. Even if it's for a bad person.'

'How can you say that? I mean, how can *you* say that. I treated you . . . horribly.'

'Yeah. You did.' She saw that he was crying. 'But I can't help that. And I can't help how I feel about you.'

'You still feel . . . you still want . . .? Don't you just think I'm just some awful bitch?'

'No, I think you made a mistake. I think about some of the things I've done. I've made mistakes too, you know.'

'Not like this.'

'Maybe I was lucky. Maybe some of them could have gone this way. Or worse. Maybe there are worse mistakes I haven't made yet. But I will. I bet you I will.'

'I don't understand, Callum. I don't understand how you can want to do this. It's not right. I can't let you. I can't let you do this to yourself. I mean, what is it? Is it pity, is that it? Do you think I'll be grateful to you? Am I the fallen woman that you're rescuing?'

The colour rushed to his cheeks. A wince of unhappiness pulled at the corner of his mouth.

'It's not that. I just want . . . I want Aimée back. I want my friend back. I know we're not going to get together. I'll get over that. That doesn't matter. What matters is I can't bear to see you like this. Hurt. Broken.'

He didn't look at her. Just hung his head. And shook his head.

And before she knew it, her arms were around him, seeking him out, consoling him.

GENERAL GAMEPLAY NOTES, I

I n life, not all psychopaths are murderers.
However, for the purposes of the game, they are. If they have not killed already, they have the potential to do so.

To put it bluntly, we are only interested in homicidal psychopaths.

Let's face it, they are more fun! And we know it's what the fans want. But is there a way to work in the chaotic, purposeless behaviour of non-homicidal psychopaths? Could these be secondary characters who pop up in the game from time to time to cause mayhem and confusion? They could provide victims for the psychopathic killers?

(Note to self: maybe we could call them Randoms? I don't know why but I like this word.)

The main thing about all psychopaths is that you cannot trust them. They are completely believable and plausible in everything they say – but none of it is true.

Naturally.

Promises are earnestly made and casually broken.

Explanations are given that have no basis in fact.

Claims are made that turn out to be utterly false.

Apparent alliances may be formed, but they are meaningless.

Each individual psychopath is always only ever working for him or herself.

Consider the possibility of having psychopaths – both homicidal and non-homicidal types – among the psychiatric and medical staff treating the protagonist. Some of them could be genuine medical professionals with psychopathic personalities, some of them could be charlatans masquerading as doctors/ nurses. (Consider the possibility of the protagonist manoeuvring himself/herself into such a role.)

It all gets very complicated and confusing, but the more complicated and confusing it is, the better. That's when the fun really starts. Also, the more confusing a situation is, the easier

it is for a psychopath to evade detection. (I would imagine –
ho, ho!)

Maybe that's why psychopaths spend so much time generating
confusion and disorder? It's not self-destruction – though it
sometimes seems like it – it's actually a survival tactic? Look
into this. More research needed? Or does it matter, for the
purposes of the game, why they do it? All we need to know is
that they do.

The main point is that the player must learn to deceive and
manipulate. That is how they progress in the game.

Deceitful/manipulative/ruthless behaviour is rewarded.

When undergoing treatment, for example, they must work
out the responses that will lead to their release. They must give
the doctors what they want or expect.

However, this is complicated by the above-mentioned refinement of having concealed psychopaths among the medical staff,
or pseudo medical staff. So no matter what the player says, it
won't lead to their release.

They have to work this out and modify their game plan. In
this case, I would say, the most effective strategy would be to
kill the psychopathic doctor (or pseudo doctor) and assume their
identity by face theft. (For the purposes of the game, face theft
is an effective disguise, though in real life we would quickly detect
someone wearing someone else's facial skin over their own. Or
maybe not? In the topsy-turvy universe of Psychotopia, maybe
everyone knows full well that an individual is wearing a mask
made from the face of a dead person but has no problem with
it? Interesting. Needs to be thought through. Could work both
ways, I think. Look into how the skin would react when separated
from the body. Would it dry out? Shrivel? Change colour – e.g.
go black? Rot? Smell? Need to get some clarity here. Does it
need to reflect what really happens or should it just be what
looks coolest? These are all things that need to be nailed down
before we progress to full-blown design. We maybe need to try
out a range of options to see which works best in game.)

Development notes for PSYCHOTOPIA VR game.
*Internal Alpha Games document. Not for release. For approved
circulation only.*

SEVEN

She had a nerve, I'll give her that. Didn't flinch. Didn't blink. Just kept staring straight at me. Course, I gave as good as I got. Nobody gets the better of me in a hard-arsed staring contest.

Especially not some ice-maiden NewsNet presenter journalist bitch. I use the word affectionately. Some of my favourite bitches are bitches.

But she wasn't giving up without a fight. 'You, sir? Perhaps you'd like to volunteer to undergo the Arbus-Lubany test so that we can all see the machine in action?'

I had to laugh. 'I don't need that machine to tell me whether I'm a psychopath or not.'

'Really? Interesting. Why's that?'

'Because I already know.'

'And? Are you?'

'That's for me to know and you to find out.'

'That rather sounds like you are.'

I shrugged. 'Do I look like a psychopath?'

'Well, I don't know. That's the whole point of the test, isn't it? Because we can't tell just by looking at someone.'

'Well, I'm not. You don't have to worry. Krystie.' I think it's always nice, if you know someone's name, to use it.

'Then you should have no objection to taking the test?'

'On the contrary. I have everything to lose. If that thing gets it wrong, I'll be publicly stigmatized. You've got to be fucking joking.'

'It won't get it wrong,' said Arbus, with that quiet absolute certainty of the incurably arrogant. I wondered if someone will ever invent a machine for detecting arseholes.

'It does raise an interesting question, the problem of a false positive.' I couldn't help noticing how quick Krystie was to pick up my point. 'Or for that matter, a false negative. Isn't there always a possibility of dangerous psychopaths slipping through the net? Couldn't your test just make us complacent?'

'There is no chance of that ever happening. If you had read the paper that I wrote for the *Journal of Criminal Psychology* you wouldn't need to ask that question.'

'Are you saying that the machine is foolproof?'

'I am saying that I have provided adequate scientific, objectively verified, peer-tested evidence that the Arbus-Lubany test is one hundred per cent reliable. One hundred per cent.'

'And it can't be rigged?'

'Rigged? No. Of course not.' But he was lying. You could tell by the way he threw the question back at her. Classic liar's stalling technique. The sudden aggressive tilt in his body posture confirmed it.

'There you are.' Krystie to me, with a cheeky smirk. A promising little crack in the ice-maiden mask.

'Well, he would say that, wouldn't he? But if you're so convinced, why don't you do the test?'

She didn't see that coming. But it only took her a moment to process the idea. I guess she saw it as a career opportunity. After all, there *was* a camera recording the event. Whichever way the test went, she'd be even more famous than she was already. 'By all means. I'm very happy to volunteer. That's an excellent idea.'

You had to hand it to her, she was certainly game. And I liked the way she went along with my proposal. It boded well for certain other things I had in mind.

'Let's do it then!' She gave Arbus an excited leer, as if she actually relished the possibility of being labelled a psychopath. Though obviously she was confident that wasn't going to happen. That said, you can never be sure, can you?

Arbus stood over Krystie and busied himself fitting the ScanCap on to her head. It was a strange kind of intimacy. Like that between hairdresser and client. Or any two strangers who are forced into physical proximity and suddenly become aware of it. You could tell Krystie wasn't comfortable. 'Can't I just put it on myself?'

'No, it has to sit in a certain way, so that all the scan points are in the right place in order that the correct areas of the brain are screened.'

'And you expect police officers to be able to do this?'

'They can be trained to do it. It's very simple really. It's just a question of getting the front of the cap at the front and the back at the back. And also making sure that there are no folds or wrinkles.'

'Will I feel anything?'

'Nothing at all. It's over in a matter of minutes. There's no physical sensation at all. Now if I can just . . .'

'What are you doing now?'

'Just connecting the ScanCap to the main unit.'

'OK. And so how does the ScanCap work exactly?'

'It uses electro-magnetic pulses to register the areas of your brain that are activated by the stimulus material, in much the same way as a traditional MRI scanner does – though obviously the technology has progressed massively in recent years, so that we're able to achieve similar results in a fraction of the time with this small, lightweight apparatus. The main difference is in this case we don't need to produce actual imaging of the brain's activity. We just need simple binary confirmation of whether certain cerebral activities occurred or did not occur. That is enough for us to get a result. That simplification of function has helped tremendously in the miniaturization.'

'What specific activity are you looking for?'

'A number of related events, located in and around the amygdala. Essentially, we are looking to monitor your subconscious emotional responses to the stimuli that I am about to show you. The images will pass before you with such rapidity that you will not consciously be able to register them – or at least not all of them. Some of the images may stand out. Also, we have had cases of individuals recalling at a later date images they were not consciously aware of seeing at the time of testing. I have even heard reports of some of the images entering a subject's subconscious, in such a way that they later recur in dreams. Obviously this is limited to non-psychopathic subjects, as psychopaths typically do not dream.'

'Whoah! Hang on! What did you just say? There was a lot there to process? Am I going to be dreaming about this?'

'There have been one or two cases reported – hearsay, to be honest – of the material resurfacing in dreams. The indications are it is the exception rather than the rule.'

'But if people aren't aware what the images are at the time they're shown them, they won't know if they're dreaming about them?'

'That's a fair point. Are you still willing to proceed?'

'I guess so. I mean, my dreams are weird enough as it is. I don't suppose this can make that much difference. Oh, and the other thing you said . . . about psychopaths not dreaming? Is that true?'

'Anecdotally. But not conclusively. We can never know. Ultimately, psychopaths are notorious liars. We can never really be sure what they are experiencing subjectively. Certainly we can't take their word for anything.'

'Well, I mustn't be a psychopath. Because I dream.'

'I have to point out that if you were a psychopath, that's exactly what you would say. We'll soon know for sure.'

Arbus clipped the main device into the VR frame and fitted it around Krystie's head so that it covered her eyes.

'What do the images consist of? Can you tell me that?'

'I'm afraid I can't. For one thing it would invalidate the test. For another, it's highly confidential and commercially sensitive material. The precise content of the images is crucially important to the functioning of the Arbus-Lubany machine. We have invested considerable time and money in researching and producing them. I'm not about to hand them over to any potential competitors who might be watching.'

'Can't you give me a rough idea?'

'Some of them are emotionally neutral images. Inanimate objects photographed in a bland way. Some are emotionally positive images. Or certainly would be perceived as emotionally positive by NP subjects.'

'Kittens, you mean?'

'I cannot confirm or deny the inclusion of kittens. But kittens would be appropriate subjects for this category of image.'

'I am sensing that there is a third category?'

'Yes, what we might describe as emotionally negative images.'

'Such as?'

'I can't give any specific details. However, suffice it to say that they are the type of imagery that many police officers here today will be exposed to in the course of their duties.'

'Atrocities? Crime scene shots?'

'I can't comment.'

'And you're proposing that children should be exposed to these images?'

'The exposure is virtually instantaneous and subliminal. They are not conscious of what they are seeing.'

'And yet they may have nightmares about it?'

'As I said before, that's just hearsay. It is perhaps an area for further research. But at the moment, it's not something that concerns me.'

'I'm not sure how reassuring that will be to the parents of children tested.'

Arbus chose not to answer that. He had finished fiddling with the machine and was standing by Krystie waiting for her final consent to activate it. 'So, are we ready?'

'I'm ready when you are.'

'OK.'

'Please keep your eyes open, obviously, for the duration of the test.'

'Oh? That raises an interesting point. What happens in the case of non-cooperation? I mean, if I just close my eyes, there's nothing you can do about it?'

'Ophthalmic specula are included in the kit, if necessary.'

'Ophthalmic what?'

'Clamps for forcing the eyes to remain open.'

'Isn't that a little brutal? I mean, again, I'm thinking of the children you propose testing.'

'I don't think it will be necessary for most children. I am confident they will be induced to cooperate by more pleasant means. For instance, the promise of treats. In adults, one could hold out the possibility of an automatic P score for anyone not complying. That is to say, refusal to cooperate will be taken as proof in itself of a psychopathic personality. After all, an NP has no reason not to go along with it.'

'There's a human rights minefield here, Doctor. Surely you can see that?'

'What you have to remember is why we're doing this. Or why we would be doing it. It's for the greater good of society. To preserve, ultimately, the cohesion of society by identifying and neutralizing individuals who threaten it. The argument can be made that that greater good trumps the rights of the individual. Especially if that individual is a psychopath. Any rational, non-psychopathic person would comply, in order to avoid the P label.'

'Perhaps you should have another designation? R – for refusal maybe? I mean I don't think you can label someone a psychopath simply for refusing to take the test. If that were the case, then our friend here is, on your terms, a psychopath.'

'We did consider something like that. However, allowing subjects that option effectively undermines the validity of the test. I mean, what would happen if everyone refused?'

'Well, that's still a possibility. You might call it the Spartacus option.'

'I think most sane people will accept that it is in the broader interests of society as a whole to weed out these individuals. We do foresee some violent resistance to testing. Which is why the kit also includes a tranquillizer pen. Fortunately, the test may also be administered when the subject is unconscious – provided the eyelids are prised open. It can even be administered to tasered subjects. But really, I believe that the carrot is always better than the stick. So positive inducements can be offered too. Rewards for compli- ance – a reduction in sentence in the case of offenders, for example. And we shouldn't rule out a further possibility.'

'Which is?'

'I'm afraid I can't say at this point in time. For this alternative to work, it's important that details of it are not leaked to the public. We have to keep our powder dry, as it were.'

'Intriguing. But also rather alarming. The conspiracy theorists will have a field day with that, I'm sure!'

'Naturally, I would rather everything was done openly and without recourse to, uh, withholding information. That's always the better way. However, I can assure you that if my proposals are adopted they will be done so on a firm legal basis. Moreover, the ethical argument is incontestable, given the scale and severity of what we are up against. The ends will always justify the means. Now, if you're you ready to continue?'

Krystie nodded. The device attached to her face bobbed solemnly.

'OK,' said Arbus. He pointed a remote at the headset and made a show of activating it.

'Oh . . . wow . . . I . . . interesting . . . It's . . . I can't . . . lots of images flashing by in front of me . . . a weird sensation . . . I feel like I'm falling into something . . . falling forwards into . . . whatever . . . But then . . . it changes . . . But I still have this sensation of falling forwards . . . I feel slightly nauseous now . . . like I'm on some kind of fairground ride. This must be what vertigo feels like, I guess. I've never suffered from vertigo, but I imagine it's something like this. It's kind of intense. A little claustrophobic. Now and then I think I can identify something that's flashed before me. But the impression doesn't last. It's a little like dreaming. Like a thousand dreams injected at high speed into my mind. There's the sense that the images are moving, but I can't even tell you if there are people in the images or just objects. Every now and then I feel a kind of . . . sadness, I think, is the best word. And then . . . Ooh. It's over. Is it over?'

'Yes.'

'How did I do?'

Arbus removed the frame from her head and detached the unit which now showed a black screen. He swiped and his finger tapped away for a few moments. Then held the screen towards Krystie for her to see.

'Thank God for that!'

Arbus now showed the result to the room.

NP.

Krystie was grinning with excitement and relief. Her face flushed becomingly. 'Of course, I never had any doubt.'

I sat patiently waiting for it. And then it came. The quick, sly, inviting glance in my direction.

I am not one to let such an opportunity pass me by.

Which is how I came to find myself with Krystie Rothwell in one of the lifts at the Bournemouth Metropole. We were on our way up to her room. She was holding it in, maintaining the professional front, the ice-maiden mask, if you like. She gave me a brisk *Sorry* as she busied herself consulting her MindPhone, dealing with calls and MindMessages.

I had to admit, the more I saw of this woman, the more I liked her. I particularly appreciated her first words to me after the event broke up. I'll hold my hands up, I was deliberately hovering as my fellow Fed reps filed out, holding my ground as I waited for her to wrap up and shake off Arbus. Why shouldn't I? I'd seen the signs. There was a definite chance I could convert those flirty little looks into something more substantial. I was not disappointed. As she drew level with me, she looked me in the eye and said, 'I just want to get one thing straight – I won't fuck in a store cupboard.'

It's good to have these things clarified upfront. Then everyone knows where they stand. Very grown-up.

So we got a taxi and headed back to her hotel. There was none of the usual your-place-or-mine wrangling. She needed to get back to her room to prepare for her next gig. So that was where we went. And frankly I didn't give a shit where we did it. Obviously.

She was a busy girl. On a tight schedule. There wasn't much slack for recreational activities. That was no reason to go without, though. It was just a question of efficient time management. For all I know, what she was actually doing on her phone was entering a new event in her calendar: *17.30 to 18.00, fuck some random police bod*. I had the feeling she wanted to get this wrapped up as soon as possible.

Anyways, I could tell she was used to getting what she wanted, and for some reason she wanted me. Who am I to deny her?

We stood next to each other in the lift, staring straight ahead, not speaking. There were a few other bodies in with us. I expect she was worried about being snapped in a compromising position. So like I say, she gave nothing away. Looking at us, you wouldn't have guessed we were together.

We both had our phones out by now. I mean, I wasn't going to stand there like a lemon waiting for her to pay me some attention. Occasionally there was the slightest, lightest bit of contact between us. Shoulder leaning into shoulder. Hand brushing hand. That shock of electricity passing between the surfaces of our skin, a promise of what was to come. We were moving imperceptibly closer to each other as we ascended.

One by one the other people got off at their floors, until we were the only ones left. I risked a palm to tentatively explore the curve of her arse. Sort of knocking on the door. Saying hello. Gently teasing a hand-edge down into the disappearingly glorious gulf at the apex of her legs. Take it as a declaration of intent.

I was rewarded with a little appreciative murmur.

I swear her hand was shaking as she swiped her key card.

Once the door was closed behind us she was clawing at my clothes and steering me towards the bed. Her hand groped appreciatively at my rigid cock, deftly untrousering me to let it out.

The sex was just the way I like it. Fast, furious and fucking

amazing. Even if I do say so myself. Start hard. Stay hard. That's
my motto. As for the speed, like I said, she was a busy girl. She
didn't mess about. I would even say she seemed to have an aversion to foreplay, guiding me into her from the get-go.

I could tell she worked out. Good body. I suppose you have
to when you're on the screens. And she was pretty handy at the
old pelvic gyrations. Taking control of her own gratification. I
liked that. Working hard at it. Single-minded. Determined. I could
see how she had managed to get on so well in the cutthroat world
of the media.

Me, I was just there to provide the means. Which was fine by
me. It's not like I didn't get anything out of it. But I can honestly
say it was the most illusion-free sex I'd ever had. On both sides,
I mean. There have never been any illusions on my side.

I kind of had the feeling it was every man for himself. In a
weird way, I'd say she fucked like a man. Not that I've ever
fucked or been fucked by another man, but you know what I
mean. It's all about running the race. Getting to the end. Yeah,
you want her to have a good time too, but that's just because it
makes you feel more like a man – *the* man.

Everybody's happy. Win-win. You know what I'm saying. But
if it came down to it, her or you, you'd take you every time.

Plus, it's a power thing. They owe you. There's more chance
of them coming back for more. Which means you've got the
whip hand. You can end it when you want to.

I had a feeling with Krystie that was never going to be a
problem. She didn't strike me as the clingy type.

For the record, I don't think she gave a fuck about me either,
to be honest. Why should she? I could look after myself.

One thing I will say for her, she committed to it. And when
it came, the big O, she gave herself to it wholeheartedly, and
wholefuckingbodily too. Half of me wanted to step back and
admire from a distance. The other half wanted to get in there
with the action. Fuck it, it was a privilege to be involved in that
spectacular undoing of a human being. The high-pitched rhythmic
whimpering building to a guttural grunt worthy of a female tennis
champion. The biting – I definitely wouldn't have missed the
biting – the swearing, the eyes closed tight on inward concentration, the welcoming moan dissolving into appreciative sobbing.
The deep gasping for air after.

It was all pretty much as I'd called it.

Afterwards, she said: 'I don't know your name.'

It was just an observation. Factual. No judgement, shame or surprise shaded in. Knowing my name had not been a priority. I must have done something to earn the question.

I reached over the edge of the bed to retrieve my jacket. Fished out a card and handed it to her.

She smiled at that. 'Thank you.'

She went through the motions of snuggling up to me but I know she was just being polite. I guess she didn't want to talk about us – there was no 'us' to talk about – so brought it back to the afternoon's events. 'What do you really think about Dr Arbus and his machine?'

'I think you've got balls of steel, letting him do that test on you, there in front of everybody.'

'I was pretty confident it would be OK.'

'I can tell you were. But there must have been a moment when you wondered, fuck, what if it goes the wrong way?'

She gave a little shrug. 'Maybe it's better to know. If you are one.' She lifted herself up to look at me questioningly.

'Do you want me to be a psychopath? Is that what this is all about? You wanted a bit of psycho action? All the girls like a bad boy, deep down.'

She smiled. 'It's weird. That test. I think it has a side-effect he didn't mention.'

'Which is?'

One of her eyebrows flicked up suggestively. She gave an almost bashful grin.

'That's probably just you. I hope to fuck it is. I would hate to have holding cells full of horny psychopaths. We don't have the resources to deal with that.'

She let out a deep, throaty, gurgling laugh. Possibly the dirtiest laugh I had ever heard.

It turned out Dr Arbus was staying in the same hotel as me, the Bournemouth Nightjar. I spotted him in the bar later, drinking on his own, around the midnight hour. As I said before, you couldn't miss him. He was a big melting slump on a barstool.

'Dr Arbus, isn't it?'

He looked up at me from his slouch and blinked. His

myopic focused look had lost its focus. Came across as simply
hostile, as if he resented the intrusion. Though all I was
intruding on was his solitude. He neither confirmed nor denied
his identity.

'I caught you at the conference today. In fact, I saw both your
events.'

He shrugged. It seemed he was done with the salesman
demeanour.

'Can I get you a drink?'

'I was just about to retire. For the night.'

'One for the road? Maybe a short? Whisky? I believe they
have some half-decent single malts here.'

He peered over at the optics behind the bar. 'Very well.
Glenfiddich. With ice. Better make it a double. How did you
know I'm a single-malt man?'

'It's my job to read people. I'm a detective.'

'Of course you are.'

I caught the bartender's eye and ordered two doubles. When
the drinks came he took his without a thank you. He didn't even
raise the glass for a toast of acknowledgement.

'For instance, I reckon I can spot a psychopath without the
help of your machine.'

'Is that so?'

'I believe so, yes. You can tell by their eyes. There's nothing
there.'

'This is true. But in any individual case, it is open to dispute.
It's just your hunch. A gut feeling. It will never have any
evidentiary force. Plus we can't roll out your gut nationwide.
So to speak. Whereas the results with the Arbus-Lubany machine
are replicable and scalable. And objectively indisputable.'

'Ever tested yourself?'

'I beg your pardon?'

'I just wondered if you'd ever tried the test out on yourself.'

'No. Obviously not. Why would I?'

I let that one go.

'It doesn't worry you that you could label some young children
as psychopaths who might go on to never break a single law in
the whole of their lives?'

'That just isn't going to happen. And if it does, I consider it
a price worth paying.'

I had to smile at that.

'Something funny?'

'Not at all. Don't get me wrong, Doc, I'm with you on this one. If what you say is true and the numbers of these psychos is on the up, then that's only going to make my job, and the jobs of my colleagues, even more difficult. We've got to do whatever we can. And any help you can offer us is welcome. I just want to be sure, before I go back to my chief constable, that this thing actually works, that's all.'

He looked at me a little differently then. As if maybe I was worth the time of day after all. 'It works, Inspector . . .?' He held out his hand.

I took it. I'm not a complete twat. Whatever else I may be. 'Parfett. Glen Parfett. And how did you know I'm an Inspector?'

'I guess I'm a good reader of people too. Besides, if I'd pitched it any lower I would have insulted you.'

He was making an effort now. He even got the next round in, signalling wordlessly at our glasses to the barman.

'It works, believe me. And I can produce more than enough research to prove it. Of course, what we really need to happen is for the government to introduce legislation to enable us to implement a programme of monitoring and . . .'

'Sterilization?'

'Exactly. So if you have any influence with the political leadership of the Police Federation . . .? It would be a powerful lobby to have on our side.'

'The leadership listens to its members.'

'That's the impression I got.'

'I take it you've had a meeting with Charles Woodbridge?'

'Your esteemed Chair? Yes.'

'Was he receptive?'

'He made the right noises. There'll be a consultation with members. So . . .'

'I'll do what I can. To be honest, you're pushing against an open door, if the colleagues I've spoken to tonight are anything to go by. Everyone wants this. Your machines. In fact, there's a worry that sterilization isn't enough. Too long to wait before we see any effect. The feeling is we'd like to go further.'

'Termination?'

I let my right eyebrow flick up in response. He could interpret that however liked. It was the only answer he was going to get out of me. 'Do you think there may be a possibility that the psychos may end up . . . in charge?'

'I think there's a distinct possibility that they already are.'

'So it may be too late? They'll never allow this.'

'It is my belief that the elite psychopaths wish to maintain order and the rule of law. I'm talking about those in government and those running multinational corporations. It's not in their interests for society to fall apart. But there is a distinct separation in their minds between legality and morality. The latter doesn't concern them at all. The former they are willing to use as a fig leaf for whatever activity is in their own interests. They are capable of changing the law to include anything that suits their ends. More than anything else, they want an infantalized, anaesthetized and utterly compliant populace that is so disengaged from the political process that it leaves them free to do what they want, which includes plundering the economy to line their own pockets. However, the challenge for them is that, as the percentage of psychopaths in the general population rises, well, that has an impact on the electorate. It may become politically expedient for unscrupulous – for which read psychopathic – politicians to actively court the psychopath vote. Fortunately we're not at that point yet. However, there are those among our present incumbents who are perfectly capable of going on record as, say, condemning all illegal immigrants as rapists and drug dealers, then half an hour later raping an underage street girl in a coke-fuelled orgy. They won't even see it as hypocrisy. So, publicly, they may well back the introduction of the machines, as they'll want to be seen as strongly pro-law and order.'

'And privately?'

'Privately they may well do everything they can to subvert it. They are, to be quite honest with you, utter cunts.'

The word both shocked and delighted me.

'And how many psychopaths do you think are in the current cabinet?'

'I haven't had the opportunity of testing them, so I couldn't possibly say.'

'What about Jackson?'
'Oh, the Prime Minister is almost certainly a psychopath.'
I had to laugh at that.

LEVEL TWO, CONTINUED

W hile still in the secure unit, the player's game persona will be subjected to various therapeutic techniques. In keeping with the game plan outlined previously – that is to say, the strategy of manipulating psychiatric professionals by seeming to cooperate with treatment – the protagonist will go along with all the therapies offered. At the same time, they must find a way to subvert and resist the possibility of a cure, or more accurately medical neutralization. (There is no cure for psychopathy in real life – but should we posit a cure for the sake of the game?)

The player's goal at this level is always to escape or effect release from the secure unit.

From the player's point of view, none of this is easy, but that's the challenge! Obviously we need to think through the detail here. Possibly this could involve not taking medication that is offered to them (concealing under the tongue and spitting out), or lying prodigiously in any therapeutic sessions, whether in a group or one-to-one.

That should be easy enough to do, unless hypnosis is involved. So yes, let's have the protagonists hypnotized. Under hypnosis, the character will regress to an earlier stage in their development. The game becomes their experiences under regression. They are a child again. The regressive experience offers another opportunity for gameplay, as the player is free to control his/her character in the new setting. (Though the inbuilt tendencies and traits associated with their dialled-up condition or disorder will exercise some kind of a pull, loading in impulses and behaviours that the player either has to resist or give into. The player is never totally in control.)

Suffice it to say, there will be siblings, there will be family pets, there will be sharp household objects that can be utilized as weapons.

How the player reacts in these regressive episodes will have a bearing on the fully developed personality of their character

in realtime play. That is to say, the formation of the game character is dynamic.

We can safely predict, however, knowing our fans as we do,
that most of them will engage in junior psychopathic serial killer
behaviour when under regression. If there is a kitten, or a gerbil,
or a baby brother, the question is not whether it will be killed,
but how. Will it be strangled? Or given broken glass to eat? Or
tied to a firework or two? These are all options that are open
to the player. Also, what will become of the animal corpse
afterwards? Will it simply be buried? Or skinned? Or eaten?

We should consult with a psychologist to explore the ramifica-
tions of these early choices in the mature psychopath. The more
authentic and plausible the pathological progression, the more fun
the game will be.

Development notes for PSYCHOTOPIA VR game.
*Internal Alpha Games document. Not for release. For approved
circulation only.*

EIGHT

He gave her a desk just outside his office so he could look at her whenever he wanted. He was aware of her expectant glances cast occasionally, tentatively, nervously, hopefully, despairingly, in his direction. But did not return them. Naturally. Naturally too, he waited until she had given up all hope, and sat with her head hanging forlornly over her *Let the Alpha Games Begin* booklet, convinced that he would never acknowledge her presence, before looming over her when she least expected it.

'How are you settling in?'

'Oh, err, I, sorry . . . I was just . . .'

He made the noise of an electric buzzer. 'Remember what we said about the sorry word?'

'Oh . . . yes. Sorry.' She winced apologetically.

'*No!* I'm going to have to take you in hand! Don't you remember our little mantra?'

'Oh . . . yes.'

'I hope you said it this morning?'

'I . . .?'

'I am a strong and confident woman?'

She laughed. It must have been pretty funny, he guessed, hearing him say that.

'I forgot?'

He shook his head in mock rebuke. 'Everything working OK? Your MindBook configured? You've found the network?'

'I guess so?'

'If you're wondering, the IT department is . . .' He gestured all around. 'Everywhere. You've fallen into a den of geeks. If you need tech support, just ask anyone. Except for Mario. Mario doesn't know shit about shit.'

Mario was his PA. Who was sitting right next to Sally. There was no doubt that he heard. 'Mario is just here to make up our diversity quota. So that we hire the politically correct number of gay fuckwits.'

Of course, he was saying this not so much to belittle Mario as to make Sally complicit in the belittling. This was her first day in a new job. She was at her most vulnerable. He was her boss. She wanted him to like her. It was more than that. A moment ago, she had been desperate for him to just *see* her. So she was in the mode of smiling at everything he said and laughing at all his jokes. If she didn't play along, she'd make an enemy of her boss. But if she did, she'd make an enemy of someone who had just as much power to make her life miserable – her boss's PA. It's what you call a double bind. It can drive people into a mental breakdown trying to navigate their way out of one of those.

At the very least, he expected it to cause her some moments of anguish, perhaps a whole sleepless night of it, when she reviewed her first day later. He'd been led to believe that people can feel pretty bad about stuff like this.

He had, in the past, from time to time, tried to imagine how it must feel when you crave other people's approval. Even harder when you want them to like you.

Neither ever troubled him at all. As far as he was concerned, the only reason for getting people to like you is so you can get them to do what you want.

In his experience it was easy enough to do, if deep down you don't really care one way or the other.

Anyhow, it was clear that her sympathy for the perceived underdog was winning out. The smile froze on her lips and tautened into a wince of pain. She looked for a moment like she was going to cry, then did all she could to avoid looking at him.

'Oh, don't worry about Mario. Like all gays, he can give as good as he gets. Besides, he's into that whole BDSM scene, like a lot of them are. He spends most weekends in a rubber suit with a ball gag in his mouth, locked in a wardrobe. It's actually written into his contract that I have to abuse him. Turns out the rougher I am with him, the more he loves it. That right, Mario?'

'That's right, Oscar.'

'Course, he had to have his rubber outfit made specially. They don't usually do them in children's sizes.'

He had to admit it, Sally really brought out his witty side. Though for one moment, he was a bit worried that he might have gone too far. He knew he had a tendency to get carried away when he was having fun. He prided himself on his self-awareness, particularly of his own faults.

'I love him really. Couldn't manage without him. He knows it. Don't you, Mario dear?'

'Yes, Oscar dear.'

He promised himself that he would get the little fag back for that sarcastic echo some other time.

'So I should take you for a tour later. Introduce you to the team. You'll notice straightaway that most of them are a little spectrum-y. Goes with the territory, I guess. I mean, we do have the best games developers in the country working here. Some of them even manage to pass for normal people. I'll let you work out which ones.'

'Thanks? I think?'

'They're not, as a rule, very good with change. Or women . . . They may actually prefer to behave as if you're not here. Don't take it personally.'

'But there are other women working here? I mean—' She broke off, embarrassed.

'Yes. Of course. We have some women in legal. And marketing. In fact, the head of marketing is a woman. Moni Samir.'

'But you don't have any female developers?'

'We have one or two. We used to have more. But you know what happens.'

'No, what does happen?'

'They leave to have babies. Or something. I don't know. I don't look into it too much.'

'And never come back?'

'Not so far.'

'I wonder why that is?'

'I have no idea? They must prefer the smell of nappies to the hormonal honk of their co-workers?' He had once again fallen back into the habit of mirroring her rising intonation.

'But everyone knows why I'm here, right?'

'Why you're here? Remind me, why are you here?'

'The thing we talked about in the interview?'

'Oh, that. Yes, sure. We should talk about that. Talk to Mario about setting up a meeting? He has control of my diary? Which is why you should always keep on his good side? Too much rising intonation?' He couldn't believe he actually said that, but what the hell. He couldn't resist it. It was funny, though it left Sally looking a bit nonplussed. It got a laugh out of Mario at least. Not that he valued that particularly.

'I'd really like to get started on it as soon as possible?'

'Yes, of course.'

'But I've been invited to a lot of other briefing meetings?'

'We've got a lot going through at the moment.'

'Yes. That's great but . . . I'm just not quite sure how I'm going to schedule in . . .'

'I'm sure you'll find a way, Sally. I have every confidence in you.'

'Well, that's great but . . .'

'You just need to have a bit more confidence in yourself.'

'Well, I think I just need to be sure that you're fully committed to it? To what we talked about? I mean, I have to be honest, it did feel a little bit like . . .'

'Like what?'

'No, well, I'm sure it wasn't . . . but you know . . . I mean, it's great . . . really great. A fantastic opportunity. I'm really grateful.'

'You don't have to be grateful. You've earned this. And, you know, it's not going to be easy. You know the old saying. Be careful what you wish for. This could end up being a case of that.'

'Yeah, yeah, sure . . . But the thing is there was no mention of it in the job description? Or in the contract you sent through. I mean, I thought there might have been something written down? So I know what the job entails? What my targets are and how I will be assessed?'

'I can do that, if you like. If you think it's necessary? I mean, I thought we were on the same wavelength? I thought we understood each other? I thought we shared the same vision?'

'We did. We do.'

'Look, the reason I didn't put anything in writing is because—' He broke off and flashed a wary glance towards Mario. 'Look, why don't we talk about this later? Are you free this evening? For dinner? I would very much like to take you out to dinner. It would be an opportunity to get to know each other better, and we could flesh out how we're going to take this thing forward. We need to get all our ducks in a row before we take it to the board. Believe it or not, this isn't a dictatorship. From time to time, I have to get the other partners to buy into my crazy ideas.'

'And you haven't talked it over with them?'

'In principle, yes. We all agree something needs to be done. The hard part is agreeing precisely what.'

He saw the despondent sag of her shoulders. The disappointment tugging at the corners of her mouth.

'Sally, there is nothing I want more than this. And, generally, I have a habit of getting what I want. You believe that, don't you?'

She gave him her brave-soldier smile. He knew he had her.

He took her to Mother Earth's, the upmarket veggie restaurant in Farringdon. He had the dim impression that she was a vegetarian. Maybe she'd told him, or he'd read it somewhere. Or he just knew. Just by looking at her.

In the cab, he warned her: 'I hope you don't mind. It's a vegetarian restaurant? You can handle that?'

'Yes! Of course! I *am* a vegetarian!'

So, he was right. He pretended to be surprised. 'You are? Me too! Well, sometimes I eat fish. But less and less these days. I try to keep it veggie. It's mainly for environmental reasons with me. You know the arguments, you've seen the films. I did have a vegan phase, but you know what I couldn't do without? It sounds pathetic but milk chocolate.'

'Me too!'

'I know it's more sophisticated to eat dark chocolate. I guess I'm just not all that sophisticated after all. I just like milk chocolate best.'

'Me too! I mean, I don't believe this? I'm exactly the same!'

He had read her like a book. She wanted to save the world, and she'd do it any way she could. As long as it didn't require her to give up chocolate. Of course, as far as he was concerned, the truth was he would eat any part of any animal. But for tonight at least, for Sally, he was going to be a vegetarian.

He could tell she'd never been to a restaurant quite like Mother Earth's before. Two Michelin stars. Immaculate table linen. Real art on the walls. Tables nicely spaced. Waiting staff who look like models or millionaires. Her eyes visibly widened as they went in. He had to admit, that gave him a kick. He liked to give pleasure to people. It placed them ever so slightly in his debt.

It pissed him off, though, the way she kept looking at the guy sitting on the next table to them. Then he worked it out. Guy's face was vaguely familiar. Some B-list celebrity. He wasn't good looking or ripped enough to be an actor, unless he specialized in slightly overweight roles. So probably a MindNet star who'd made a name for himself by sharing the tedious details of his meaningless life with millions of MindLess followers.

He decided to have some fun.

He leaned across and pointed a finger at the sleb. 'I love your work.'

'Thank you.'

'I mean, it's so brave what you do.'

'Thank you.'

'For a guy with such a tiny dick to do porn, it takes a lot of guts. But God knows you've got plenty of that.'

'Fuck you! I'm not a fucking porn star. And I don't have a tiny dick.' The guy had reached full off-the-scale shouty without even realizing it.

'Are you sure?' He made sure to keep his own voice level and polite – and just a little bit sceptical.

'Yes!'

He turned to the MindNetter's friend, a girl who was visually way out of his league. 'It's gay porn. I guess that's why he's denying it.'

That didn't go down well. 'Who the fuck are you? Joker! Fucking joker.' The guy's shouting went so far off the scale it broke the shout-o-meter.

One of the waiters came over and had a quiet word.

'No way! No fucking way! Why the fuck should *I* leave? He fucking started it.'

'All I said was, I love your work.' Ever the reasonable one.

The B-lister's dinner date was on her feet, grabbing her bag and phone. 'Come on, Raj, it's not worth it.'

He could always count on the women to avoid a scene.

'Why did you do that?' said Sally.

'Do what?'

'You know what.'

He gave an excellent impression of an honestly bewildered

man. Then remembered. 'Oh, that! Case of mistaken identity, I guess. I genuinely thought he was a gay porn star with a tiny penis. Little Will is his *nom de guerre*. Is he not?'

'You know very well he isn't.'

'I don't know. Those MindNet celebrities piss me off. I mean what have they ever done? I really would have more respect for him if he *was* a gay porn star with a little dick.'

'Well, I think it was mean, what you did.'

'He was asking for it. The way he was looking at you.'

'He wasn't looking at me.'

'*You* were looking at him.'

'I wasn't. But even if I was, that wasn't a reason to take it out on him. And another, you can't tell me who I can or can't look at.'

'OK, don't get all feminista on me. Look, he was the one who started shouting. He could have just said, "I'm sorry I think you have the wrong person".'

'It's not very sensible, from a PR point of view, to go round making enemies of MindNet stars. They have a lot of influence with gamers. Did you even know who he is? He's Raj Sandeep. A big game reviewer. He can make or break a game. If he recognized you . . .'

'He didn't recognize me. I've made a point of keeping a low profile with the public. I'm a backroom boffin. Nobody knows my face. That's the way I like it.'

She stared at him for a few long minutes. 'I've got a feeling I know you.'

'Duh, yeah? I'm your boss.'

'No, I mean from somewhere else. I can't help feeling we've met before.'

'Very probably. At some gaming convention or other. I do panels. You probably saw me speak at one.'

'I thought you like to keep a low profile.'

'I make a point of only appearing on panels that nobody comes to.'

She couldn't help laughing at that. He'd won her back.

Though he came close to throwing it away immediately. 'I love it when you laugh. It's like I can feel your throat vibrate inside me. In my loins. It's the most sexually arousing sound in the universe.'

'What the fuck did you just say?' Sally was trying to hold on to her outrage, but laughing. The laughing showed he was winning.

'I said I love the food here. I love the taste of it in my mouth. It's the most exciting vegetarian food in London.'

'Yes. OK. That's what you said.'

He tilted his head to one side and gave her a bland, innocent face.

He ordered for her. Of course he did. 'It's all good,' he told her. 'But this is the best. Trust me.'

The starters arrived. A salad of soya curd, beetroot and nasturtium. She had to agree he had chosen well. 'It's amazing. I've never tasted anything like this.'

'I would be disappointed if you had.'

She looked down and smiled, flattered, he didn't doubt, by his attention.

'I don't usually do this.'

'Eat nasturtium petals?'

'No. Go out for dinner. Like this. With . . .'

'Careful.'

'My boss.'

'I'm not your boss here. Now. We're just two people having dinner together. Two friends. I hope.'

She gave a little shrug. 'I guess. Are these really nasturtium petals?'

'That's what it said.'

'They're very strong. Peppery.'

'Do you hate them?' He made a show of being devastated.

'I love them!'

'Thank God!'

They laughed. And then, for a moment, it seemed like she was going to cry. 'If . . . I . . . *Oh!*' Her face was an exquisite picture of anguish.

'Sally?'

'This is all happening so quickly!'

'Is it? Or is it just happening? You know? At the speed it's supposed to happen?'

'What am I even doing here?'

'Is there someone else?'

'No . . . I . . . I've just come out of a long-term relationship.

I'm not ready for . . . I don't think I'm ready for this. Whatever *this* is.'

'This is just dinner. Just two people. Colleagues. If you like. If that's less problematic for you. You know, than friends. Getting to know each other better. And besides, I've got an idea for a new game I wanted to bounce off you. It came to me just then when that guy was shouting at me. I mean, I seriously was a little bit worried that he was going to pull out a shooter or something. I mean, I looked in his eyes. I could see it.'

'See what?'

'Psycho. The guy's a psycho. So my idea, it's a little sketchy at the moment. But hear me out. Let's brainstorm it together. My idea is a POV role-player game about a psychopath. Maybe he looks like that guy? Or you have this mask that is his face. And when you put it on, you become a psychopath. There are things you can only do while wearing the mask. It kind of liberates the player. It's a licence to . . . behave in a psychotic way. I know there was a film like that way back, but this is different. The mask isn't a mask, it's actually his face. The face of a psychopath who you have killed and whose power, and negative life force, you take on when you wear the skin of his face as a mask.'

'And this is fun – why?'

'Oh, it's fun because it's fun to be a psycho. I imagine. I think it should be very dark. An eighteen.'

'What happened to changing the world?'

'But redemptive. Dark and redemptive. Could you architect a dark and redemptive player experience?'

'I don't know . . . I mean, are you even serious? I can't tell. I don't think he'd be very happy about us using his face.'

'Why not? We're Alpha Games. The fucking number one games producer in the world. He should be honoured.'

'Would you pay him?'

'We could pay him. If legal thought it was necessary.'

'I can't make you out,' said Sally.

He gave a *who-me?* shrug.

'Why do you play all these games?'

'I like to make things interesting. Fun.'

'But it's kind of unsettling . . . for other people?'

'Is it?'

'Yes.'

'I think it's good to be unsettled now and then. Settled is . . . well, settled is dead. If you're unsettled you know you're alive. You are alive, aren't you, Sally?'

'Yes, Oscar. I am. I'm pretty sure I'm alive.'

'Good. That's all I want to hear. I don't want any dead people working for me.'

'OK? I think . . .?'

The main course arrived. Fried porridge, wild garlic and broad beans, dressed with a courgette flower. Again, they were having the same.

When she pointed this out, he explained it to her like this: 'If I know what the best thing on the menu is, why would I let you order something not as good?'

'What if I don't like the same things as you do?'

'You have to trust me. You just have to trust me.'

'You keep saying that? And to be honest, the more you say it . . .?'

'The more you trust me.'

'I wasn't actually going to say that. The truth is I don't really know you. I mean, I know you're my boss. And I've heard of you, of course. Read about you. But I don't really know *you*, who you are, do I? The same way you don't know me?'

'I hear what you're saying. Can we ever really know another person?'

'That wasn't really what I meant? But, yeah, I guess that's true. Scary thought.'

'What do you want to know about me? Ask me anything.'

'I guess, where are you from? Your family? That sort of thing?'

'Hertfordshire.'

'Where in Hertfordshire?'

'North Hertfordshire.'

'Where in north Hertfordshire?'

'Letchworth Garden City.'

'I honestly don't know whether to believe you or not?'

'Why would I lie about a thing like that?'

'I don't know. Because it seems to be like a mask you're hiding behind, all this game-playing. Messing with my head. It's like a tactic to keep the real you hidden from me.'

'Quite the trick cyclist, aren't you?'

'I like to work people out. Find out what makes them tick.

Get under their skin. I think that's what makes me good at my job.' She blushed again, in that startled-squid way of hers, then said, 'Sorry.'

'For what?'

'Boasting.'

'It's not boasting if it's true.'

'Well, *I* think it's true. But I don't want to . . . come over like a dick.'

'You could never do that, Sally.'

'It doesn't come naturally to me, bigging myself up. But when I look at some of the men I've worked with who don't seem to have any problem, you know, telling people how great they are . . . But honestly, when you work with them, some of them . . .'

'They're shit?'

'They're not as good as they think they are or say they are. But that's what people take notice of.'

'Exactly. That's why I wanted you on my team. Because I know you're better than the whole lot of them put together.'

'But how do you know that? I haven't done anything yet?'

'I just know. I can tell. It's gonna be great. It's gonna be awesome. You're gonna be awesome.'

She looked at him like she might say something. But in the end she just smiled and shook her head and kept whatever she was thinking to herself.

PROGRESSING FROM LEVEL TWO

At this stage of the game, the player's objective is to escape from the secure unit to the outside world. There are several means of achieving this available to them.

EITHER:

1. The player must convince the psychiatrists and other medical staff that they present no danger to others – either because they have been cured of what ails them or because they were wrongly incarcerated in the secure unit in the first place. This would be fairly straightforward if the player did not have to contend with the strong (not to say uncontrollable!) psychopathic urges programmed into the game protagonist.

OR:

2. Consider the possibility of a do-gooder civil rights-type character who lobbies on behalf of the protagonist. How does the player access this character? They are visitors to the unit. The player encounters them. Convinces them that a massive injustice has been perpetrated – that they (i.e. the psychopath) are the victim. Player has to decide how to manipulate them – and be careful not to kill them!

OR:

3. The protagonist kills their way out. For example, they kill and steal the face off the do-gooder civil rights-type who came to help them. The stolen face is how they manage to get out. Remember, however, that the player is not provided with any firepower. And therefore has to either manufacture or purloin potential weaponry. The protagonist must work themselves into a position of trust, working in the kitchen perhaps, or an engineering workshop, or a laundry detail.

OR:

4. There is some kind of route out through the regression therapy sessions already discussed. The experiences unlocked by regression create an alternative reality – the protagonist finds a door or window or portal of some kind in the flashback sequence – a symbolic way through that actually results in them being physically transported out of the secure unit.

OR:

5. There is a game cheat. A completely random way of getting out – a development of the spider storyline. The player needs to keep the spider alive. The spider is the protagonist's only true friend. What does the spider do? How does the spider help now? Here's a thought. The spider continues weaving a web – naturally, that's what spiders do. Twisted and weird as the web is, it is still moderately effective at catching flies. These are the spider's gifts for the protagonist. So the protagonist naturally is grateful and eats the flies that the spider has caught. This is the cheat. If the protagonist eats enough of the flies, the cell door springs open and they are able to walk out of the secure unit without being challenged. We could leak a hint on gamer forums. But we don't want to make it too easy for them! The fans don't like it when we make it too easy.

Development notes for PSYCHOTOPIA VR game.
Internal Alpha Games document. Not for release. For approved circulation only.

NINE

I t was a couple of years after that interesting Fed conference when – well, I won't say all hell broke loose, but a small part of it leeched out and spread itself across my little corner of the world. Of course, it didn't happen overnight. We had been building to it.

PGD was a thing now. The NewsNet was full of it. PGD here, PGD there, PGD every fucking where. It wasn't just happening on our watch. It was all over the country. In fact, it was global.

The government was calling COBRA meetings virtually daily. World leaders were convening special summits to discuss the spread of disorder. They were all putting their heads together and coming up with nothing.

The time was surely right for Dr Arbus to step forward. But weirdly, I hadn't heard any more talk of him and his machines since the conference. Maybe some problem with the technology had come to light. Either that or the human rights issues Krystie had raised turned out to be a major stumbling block. Mind you, the powers that be were getting pretty desperate. (So far, no politician had openly declared themselves of the P tendency. No doubt they were all watching to see which way things were going to go.) I think they would have clutched at any straw available and fuck the consequences. There were more important things at stake than psycho rights.

People were stockpiling tinned goods and bottled water. Public services were falling apart. Except for the police, of course. We were soldiering on. (Ha ha. Hollow laugh. That was the official line. Don't forget, I was on the inside. I could see what was really going on.)

Even some private sector companies were feeling the attitudinal shift, let's call it. It's very difficult to motivate your average psychopath to stick to the old nine-to-five routine. It was getting to the point where there were enough psychopaths in the workforce to really fuck things up. Talk about a spanner in the works. That's nothing compared to a psychopath in the open-plan.

The more imaginative companies were trying to come up with innovative work-arounds. Flexible working practices. In the hope of . . . well, do you know, I'm not really sure in the hope of what . . . Maybe in the hope that if you are nice to people they will be nice to you back. A basic misunderstanding of the psychopathic MO.

You cannot negotiate with a psychopath.

People were very reluctant to use the P word. Not openly; not if it was someone you knew. I mean, we all talked about PGD but I don't think a lot of people knew what it meant. They hadn't worked out that the P stood for Psychopath. I heard it said that it stood for Panic. Panic Generated Disorder. All the erratic behaviour was being blamed on the stress of living in such difficult times, you see. The old social bonds were loosening. Families, neighbourhoods, communities, religion, class, culture, business, even country – the old certainties were letting us all down.

I have to say, those things had never meant that much to me in the first place. Which meant maybe that I was better prepared than most for the way things were shaping up.

People were cast adrift. Forced to rely on themselves. And generally not coping very well.

So it wasn't called psychopathy. It was called the New Individualism. Every fucker for himself, in other words.

PGD. To be honest, you might as well say the P stood for People.

I heard of perfectly decent middle-class families in suburban neighbourhoods shopping for guns and ammo. Everyone who could was installing panic rooms. One guy we pulled in had a cache of weaponry in his cellar, specially reinforced for the purpose. He had a theory that this was going to become some kind of currency. He paid the workmen in Kalashnikovs, which is a dangerous thing to do if you think about it. The surprising thing was the guy with the cellar turned out to be some kind of economics professor and government adviser. So maybe he knew what he was doing after all.

One thing he had right: the pound was in free fall. Correction. Every currency in the world was losing its value against . . . against what? That was the point. I could say gold. But people didn't give a shit about gold any more. The only things they seemed to value were alcohol and drugs – and prostitutes, of course. The younger, the more valuable. So maybe your future currency was going to be twelve-year-old virgins? We weren't there yet but I could see it coming. In the meantime, more and more people were switching to MindCoin.

People called me a doom merchant and scaremonger when I said stuff like that. 'It'll never happen,' they said. 'The government will sort it out. They'll send in the army if necessary. If the police aren't up to the job.'

I'm paraphrasing, of course. There wasn't a whole chorus of people talking shit at me with one voice. But I heard that kind of thing a lot. Surprisingly even from some of my colleagues in the force.

Some people still kept the faith. The older people. Hung on to their belief in money, for example. But what's the point of money when theft becomes a viable consumer option?

But, yeah, as far as I could see, Arbus had dropped off the radar completely. Maybe he was playing the long game. Waiting for things to really turn to shit before he offered himself as the saviour. The more desperate the authorities were, the more likely they'd be to welcome him with open arms. If so, I had to hand it to him. That was a pretty cool calculation to make. You might even call it cynical. The sort of thing a true psychopath would do.

Of course, there was another possibility. Things were happening behind the scenes. The authorities and Arbus had already got a plan in place. They were both biding their time, waiting for the shitstorm to really set in before they unleashed the machines on a grateful and unsuspecting public. Which meant it wasn't Arbus who was the cynical psychopath in that relationship.

I had been co-opted into a new force-wide anti-PGD unit, working out of Reading. It was a joke really. I mean, we were a team of six officers for the whole of the Thames Valley area. I was the de facto lead. The whole thing had been set up just so the police commissioner could say he was doing something about PGD. Not to actually do anything about it. If you understood that – that basically nothing was expected of you – you were fine. Naturally we had to work with the local bobbies, who were the ones on the frontline, if you like. Our role was advisory. Basically, we'd hot-tyre it over to a borough where something bizarre and destructive had gone off to basically say, 'Yeah, that looks like the work of a psycho.' Which the locals pretty much knew already.

We had some basic psych training. A three-day course on 'Identifying and Neutralizing Psychopath-Generated Disorder (PGD)'. I love those three-day courses. They make everything seem so easy and manageable. I mean, how big can this problem be if you can learn everything you need to know about it in three days? They give you this big fat comb-bound document to take away. I think the idea is if you see a genuine psychopath you're meant to whack them around the head with it.

Yeah, it all makes perfect sense when you're on the course. They show you these MindPoint presentations with slides full of bullet point lists headed things like 'WHAT TO LOOK OUT FOR', 'IDENTIFYING JUVENILE PSYCHOPATHS', 'EXAMPLES OF PGD'. They play you some clips of psychos talking, like the ones Arbus had. So that if you ever meet someone who says exactly the same thing, you'll know you've got a psycho on your hands. And you get those coffee breaks with biscuits. And a choice of sandwiches for lunch, including little tiny wraps you can eat in one mouthful. Everything seems so containable. And reasonable. Nobody panics.

It's only when you get out there on the street, face-to-face with some guy who may or may not be a P. May or may not be the one bundling schoolgirls into the back of his van for purposes that you really don't want me to go into. Then suddenly everything you learned on your three-day course goes out of your head. Except maybe how good those tiny wraps tasted. Duck with hoisin sauce if I remember rightly.

So you fall back on your tried and trusted police instincts. Something doesn't look – or smell – quite right. I mean, what's with the upside-down sun visor? Probably is a psycho.

They partnered me with this Asian Muslim guy, Rashid Ali. The joke went around that they'd teamed up a psychopath and a terrorist. Using a process of elimination, I guess that made me the psychopath. I don't know where people get these ideas from, I'm telling you. I admit, I have an unusual sense of humour, which my colleagues don't always get. But can I help it if they're stupid?

You may not believe me, but I liked Rashid. He was actually more like an accountant than a terrorist. I think he had actually studied accountancy at university, or something. That's what he told me anyhow. He may have been lying, of course.

'Why the fuck did you study that?' I once asked him.

'You never know when it might come in useful.'

In that one sentence you have everything that I liked about him. I mean, people used to say that they could never tell whether I was joking or not. Rashid was the same. My own view was that he had ambitions. I reckoned he wanted to be the country's first Muslim chief constable. Running a force is a lot like running a business these days, so some accountancy expertise was never going to go amiss.

So back to the typical day.

We got this PolNet alert in of a suspected PGD incident in Milton Keynes. Some nut job had pushed a cyclist off his bike on Tongwell Street just north of the Brinklow Roundabout. The cyclist worked for one of those takeaway food delivery firms, *Veloci-fed* – you've probably seen their livery. The riders dress in brightly coloured lycra racing kit like they're on the track in some velodrome, except they have these big square boxes on their backs. Their USP is speed. The bikes are aero-dynamically designed with lightweight frames and special wheels. It's a bit of a gimmick, because honestly how much time can you save around town? I tried them once. Waste of money, if you ask me.

According to the cyclist's statement, he had no idea who the guy who pushed him off was, or why he'd done it. He was rattling along the road at his usual high speed, you know, minding his own business, when he felt this force hit him from one side. He went down, *wham!* Luckily, the driver of the car behind him saw what happened and managed to brake in time and there was nothing coming on the outside of him. It's a dual carriageway there, of course, so there was never any danger of him going into oncoming traffic.

Still the cyclist was pretty badly shaken up, lots of scratches and bruises, his lycra ripped to shreds, but nothing life-threatening.

When he looked around to see what had hit him, he saw this guy standing there just laughing, as if the whole thing was a big joke. The guy saw the rider looking at him and shouted, 'Veloci-fucked!' Which he seemed to think was the height of wit. Obviously the delivery rider didn't appreciate the joke. I can get that.

He was still pretty shaken when we spoke to him. His face was a swollen purple mess. I think he'd broken his nose in the fall. He had that kind of shocked, uncomprehending anger that victims of PGD often feel, unless they're psychos themselves of course. If they're psychos, they just kind of take it in their stride. To them, it's just like going out without an umbrella and getting caught in a storm. These things happen, is how they view it.

But our delivery rider was obviously not a psychopath, because he was trying to make sense of what had happened to him. 'What kind of person does a thing like that?'

First thing you always try to do, with any crime, is try to work out a motive. Maybe the perpetrator was a commercial rival. Or maybe it was a disgruntled customer, who'd got food poisoning from a dodgy meal. Something like that. Of course, when you're dealing with psychopaths, that's a complete waste of time. They don't, generally, have any reason for anything they do, or at least not something that any normal person would call a good reason.

The driver of the car took some pictures of the offender, from which we were able to identify him. No previous criminal record. In fact, you might even say he had been up to this point a respectable member of society. He was a fucking solicitor! It's this kind of thing that made people think there was some kind of virus going around. I mean, what makes some guy who has never shown any signs of psychopathic behaviour suddenly push an innocent cyclist into the road?

So we tracked him down and pulled him in and questioned him. He denied it of course. Claimed to know nothing about it, to have been nowhere near the scene when it happened. We showed him the pictures of him there, gloating over the injured cyclist.

We even put him in a line-up and had the driver pick him out.

'OK, yeah, I was there. But I didn't do it.' The fact that he'd been caught out in a lie didn't faze him at all.

'We have a witness who says you did. The witness who took these pictures.'

'She's lying.'

'How did you know it was a woman?'

'I saw her taking the pictures. She got the wrong person. It wasn't me. This black guy did it. You should be looking for him.

She and him were in it together. Obviously.' The woman driving the car was black.

'It was you who shouted "Veloci-fucked" at the victim. Why did you do that?'

'It wasn't me.'

'You were filmed shouting it.'

We played him the clip. Again, no embarrassment at being caught out in a lie. In fact, he was smirking all over his face. 'That's not what I'm shouting.'

'What *are* you shouting then?'

'*Do you need any help? Shall I call an ambulance?*'

'No . . . it sounds more like "Veloci-fucked" to me,' said Rashid.

The pusher-off didn't bat an eye. 'Play it again.'

We did. He went through the motions of straining hard as if he was trying to make out the words.

'It's jihadi to tell,' he said at last with a deadpan stare at Rashid.

'You're very funny,' I said. 'Veloci-fucked. Jahadi to tell. You should do stand-up.'

'Yeah, I reckon I should.'

'You could tell the story about the guy you pushed off a bike. Observational humour. You were observing him riding along the street and you pushed him off.'

'Is that supposed to catch me out?'

'Damn. You're too clever for me. I'll have to resort to Plan B.'

'What's that?' It was like we were playing a game. Bantz. He knew I was going somewhere with this and he was giving me the feed-line. We could have been a double act.

'I beat the shit out of you until you confess.'

'You can't do that. I have rights.'

I sort of made him understand that the whole him-having-rights thing was maybe a bit overstated.

'New laws have been brought in that basically mean if we catch a cunt like you we can do what we like.'

There was blood streaming out of his nose. He looked at me like I'd let him down somehow.

'You should be more careful,' I advised him.

'Why the hell did you do that?' he shouted.

'Why the hell did you push that guy off his bike?'

'I had a reason! I had a *good* reason!'

Me and Rashid exchanged a look. 'OK, explain it to us,' I said. 'We'd like to know.'

'It's a fucking stupid name. *Veloci-fed.* I hate it! For fuck's sake, it's horrible.'

'So that was why you pushed him off?'

'Yes! You can't go around riding a bike with a big box on your back with the name Veloci-fed on it. It shouldn't be allowed. I mean, it really upsets me. Really.'

'Obviously.'

I remembered enough of the three-day course to be pretty sure we were dealing with a certifiable psychopath. I didn't need one of Dr Arbus's machines to tell me that.

The weird thing about this case was that almost immediately we started to get other alerts on PolNet of copycat incidents. The clip of him shouting somehow got out. The woman who filmed him no doubt intended it as a shocking indictment of the level of callousness now prevalent in society. Or some such thing. And yes, there were some who expressed their outrage. But a lot more just thought it was funny. Pretty soon #velocifucked was going viral on MindNet. Psychos all over the country were now pushing hapless Veloci-fed cyclists off their bikes. And posting shots and clips of the mayhem they were causing on MindNet.

It wasn't long before we had our first velocifucked fatality. One of the riders was pushed under the wheels of an oncoming lorry. The shots of his crushed and mangled body went straight on MindNet and garnered over a million likes. Which kind of made us realize the scale of the problem we were up against.

There were going to be some long days ahead.

LEVEL THREE

Once outside, the player's aim is simple: to express the full, florid psychopathy of their character's nature without being captured. At the same time, they have to keep their character alive and so the basic necessities for living must be met, i.e. the character needs to eat and drink, and find shelter. Therefore the character will need money. The income-generating options available to the player are the same as those open to any psychopath in the real world. They may con their way into a job for which they will have no qualifications. They may perpetrate frauds, or even thefts on vulnerable victims. They may get involved in drug dealing. Or they may play for higher stakes and set up some kind of high-profile business (a total scam, of course) which will attract mucho attention and investment. Consider crowdfunding a computer game that never gets made. Consider setting up a film investment company for films that never get produced. That sort of thing. Here's one that could work: the character could pick up sexual partners (men/women/both) and rip them off. You know, building trust, pretending deep love, then clearing out their bank accounts and moving on to the next victim. Could be fun, especially as it gives the opportunity for some kind of porno interactions – always popular with fans.

These are just options that are offered to the player. They choose what appeals to them the most. However, as ever, the inbuilt disorder of the game character may subvert the player's aims and ambitions. You know, killing someone at an inopportune moment. That sort of thing. Adds to the fun.

But to return to the immediate release/escape. First things first, so to speak. It is a question of basic survival.

The setting of the game outside the secure unit is a rundown urban neighbourhood. Gangs of youths roam the streets. These provide a threat which the psycho character has to contend with – or maybe they are an opportunity to be exploited? Consider having the psychopath gain some kind of control over a street gang?

The key is to pick your battles. Choose easy targets, like the homeless. We need lots of homeless on the streets to provide victims for the psychopaths. Gameplay benefit is they will not be missed or investigated? Also the player will be rewarded with some kind of psycho boost with every killing. There will be a scale for this. Character could start with small animals. Cats are the obvious ones. Relatively small reward for that. Greater reward for bigger or harder to catch animals. Foxes, for example, provide a bigger reward.

The downside of killing the homeless (and animals) is they do not have any monetary (or other) value. They do not help the psychopath to survive. Unless they turn to cannibalism. But then killing them would have a purpose. Is it a twisted enough purpose to qualify as psychopathic behaviour? We probably need some advice on this. My gut feeling is, yes, it's OK. I mean killing a homeless person to eat them is not the normal reaction to feeling a bit peckish.

That said, I would like to explore the possibility of a little more complexity here. One to return to.

Development notes for PSYCHOTOPIA VR game.
Internal Alpha Games document. Not for release. For approved circulation only.

TEN

She took him to her bed. That bed. The same bed that had been the site of her recent shame. Though it hadn't felt like shame at the time, of course.

It was not out of pity, or gratitude, or despair that she did it.

It was done as a healing act. To heal them both, in fact. To heal what had once been between them, which she had broken.

To heal the world, even. For in the days since that hateful party, the world had grown sick and strange and frightening. She'd stopped watching the news. It was too much on top of her own misery. And somehow she felt responsible for all that was happening out there too. She'd let that beautiful monster into her own home, and in so doing, somehow, she had unleashed something terrible on the world.

At the very least she did it to heal the bed. To obliterate from it all memory of what she had done with . . .

But she could not bear to form his name, not even in her thoughts. How did she know it was his real name anyway?

Some traitorous part of her mind was still showing porn-film flashbacks to her couplings with him. Even while she was trying to record over them with Callum. And part of her also imagined him looking down on them now and delighted to think that he might be stung with jealousy. But that was ridiculous, of course. She knew that. If this was done to get back at him, then it wasn't going to work. There had to be a better, nobler reason for it.

And as she had with him, so she did with Callum – no condom.

She wasn't going to deny good, loyal, loving Callum anything that she had given freely to that monster.

The slow, inescapable changes to her body, the life growing inside her as silently as salivation, were another part of the healing process. Callum's baby. That's what she told herself.

Callum's eyes grew wide with wonder and joy when she broke the news. He hugged her to him and wept into her hair.

They were on the way to being healed.

Of course, the timing wasn't perfect. She'd have to put her architectural career on hold. It was a shame as she was so close to completing her training. But they would find a way. Callum promised to support her in whatever she wanted to do. She looked into it and found out that she would only have to repeat the second year of her professional placement, and could possibly even get by without that if she was prepared to lower her sights.

She moved out of the grotty shared house in White City and into a two-bedroom flat Callum found for them in Hoxton. He was on pretty good money as a software developer. He even showed her his payslip to prove it.

She didn't want to look at it, but she had to admit it was more than she expected, considering he was so soon out of uni. He told her he was due a bonus too, and maybe even a rise. He told her that once the baby was born they'd be able to afford childcare and she could carry on her career where she'd left off.

She started to cry.

'What's the matter? *Aims?*'

'Don't you understand? I don't care about any of that. I don't care how much you earn. That's not why . . .'

'I know that. I'm just trying to show you . . . we're going to be all right. I think we're going to be all right. You and me. Together. We'll be OK. I promise you. Everything will be OK. The baby. Everything.'

'I don't deserve you.'

'Shut up.'

A lump of anxious emotion exploded into happiness inside her.

What they had created together was a small good thing in a world that was increasingly turning rotten. They owed it to each other to nurture it. Hate was very much the current thing these days. Hate and fear. Love was in desperately short supply. So, the way Aimée saw it, they had a duty to love. Simple as that. Anyone who was capable of love, who had the opportunity of loving and being loved, they simply had to do it. It wasn't just a personal thing any more. It seemed bigger than that. Bigger than the two of them. It was a biological imperative. It was for the good of the species.

Love had to win.

They talked about whether this was a fit world to bring a child into. It was Callum who brought it up. The NewsNet was buzzing with the latest mass craziness. Every day things seemed to get a little bit more stupid, a little bit more dangerous.

The way she saw it, they didn't have any choice. There was no other world available to them. This was it. They had to make the best of it.

It wasn't just the unconscious vestiges of her Catholic upbringing. It was a matter of principle. If you wanted to change the world, you had to be part of the world. You had to make a contribution to it, and their contribution would be a child. A child of the light, who would grow up to be on the side of the angels. You couldn't leave the world to the crazies and the cynics, and the heartless, soulless, loveless monsters. You just couldn't.

Now, if she ever thought about what had happened with . . . *him*, the one she wouldn't name, she almost felt sorry for him. Pity: she found it in her heart to pity him. She had spent so long trying to understand why he had treated her the way he had, how he could have said those things, professed his love for her, shown it in so many ways, how he could have done all that, and yet also do those other things. Stolen her money. Ripped off her friends. Ripped out her heart. Vandalized her emotions. Made a mockery of her love. She had come to the conclusion that the reason was he was simply incapable of love. He didn't even understand what love was. To him it was just an empty rigmarole, a game you played to get what you wanted out of people.

Life must be so empty for him, and people like him. There was nothing there. Nothing behind the eyes. Nothing in the heart. Nothing to come home to. Nothing to go out for. Except prey. And the icy satisfaction of predation. She had been prey to him. That was all. She still flushed with the heat of shame and embarrassment to think of herself in those terms.

But mostly it was pity she felt now.

He could never experience what she had with Callum. This, this wonderful love was real and it was hers. And she was so lucky to have it. In some ways she owed it to *him*, the unnamable one. He had made it possible not only for their love to exist, but also for it to reveal its full power and beauty. Had she got together with Callum at the party, might there have been some sense in her that she was settling for the easy option? That there were still possibilities she had not explored? Experiences she had missed out on?

Callum now was not the easy option. Callum now was hard won and suffered for. And Callum now was everything to her. There were no possibilities or experiences – none that she had any desire for – outside of him.

She was not deluding herself. What she had with Callum was real and precious. Something worth fighting for.

There was only one thing that threatened it. One thing that could undo it. But she pushed that thing deep down into the murk at the bottom of her consciousness.

She layered it over with thoughts of Callum and the life they were making together.

That life grew inside her. Rearranging her internal organs as it muscled its way into existence. Changing her shape, her walk, her moods, her appetites and her identity. She had a sense of herself as two beings now. One was the old Aimée, the persistent presence, there since she had first been aware of herself as an independent entity, who looked on now with something like awe and bewilderment at what was being wrought inside her. The other was some kind of supra-Aimée being, a kind of atavistic instinctual spirit who knew exactly what was going on and what to do. As the pregnancy progressed, the old Aimée dwindled and dimmed. The supra-Aimée took over. It was like the supra-Aimée was some kind of by-product of the growing foetus. And maybe that's just what it was – the readjustment to her personality created by the shifting tides of hormones surging through her.

It was a voice inside her reassuring her that everything would be OK. It was her body taking over. She just had to surrender to it.

Suffice it to say, she surprised herself. She became this wise, all-knowing goddess of maternity, emanating serenity and strength. She took everything in her stride.

Whenever they went for a check-up or an ultrasound scan, she was sure everything would be all right. And it was.

They pored over the throbbing image on the screen, as the nurse interpreted the thumbprint smudges for them. The tadpole head, the tiny heart beating, the fishbone-fine fingers grasping, all the necessary internal organs immaculate and in place. She marvelled at the intricate structures that took shape before her.

She was unconsciously – almost effortlessly – creating an architecture more amazing than any she had given shape to in her years of professional training. And no engineer could ever build a system as perfect as this.

'Do you want to know the sex?' the nurse asked.

They shared a look, a smile, and nodded.

'It's a girl.'

Aimée felt the bounce of her heart. A girl. She'd known it would be. Of course. Supra-Aimée knew everything.

'Perfect,' said Callum. 'We particularly wanted a girl.'

She shot him a questioning glance. He winked back at her.

She even stayed calm when her blood pressure spiked a little at week thirty-two. She just rested up and sent Callum out for some dark chocolate, anchovies and bananas. Not so much because she thought they'd help her hypertension, or even because she was craving them, more because she realized he needed something to do.

She could taste her own delight at the drum-skin tautness of her torpedo bump. And when she saw and felt the probing jabs of the baby limbs punching out against the prison of her womb, she gasped with amazement. She'd call Callum over to share in the moment. And be both lifted and humbled at his gentleness and awe.

Towards the end, she was frequently hot and tired, but never anything other than happy.

Even when her waters broke she didn't panic. She simply said, 'Cal.' And from all the freighted inflection that she put into that single syllable, he knew that it was time.

Callum had optioned a CarClub rental for two weeks either side of her due date. It was typical of him. A good, sensible plan, except that in the CarClub depot round the corner from them, all the cars had been vandalized. Tyres slashed and windscreens shattered, with faeces smeared over the door handles, just in case you still fancied driving one of them. There was another depot about three miles away. There were two buses he could take, but it seemed that one of them had been suspended. No reason was given, of course, though he knew from bitter experience that the likeliest explanation was simply that no drivers had turned up for work. When the other bus came, it was packed, and there was a gang of morons goading anyone who looked remotely foreign. Callum didn't get involved. He wouldn't anyhow, but today of all days he couldn't afford to get mixed up in any trouble. He just kept his head down and his mouth shut. Even when one of the morons threw an open bottle of what turned out to be urine at him.

'Ginger!' It was not a taunt, so much as an explanation.

He got off the bus early and ran the rest of the way. At least the fresh air would help to dissipate the stink of his dousing.

All in all, it was a tense three miles. He'd seen on the NewsNet how acts of mindless destruction like this often spread, like some kind of virus of stupidity. He could hardly bear to think what awaited him at the CarClub. But fortunately he got to the second depot before any of the local psychos had.

By the time he got back to the flat, Aimée's contractions had started. She still managed to appear amazingly calm and organized. A little bit distracted maybe, but not panicky at all. She didn't comment on the time it had taken him to pick up the car. Just pointed him to the bag she had ready and waiting.

He said he needed the loo quickly, which was an opportunity to rinse his head under the shower and change out of his smelly hoodie. He reckoned his jeans were OK.

She raised an eyebrow at his change of top. 'In your own time, mister.'

'I just . . .' But he couldn't think of an explanation that made any sense, so he just left it hanging. He was not about to tell her what had happened on the bus. Not unless she pinned him down, which was always possible with Aimée. There wasn't much that got past her these days. She was particularly attuned to random psychopathic behavior – after her own experiences, he guessed.

In the car, she sniffed the air and said, 'It smells like someone's pissed in here.'

'It's always possible,' he answered. There must have been a splash on his jeans after all, or maybe he hadn't got it all out of his hair. He reckoned the best thing to do was distract her. 'Are you still timing the contractions?'

'The last one was nearly five minutes ago. They're not regular yet. It's fine. We've got plenty of time.' She pulled a face. 'Ugh! That smell is getting worse.'

'I'll open the window.'

North London Mega-Hospital occupied a sprawling site off an inaccessible roundabout on the North Circular. It was sandwiched between a Sofa Universe and an abandoned self-storage facility that had long ago been taken over by an army of squatters. The rumour was some of the squatters had come over into the NLMega itself and were slowly taking over the hospital buildings, slipping in alongside the patients and staff who had a right to be there. Apparently, some of them had forged Health Corp ID and scrubs to wear, while others wore fake surgical dressings and even had dummy IV drip trolleys to push around.

NLMega had been built at the merger of the failing Whittington, Royal Free and North Middlesex hospitals. The area and population it served was vast. Which was perhaps why the architect had designed the central building as a towering block visible from miles around. Or perhaps he just liked the idea of blocking out the sun.

One consequence of the enlarged catchment area was that a considerable number of patients with serious or life-threatening conditions died before they ever got to hospital. On paper it looked like the NLMega had much better outcomes than all the previous hospitals put together. Certainly that was the way the new Health Corp represented it.

The car park was vast. It was organized so that the cheapest spaces were the ones furthest away from the hospital building, so those were the ones that usually got taken first. There were banks of coin-release wheelchairs, rusted and rammed together like supermarket trolleys, for ferrying patients from the peripheral zones. Callum circled in to slot the car into a space right by the main entrance.

'Are you kidding?' said Aimée. 'It's going to cost a fortune to park here!'

'I'm not fucking about. Not today. We're parking here.' One thing that clinched it for him was that the security cams nearer the hospital tended to be the ones in working order. So the closer they parked to the building, the more chance there was of them having a functioning car to return to.

She didn't argue.

They followed colour-coded signs and lines on the floor through the labyrinth of the mega hospital.

They walked into a gleaming reception area, which inspired

confidence with its plush hotel lobby-style armchairs, thick fashion magazines and tasteful, calming prints on the walls. There were even what appeared to be fresh cut flowers in vases on the highly polished wooden tables. All around them, stainless steel fixtures glinted almost as brightly as the receptionist's teeth.

The brilliant facade didn't hold up to extended scrutiny. The armchair Aimée sank into tilted over vertiginously to one side. Callum discovered that one of its legs was only loosely connected. The same was true of the next chair she tried.

'This is ridiculous!' said Callum, loudly, to the room in general. The room in general was unmoved.

Some of the armchairs were obviously capable of supporting the weight of a human being. But these were already occupied, and not all by heavily pregnant women. The birth partners who were there with them saw no reason to give up their seats. Not for any of the obviously pregnant mothers who were roaming the floor like caged lions, or leaning with their backs against the wall, or sitting on their haunches on the floor.

Callum couldn't understand the attitude of the non-pregnant people who had seats, particularly the men. But they were untroubled by his agitation. Somehow with their body language they seemed to indicate all the empty chairs around them, as if they couldn't understand why anyone would choose to stand when there were so many seats available. Of course, it was no business of theirs if all these chairs were broken. They had no way of knowing that, as they hadn't personally tried them out. And even if that was the case, it was hardly their fault.

Callum was on the verge of having a go at one particularly smug individual. Aimée cut him off with a brave stab at a smile. 'It's OK, Cal. I prefer to stand anyway.'

They were given a form to fill in, which was the same as the form they had filled in every time they had an appointment with anyone connected to Health Corp. In short, their details should have been on the HealthNet by now. They had a Health Corp number. It should have been enough just to give that. You would have thought.

Callum vented with another 'Ridiculous.' The stress of the day was getting to him. It was hard enough without all these wind-ups.

How Aimée managed to stay so calm, he didn't know. She

must have felt it more than him, and yet she held it all in. She never went off on one. Or turned on the waterworks. Or even let slip the occasional, *'Fuck!'*

She just had this look of absolute inner peace. She was amazing. He knew she was focusing on a point beyond the present. On the moment when they would take their baby home and begin the next phase of their life together.

He reached out and took her hand, which was hotter than he had ever known it.

She gazed for a moment into his face, blinking as if she were startled by this sudden reminder of his presence. *Don't worry,* she seemed to say. *We'll get through this.*

He gave her hand a little squeeze. And felt the answering squeeze from her. And knew it would be OK.

Aimée couldn't wait to get out of the reception area. She hated the superficial glitz of the place. It was a mask. It treated them like children. *Look at the shiny glass!* it said. *Don't look at all the broken fucked-up shit going on everywhere else.*

Besides, she was desperate to lie down on a bed, and anxious to be seen by a doctor. She did her best to hide her anxiety from Callum. She knew he was on edge. Something had happened when he had gone to get the CarClub car. She allowed him the privilege of keeping it from her. And felt grateful to him for that. He was protecting her. They were protecting each other. Maybe it would be better if they shared their fears. But then, no . . . She had long ago decided that there were some fears she would never share with anyone. Not even Callum.

At last their number was called out and they were allowed to go through the entry-coded door into the maternity ward itself.

It was a shock to see how little effort Health Corp made to keep up even a pretence of giving a shit. The ward was so rundown and dirty, they may as well have had signs up saying, 'PATIENTS REMAIN AT OWN RISK'. In fact, they probably did use to, but they had all fallen off by now.

The message seemed to be, *You're in here now, what are you going to do about it?*

No doubt the staff were all doing their best, though why did everyone always say that? The only evidence she had to suggest that was the edge of panic and hostility she detected in the eyes of the midwives and nurses. As if the last thing they needed right now was another pregnant woman about to give birth. If they didn't care at all, they wouldn't look so harassed and bad-tempered. The ones who were really trying to do their best looked downright frightened.

She remembered her parents telling her about her own birth, when they had been advised to take cleaning products into the hospital with them to clean the bath before her mum used it. That was no longer necessary. The NLMega had neatly got round the problem by removing all the baths from the maternity wards. No more complaints about dirty baths.

Well, at least she had a bed. That was something. From what she had heard, you couldn't always rely on it. There was a bedside cabinet too. With a patina of dust over the top of it. She picked up a tumbler that was there, and held the lipstick smear out to Callum.

'I've got you a bottle of water.'

She nodded and looked around for a bin to drop the tumbler into. There wasn't one. It seemed that the previous occupants of the bed had used the space beneath the bedside cabinet. She didn't want to look too closely, but even in one quick glance she could distinguish, amongst the balls of grey fluff, screwed-up tissues, nail clippings, cotton buds and even some discarded syringes and bloody dressings. So maybe it wasn't just the patients who stuffed their rubbish under there.

She closed her eyes on the grimness of it.

She visualized herself opening the door to their flat, Callum behind her carrying their baby daughter asleep in her car seat. The mental image fortified her enough to face her surroundings again. That was why she was here, to make that image a reality. Whatever she had to endure was worth it.

She clambered on to the bed. There was something a little self-conscious about the sigh she let out. She was willing herself into the relief it expressed, rather than genuinely feeling it. In some ways, it was a statement of intent. For Callum's benefit as much as her own.

It was odd that she was thinking of him so much right now when really everything ought to have been revolving around her. She acknowledged the irony of it with a smile. If there was one time when she ought to put herself first, it was now.

It was as if she believed the only way she could make amends was through self-negation.

Maybe there was something a little unhealthy about this. But it worked for her.

She lay back and let her gaze wander over the network of cracks and watermarks that covered the ceiling. It looked like there had been a leak once immediately over her bed – not a comforting thought.

A mass of cobwebs hung in the cornicing. She didn't like spiders. She certainly didn't like the idea of them over her head. She had an irrational fear of one crawling into her ear while she slept and laying its eggs. However, she had to face the fact that there was little likelihood of her getting any sleep while she lay on this bed.

She closed her eyes and summoned up the motivating visualization again. It seemed a little fainter this time, somewhat dimmer, as if one of the lights illuminating it had gone out.

As if on cue, she was hit by her most violent contraction yet. The ones she had felt up to now were nothing compared to this. Shadow contractions. Her body warming up for the main event. And yet she knew that even this one was nothing compared to the pain that was yet to come.

The pain that would rip her apart and make her anew.

That would erase all the other pain she had ever suffered.

She longed for it to begin.

The system was not entirely broken. Or at least, it had the presence of mind to act as if it wasn't. For example, she was visited by someone who called herself a Pain Relief Practitioner. Petite and extraordinarily beautiful, with perfect skin and an immaculately starched uniform, her very presence reassured you. She gave off a scent of deep, almost inhuman cleanliness and spoke with a delightfully uplifting Nigerian accent. Her smile alone might have been enough to make you forget your pain, as long as your pain was not that of parturition. For that she pushed a trolley of goodies in front of her.

She pulled out a slim black box with two electrodes hanging from wires. 'Would you like a TENS machine, my darling?'

'Yes, please.'

'That will be fifty MindCoins, my darling.'

'Oh, I see. What other options are there?'

'You may have gas and air.'

'How much is gas and air?'

'It is fifty MindCoins to activate the gas and air dispenser. And then there is a meter which will measure how much gas and air you use. It should not come to more than two hundred MindCoins, if you are not wasteful.'

'What else?'

'You may have a pethidine injection.'

'How much is that?'

'A pethidine injection is three hundred MindCoins.'

'What else?'

'You may have an epidural.'

'And that is?'

'And that is very good, my darling. It is the best one.'

'No, I meant how much does it cost?'

'It is the most expensive because it is the best. I am sure your husband will not object to paying it for you.'

'We'll have them all,' said Callum.

'Very well, sir.'

'It was a joke.'

The deliciously scented woman blinked and smiled happily. 'I see. It is very funny.'

'How much is the epidural?'

'You do not need to decide yet whether you have the epidural. You can wait to see how bad the pain gets. You may try the other less costly methods first. A lot of the ladies are very content with the TENS machine. It is a very good machine.'

'If we need to upgrade to one of the other methods, do we get what we spent on the TENS machine back?'

'No, sir, we cannot do that.'

'We don't even get a discount?'

'It is not the time to be haggling over money, sir, when your wife is suffering from the pain of childbirth.' The Pain Relief Practitioner turned to Aimée. 'If it was he who experienced the pain, he would not think twice about paying.'

'We'll get whatever you want,' said Callum, stung by the implication.

'But there must be some people who can't afford any of it?' said Aimée.

'You need not worry, my darling, they are not on this ward.'

'But what happens to them?'

'There are many parts of the world where this technology and these medicines are not available. I think people still find a way to have babies!' The Pain Relief Practitioner offered up her most cheerful smile yet.

'What do you want to do?' asked Callum.

'I suppose we could take the TENS machine.' She couldn't help feeling guilty about all those parts of the world where this technology was not available.

'You may always buy some gas and air later, if you wish,' said the Pain Relief Practitioner, handing over the unit. 'Do you know how to use it?'

'No . . . I . . . I've never had to use one before.'

'I will show you.'

Aimée had to give the woman her due. She patiently explained how the machine worked, fitting the electrodes to Aimée's lower back and demonstrating the controls. She even waited for Aimée's next contraction so that she could help her set the level of relief. The tingle was a pleasant wash of sensation laid over the spasm of her flesh, somehow melting its intensity. It didn't get rid of the pain entirely, but it helped.

The only problem was that as soon as the woman and her trolley were out of sight, the lights on the front of the box blinked and went out. The TENS machine stopped working entirely. Callum unplugged it and ran after her, but she was nowhere to be seen.

They hadn't seen a midwife for four hours now. Aimée's contractions were lasting longer than the intervals between them. Time was being measured out by pain. And the unit of pain was elastic. Time didn't exist any more. Just pain.

She held on to Callum's hand and squeezed tightly with each contraction, transmitting some of the pain to him. He absorbed everything she had to give him.

He was doing his best not to panic. The hand squeezing seemed to calm him, or at least distract him from his anxieties. But he was increasingly on edge. He didn't want to leave her on her own. At the same time, surely by now someone should have come to check up on her?

Just as he was about to abandon her to go looking for a
midwife, the inanely smiling Pain Relief Practitioner came back
round with her trolley. This time, they took everything she had
to offer apart from the epidural. They opted initially just for gas
and air, but she offered them a deal on pethidine if they paid for
it now. Aimée was nervous about the synthetic heroin, not least
for the potential impact it might have on the baby. Also because
she'd heard rumours that some Health Corp managers were
purchasing counterfeit drugs. But given the increased regularity
and severity of her contractions, she was reluctant to rule it out
entirely. Yes, she longed to be purged by the pain, and, yes, she
felt guilty about the women who couldn't afford any pain relief
at all, but there were limits.

'Can we order it and make our mind up later whether we use
it?' asked Callum.

'Yes, sir. Of course, sir. That is a very good idea, sir.'

'And what if we end up not needing it?' wondered Callum.
'Do we get our money back?'

'Regrettably, sir, if you have ordered a treatment and in the
event do not avail yourselves of it, we cannot give you your
money back.'

'Cannot?'

His question was answered by a sharp shriek of pain from
Aimée.

'It doesn't matter. We'll take it. I'm sure we'll use it. If she
doesn't want it, I'll take it.'

'That is not permissible, sir.'

'It was a joke.'

'It is very funny.'

Needless to say, there was no possibility of a refund for the
broken TENS machine. The terms and conditions which they had
automatically agreed to (sight unseen) made that clear.

Once again, the Pain Relief Practitioner stayed to show them
how to use the gas and air mask and waited to check it was
working. But somehow her seeming diligence was less reassuring
this time than it had been before.

But Aimée had to admit, the gas and air seemed to hit the
spot. It was certainly more effective at melting the pain of her
almost continuous contractions than the broken TENS machine.

'How are we doing here?' At last, a midwife. Although,

somewhat disconcertingly, it was a man. She accepted it shouldn't have been disconcerting. But Aimée had reached a point where she found it difficult to trust any man apart from Callum, especially when it came to letting him look into her vagina.

The male midwife held up both hands and spread his fingers, displaying their marvellous extent. As if this in itself was a mark of his competence. *Don't worry*, he seemed to be saying. *I'm not going to drop your baby with hands like these.*

'OK, let's have a look at your cervix, my dear.'

She shifted her legs to allow him to do the examination. It was the closest she came to losing it during the whole of the pregnancy. All the fears and anxieties that she had been keeping a lid on suddenly rose to the surface and threatened to blow. What if this guy, this male midwife, was just like *him*? A complete fraud. What if he was one of the squatters she'd heard about? He wasn't a midwife at all. There were people who did this. Who faked Health Corp ID and wormed their way into hospitals. Some of them even pretended to be surgeons and carried out operations. In a vast organization like NLMega it was impossible for them to keep tabs on everyone. For one insane moment, when his head was between her thighs, she even thought it was *him*. Rationally, she knew it wasn't, of course. But the top of his head there . . . it brought on unwelcome flashbacks.

It was all she could do not to squirm away from him up the bed. She squeezed Callum's hand more tightly than she had during any contraction.

'Yep, OK. That's ten centimetres. We need to get you into a delivery room, pronto.'

At least things started to happen now that the midwife was on the scene. He helped her on to a wheelchair and raced her through the ward, shouting, 'Out of the way! This mother's set to pop.' Callum ran after them with the gas and air canister.

She gave birth almost as soon as they got into the delivery room. There was just time for her get off the wheelchair and on to all fours on the floor. The contractions had stopped being contractions and were just one long continuous upheaval of her whole physical being. It felt not so much like she was being split in two as turned inside out.

'Push! *Push!*' shouted the midwife.

She swore back at him. 'What the fuck do you think I'm doing?'

He was there behind her, ready with his big hands to catch the baby when it came out.

And then she really was ripped apart by one intense wave of pain and bliss and release and relief and fear and joy and wonder. And echoing waves of sensation.

Suddenly she was aware that there was another life in the world. Tiny, new-forged lungs breathing in air for the first time. Fresh eyes unimaginably startled by the bombardment of light and movement. Limbs stretching out to make their first unfettered grasp at freedom. A new voice adding to the clamour of the world.

And a world irrevocably changed because of it.

She heard the midwife say, 'It's a girl. A beautiful, beautiful girl.'

Callum helped her into the bed. And the midwife handed her the naked perfection of her daughter.

It was strange. She could not have predicted it. After all that she had gone through to get to this point.

How little she felt. No, it was worse than that. Not that there was an absence of feeling. But that the only feeling she felt was a visceral coldness. A physical repulsion.

In the very instant that the baby was lain on top of her, she realized that she hated it. She could not bring herself to hold it.

And the worst thing was, she knew that this feeling was not irrational.

LEVEL THREE, CONTINUED

S o, yes, to return to the issue of killing the homeless.
I'm going to let my thoughts just drift free form for a
while here. See where it takes me. Uncensored ramblings.
So bear with me.

And, you know, don't judge . . . I'm trying to reach a point
beyond the normal 'civilized' responses. The polite lies we tell
ourselves and each other. I'm trying to reach the truth. It seems
to me that's what psychopathy is all about, reaching a truth that
ordinary people won't acknowledge because it scares them. They
don't have the courage to face up to their true natures.
They don't have the courage to be who they are. To be true
to themselves. So they wrap themselves up in all these manners
and customs and modes of behaviour.

And they care what other people think.

They are not free.

The great, deep appeal of our game is that it will give them
a chance to be free. They will experience the wild, soaring
freedom of the psychopath.

Freedom is power. Power is freedom. That is a truth that all
psychopaths instinctively grasp.

Power multiplied by freedom equals truth. Or freedom to
the power of power. You could probably express it as a formula:
$f^p = t$.

There are no rules. The truth acknowledges no rules, no
etiquette, no manners, no code of conduct.

The truth simply is.

That's what this is all about.

So the question is not why would the protagonist want to
kill homeless people, but what is it that stops a normal person
from killing homeless people?

Cowardice.

I mean, let's face it, doesn't everyone when they see a homeless person just feel *what's the point of this person?*

Back me up here.

I mean, deep down, on a level that we don't ordinarily acknowledge. We think this person is doing no one any good. Not even themselves. Even they would be better off if they did not exist.

Now I know the average psychopath is not overly exercised by what does or does not benefit the common good. So that argument would not hold much sway. But I think on some level they would just get annoyed by the whole pointlessness of these people.

I mean, we have a nice life. We buy our coffee from our favourite coffee chain. We shop for clothes and games. We go to bars and pick up fuck partners. We have our gadgets that let us plug into the MindNet. It's all great. It's all fucking fantastic.

And then there are these fucking dirty tramps all over the place messing everything up with their grubby clothes and matted hair and their begging. The fucking begging is enough of a reason to kill them, surely! I mean, how does that work? You just hold out your hand and people give you money? Earn it, fucker! (Possibly build in some secondary game play where the psychopath makes the homeless one perform some sort of task in return for change – before killing them. Naturally. Maybe it could be along the lines of *suck my dick* kind of thing. The distaste of having this done by some stinking dirty tramp is outweighed by the fun of humiliating said stinking dirty tramp?)

But anyhow, these homeless people, basically they're spoiling it for the rest of us. Trying to make us feel bad about how great our lives are. Of course you're going to kill them.

The government would even back you up on this. The government doesn't want all these homeless people all over the place. So there could be some in-built leniency in the policing, etc., of these crimes. A blind eye is turned to some extent, which gives the protagonist leeway in which to commit these 'crimes'.

So, yeah, on that level, I think there is sufficient motivation for the protagonist to spree-murder tramps.

Why does any of this matter? you may be wondering. After all, the only issue that should be concerning us is whether or not a particular game element is *fun* for the player. But what I'm trying to do is get to the bottom of that question.

In other words, is it fun to kill homeless people?

Yes, I think it would be. But what I'm trying to do is work

out why I think that, and to offer some kind of justification for that view.

To recap, the difference between psychopaths and so-called non-psychopaths is that the psychopaths are free. If the non-psychopath could find a way to become free, they would behave in exactly the same way as the psychopath. Which is to say there is no fundamental difference between a psychopath and a non-psychopath.

Or to put it another way, there are only two types of people: psychopaths and latent psychopaths.

Or to put it another way again, there is a psychopath inside us all.

That is the core truth upon which the game's success depends. If the game is a hit, then I am right and that is a truth. If the game is a flop, then I will have been proven wrong. The logical conclusion is that there is a difference between psychopaths and non-psychopaths, after all. (Who knew?!)

But for this premise to be properly tested we have to character-engineer the protagonist to be psychologically true, so that the character's persona resonates with the inner psychopath in the player. The motivation has to stack up, which is why I am expending a certain amount of energy in thinking it through.

The truer it is, the more it will resonate. The more it resonates, the more fun it is.

And the more successful the game will be.

It may not seem like it, but this is all about business, folks.

Development notes for PSYCHOTOPIA VR game.
Internal Alpha Games document. Not for release. For approved circulation only.

ELEVEN

'Oi, you two – Parfett, Ali. In here now.'

Rashid gave me a quick, questioning look. 'What have we done now?' But the chief super's back was already turned as he headed back into his office. It was impossible to read his expression.

But Rashid was right. The chief was very much a laissez-faire boss. You'd get the initial briefing, which was often little more than an access code for a new case on PolNet. Then he was usually happy to walk away and let you get on with it. He didn't want to hear from you until a case was wrapped up or certain targets met. Which they never were, because he had a knack of not defining them clearly, or moving the goalposts just when you thought you knew what you were supposed to be doing. He called it keeping us on our toes. I called it bullshit.

Generally his management style could be summed up thus: keeping himself as detached from the day-to-day stuff as possible so that when the shit started to fly, none of it ended up on him. If you were called into his office it was invariably for a bollocking. He did not do pats on the back. And he did not do desk-to-desk walkabouts dispensing words of encouragement and appreciation.

He was an old-school hard arse, in other words. A great one for taking the credit when things went well and hanging you out to dry if you fucked up. Or even if you didn't.

If I didn't know any better, I might have said he was a psychopath.

Mind you, it was nothing I couldn't handle. I jumped up and followed him into his office with what Rashid called my bring-it-on swagger.

'You should have been a rock star,' he often said to me.

'I am, mate,' was my stock reply.

But it was something of a shock, I can tell you – almost stopped me in my strut – to find Dr Arbus waiting for us in the chief super's office. He wasn't the only one there either. Ronson, our esteemed chief constable, was standing by the window watching us come in with a determined if somewhat pensive expression. As if he was trying to project 'leadership' while at the same time being aware that deep down he didn't have a fucking clue what he was doing. Ronson was a slick operator. Or at least that was his reputation. A great one for getting in front of the cameras and spouting soundbites. He gave good speech. Something to do with his strong jawline, I guess. And his knack of looking straight down the lens with his trust-me-I-know-what-I'm-doing eyes. To be fair, he knew all the theory. Was a real high flyer at university. Top of his year on the Strategic Command Course. A great one for drawing up a plan and getting everyone on board. And provided everything went according to plan, he was fine. If it didn't, his face took on the expression of a baby who had just filled its nappy.

And you know, in our business, things rarely go according to plan. Which meant he looked like that quite a lot of the time. And weirdly it didn't ever stop him drawing up more plans.

Arbus had tidied himself up since the last time I'd seen him. The bird's nest hair had been cut back drastically, and the orthodox priest beard, though longer and greyer than before, somehow gave the impression of being actually groomed. His moustaches were certainly more defined. I had the feeling that someone had told him that the key to getting his machines adopted was to run a comb through his face hair. Seemed like it had worked.

He sat up a little when he saw me come through the door. Narrowed his eyes like he was trying to work out where he'd seen me before. I decided not to help him out. Not sure why really. It was a test, I suppose. To see if he remembered me. And also, I just couldn't be arsed.

'Gentlemen, allow me to introduce to you Dr Simon Arbus. The chief constable, you know. Dr Arbus is here as part of a Home Office initiative to help us try out some new technology which, it is hoped, will enable us to rein in the current phase of public disorder with which we are contending.'

'It's not a phase,' said Arbus grimly. 'It's the future.'

'Well, let's hope it's just a phase,' said Ronson with a nervous smile.

'Otherwise we're all fucked,' I threw in, just to contribute to the debate.

The chief super's expression soured a little, though he pretended he hadn't heard me. 'We're to be a pilot scheme. And you two are going to be our head guinea pigs. I'll let Dr Arbus explain.' He shook his head despairingly at Ronson as he sat down behind his desk.

Arbus gave us a top-level rundown of his machine. I'd heard it all before but it was interesting to watch Rashid's reaction.

'Can you do that? I mean, is there a legal basis for it?'

'The recent amendment to the Terrorist Act covers it,' said Ronson smoothly. 'Any means necessary, I think is the wording. We'll leave it to the lawyers to argue over the meaning of the word *necessary*.'

'Just make sure your Fed dues are up to date,' I told my partner. 'In case you need any legal advice yourself.'

'It won't come to that,' said the chief super tetchily. 'The procedure that has been drawn up requires that we secure a suspect's consent before we administer the test.'

'And what if they don't consent?' asked Rashid.

'Oh, they'll consent.' Arbus seemed very sure of himself.

'By law, they are required to give their consent,' explained Ronson.

'That doesn't make sense,' said Rashid.

The chief super made a vague flapping gesture with one hand. 'It's not something you need to worry about, Ali. Above your pay grade.'

'But it doesn't make sense. You can't *require* someone to give their consent. The whole point of consent is that it is given freely.'

'What you have to understand, colleague, is that we are living in exceedingly challenging times. A time of unprecedented lawlessness and disorder.' This was the chief constable. It sounded like it was an edited version of some speech he'd already made. It was weird the way he called Ali 'colleague'. I'm guessing in the original speech he'd said 'colleagues'. Either that or he was just covering for the fact that he couldn't remember Ali's name or rank. 'We must formulate innovative, imaginative solutions to meet the new challenges we face. The law has been framed in such a way that consent is presumed. That is to say, consent must actively be withheld by the suspect. And in the event of that happening, the law allows for the test to be administered SJV.'

'SJV? What the fuck is that?'

'*Sub judicis vi*. Under force of law.'

'That's not a thing.'

'It is now.'

'But . . .' Rashid was genuinely lost for words.

'It won't be a problem,' said Arbus. 'As I say, they will give their consent. They won't be able to resist. You see, the thing about psychopaths is they don't believe they are psychopaths. So they will be convinced that they'll pass the test.'

'But what about the ones who aren't psychopaths?' It was a fair question, though everyone looked at Rashid as if he was the guy who'd farted in the lift.

It was left to the chief super to explain. 'We're not worried about them. Obviously.'

Rashid's problem, basically, was that he was still of the mindset where he expected things to make sense. I had long since gone past that point.

'So, Dr Arbus here has kindly agreed to train your team in the operation of the machine. All we need from you is a psychopath to play with.'

We had the fucker who had pushed a delivery rider under the wheels of a lorry.

I explained the case to Arbus as we headed down to the custody suite. He was carrying an aluminium briefcase like the one he'd had at the Fed conference that time. For all I knew it was the same one.

'He'll do.'

'It's a girl.'

Arbus flicked up an eyebrow and pursed his lips as if he was impressed. But quickly recovered with a nod. 'It makes no difference.'

We got to the basement where the holding cells are, to be met by that funky waft of unwashed, troubled humanity that lingers around the cells of every police station I have ever visited.

Arbus sniffed the air and narrowed his eyes, as if psychopaths had their own distinct odour. Maybe that was how the machine worked and all that talk about stimuli and brain patterns was just a cover story.

Arbus checked out the prisoner through the hatch. He stayed

looking at her for a long time. I'm not sure what he was looking for, or whether he just got fascinated by her. Because, to be honest, she was pretty fascinating to look at. Anyhow, eventually he pulled his face away from the hatch and nodded.

I had the custody officer open the cell door.

She was seated on the bed, staring into space, dressed now in a white paper boiler suit as her clothes had been taken off for forensic examination. There was no doubt she had pushed the guy under the lorry. But that didn't rule out her being linked to some other mayhem. She looked up at us and gave a broad, attractive smile. 'Finally!'

To this day, I still don't know what she meant by that.

Her name was Annalise Carpenter. She was thirty-seven years old. So no, not one of your juvenile delinquent idiots who didn't know any better. She had a pretty face and an unembarrassed eagerness to her look that was really quite engaging. She was well spoken, well educated and, to use an old-fashioned phrase, came from a good family. She worked as a PA to a company director in some kind of marketing firm. Her mum and dad had been in to see her. They put on a good show of being shocked by her behaviour, at first refusing to believe it. But when we showed them the footage we had, they had to accept it. The incident had been picked up by CCTV and the Veloci-fed rider's own in-helmet camera. There was no doubt.

Despite their protestations of shock and dismay, there was something about their reaction that struck me as phoney. I reckoned they'd been dealing with shit like this their whole lives. Maybe not so spectacular and off-the-scale. But waywardness of some kind. Their relative wealth and position enabled them to keep a lid on it. I was pretty sure I saw the old man give a little smirk when he'd first been told what the charge was. OK, he suppressed it immediately. But I saw it. My interpretation? It was a that's-my-girl kind of smile.

Maybe I should suggest to Arbus that he test the father as well? But I wasn't quite sure how the law stood in regard to extending tests to relatives of suspects in custody.

'Hi, Annalise, how are you doing?' I liked to keep things friendly with the suspects. She, in particular, seemed to respond to this approach.

'I'd really like to get out of here now.'

'Yes, I'm sure you would. But you know, what you did was very serious. You killed a man. I'm afraid you're going to be locked up for a very long time.'

'I didn't kill him! The lorry killed him.'

'But it was you who pushed him in front of the lorry.'

'Oh, that! That was just a joke! Everybody's doing that! It's a meme, you know? It was trending on MindNet. I mean, come on! You can't lock someone up just for joining in a meme!'

'You can if someone dies.'

'But it wasn't me who killed him! How many times do I have to explain that to you? You've seen the video clips. They clearly show that the lorry ran him over. Now if I'd been driving the lorry, that would be a different matter.'

'I'm sorry, Annalise, that's just the way the law is. You're held responsible because what you did caused him to fall under the wheels of the lorry.'

'But that's just stupid! I mean, it's just not fair. I shouldn't be in here. I've got work to do. My boss is flying to New York on Friday. If I get fired because of this I'm going to sue you lot. And another thing. When am I getting my clothes back? I mean, come on. Look at this outfit they've given me. I can hardly post a picture of myself on MindNet looking like this!'

'There won't be any pictures on MindNet, Annalise. That's why we took your MindPhone off you.'

She was genuinely outraged. 'Yeah, what's that all about? I meant to talk to you about that! You can't do that! That's denying me a basic human right!'

Dr Arbus, you can imagine, couldn't wait to get his machine out of the case and start testing her. She kept one wary eye on him as I kept up the banter. 'I don't make the rules, darling. I just enforce them.'

'The sooner I get out of this place the better.' She genuinely didn't seem to understand that she wasn't going anywhere. Or if she was taken out of the police cell, it would only be to go to court. Then jail.

Arbus consulted some notes on his phone, then turned his attention to the psycho. 'Annalise, good afternoon. My name is Dr Arbus. I'm not a policeman. I'm not a psychiatrist. I'm an anthropologist. A psychoanthropologist, to be exact. I'm conducting a study into cultural attitudes to law and order across diverse groups and I was wondering if you'd be willing to help me?'

'I'd love to. I studied anthropology at university.'

'So you give your consent to take part in the study.'

'Sure, fine.'

'Don't you want to know more about what's involved first?' That was Rashid, who seemed more concerned with Annalise's rights than she was herself. 'I don't think you can count that as her giving consent. She hasn't been fully informed about the nature of the test.'

'It's a test?' Annalise was all wide-eyed and eager.

'Yes.'

'I like tests.'

Dr Arbus consulted his notes again. 'The purpose of the test is to aid the police in assessing and processing the individuals who are detained in police custody, so that they can decide more quickly whether or not an individual should be charged or released. That is to say, it is designed to speed up the release of those who are wrongly held.'

'So I'll get out of here quicker?'

'If you pass the test, yes.'

'That's bollocks,' said Rashid. 'Besides, she's already been charged.'

'Rash, leave it,' I advised him.

Rashid spelled it out for her. 'The test is to see whether you're a psychopath or not.'

'Can have a word with you, please?' Arbus took Rashid to a corner of the holding cell. I naturally followed. 'I'd appreciate it if you'd allow me to do all the talking here. Once you have been trained in the operation of the machine, you will be provided with a script for use when interacting with test subjects. This script has been created with a great deal of thought in order to elicit the cooperation of the subject. It has been through many levels of approval, including by senior government lawyers. You will learn the script by rote and never deviate from it. Not by a single letter.'

'And don't tell me, it never mentions the P word?'

'It has been discovered that the use of that word may inhibit compliance in certain cases.'

So. This was the alternative Arbus had hinted at in his interview with Krystie at the Fed conference. Compliance by deceit. You would get people to agree to the test by not telling them what the test was for.

'That's bullshit,' was Rashid's opinion.

'Nevertheless, that is the procedure.'

To be honest, I don't think it made a blind bit of difference to nut jobs like Annalise. But now that the cat was out of the bag, Arbus was obliged to offer her some sort of explanation. And inducement.

'If the test shows you're not a psychopath, it may help your defence, because your lawyer will then be able to argue that your offence was an aberration, perhaps caused by stress. Which means that you're less likely to present a danger to society in the future. Therefore your sentence will be reduced.'

'Oh, I won't do it again! I've learned my lesson.' The passion with which she made this plea was somewhat undermined by what she saw as her clinching argument: 'I don't want my MindPhone taken off me again.'

'That's good. However, the test will convince the court of your sincerity. On the other hand, if the test shows you are a psychopath—'

'That won't happen—'

'Well, if it does, that's a good thing too, because it will show the court that you're not responsible for your actions. You're suffering from a personality disorder to which the appropriate response is therapy, not incarceration.'

'So I'll be released?'

'You won't be sent to prison. You will be released into a secure psychiatric unit.'

'OK, let's do it!' said Annalise brightly.

Arbus turned to me. 'You've seen me demonstrate the Arbus-Lubany machine before, haven't you?'

So. He did remember me. 'Yes.'

He handed me the unit, to which he had already attached the shower cap thing. 'It's very simple. We've made a few modifications to the interface to make it more user-friendly. The machine now virtually talks you through the stages. Would you like to have a go?'

'Sure.'

A pictogram of the cap was flashing in red on the screen of

the device, with the words PLACE SCANCAP ON SUBJECT'S
HEAD.

I did as I was instructed. Words on the screen, and a wireframe
picture of the ScanCap in place, continued to guide me.

ROTATE SCANCAP TO RIGHT.

PULL SCANCAP DOWN AT BACK.

ENSURE SCANCAP IS FREE OF CREASES.

You get the idea.

When the device was satisfied I'd fitted the ScanCap correctly,
it talked me through the rest of the set-up, until I had it in its
frame and in place in front of Annalise's eyes.

'Now what?'

Arbus handed me a second contraption, a small black remote
control with a single button on the top. 'You point this at the
machine and press the button to activate the test. But first you
have to read this to the subject.'

He held his MindPhone up for me to see the words on its
screen. I read out his precious script that had achieved all those
many levels of approval.

'You are about to take the Arbus-Lubany demographic survey
into subconscious attitudes towards violence and disorder. Please
keep your eyes open at all times from the commencement of the
test to the end. Try to avoid blinking as much as possible. If you
close your eyes or blink excessively, the test will be void. In the
event of a void test, you will be detained for a further day for
the test to be repeated. Every void test will result in an extra day
of detention. Three void tests will result in the presence of a
doctor who will medically ensure that your eyes remain open
sufficiently for the test to be successfully completed. Do you
understand?'

'I get it. Keep my eyes open.'

I decided to go a little off script: 'The thing is if you cooperate,
we get this over and done with.'

'And I get out of here?'

'Something like that. But not exactly that.'

'Do it.'

'OK. Here we go. Eyes open wide please.' I pointed and
pressed. There was a beep from the device. A few seconds later,
a second beep, a minor third lower.

'That's it,' said Arbus. 'Take the machine off her now.'

'That was weird,' said Annalise. 'I kind of liked it? I kind of wanted it to go on for longer? You should make that into a game, you know. People would go mad for it. I can talk to my boss about it if you like. He can help you with the marketing.'

I had the machine off her face now. The wording on the screen announced:

TEST COMPLETE. SWIPE FOR RESULT.

I held it out to Arbus.

'No, you do it.'

So I did.

She was a P. Naturally. I mean, what else was she going to be?

'How did I do?'

I showed it to her.

'P? Is that P for pussycat?'

'I think it actually stands for psychopath?' suggested Rashid.

'And that's a pass? Right?'

'If you want to see it that way.'

'So I can get out of here now?' She started to loosen her paper overalls, as if she was getting ready to get changed. In the process, she gave all three of us a flash of her tits. She directed a foxy smile at me specifically, letting me know the flashing had been deliberate and, I guess, for my benefit. I remembered what Krystie had said about the test making her feel horny. It seemed Arbus hadn't quite ironed that one out yet, if he was even aware of it.

'These officers are certainly now in a better position to progress your case,' said Arbus.

'Do I get my clothes back? So I can look nice for you boys.' I swear she was touching herself up through the overalls.

'I'll see to it.' I banged on the door for the custody officer to let us out. To be honest, she was getting on my nerves. They always did, eventually.

GENERAL GAMEPLAY NOTES, II

In every death there is a release of power (traditionally termed the life force). In a murder, this power is transferred from the victim to the killer. There is an old saying: *what doesn't kill you makes you stronger*. The truth (for the purposes of the game, people – do I need to remind you, it's just a game I'm talking about here!) is actually: *what you kill makes you stronger*.

A prolific serial killer is a receptacle of tremendous power.

The killer who kills a serial killer receives all that power.

So a good game plan would be to seek out and kill other psychopaths, or certainly those who have made the progression to killing.

A victim who has not killed relinquishes only their own life force.

A victim who has murdered someone relinquishes their own life force, plus the life force of their victim.

A victim who has murdered ten people relinquishes eleven life forces.

And so on.

What this means is that as the protagonist becomes more successful and prolific as a killer, they themselves become of interest to the other psychopaths who are in the game.

They are under threat not just from the forces of law and order, but also from other psychos.

Fun, hey?

Development notes for PSYCHOTOPIA VR game.
Internal Alpha Games document. Not for release. For approved circulation only.

TWELVE

He took her dancing afterwards. Never let it be said that he doesn't know how to do romantic.

They went to Out in Camden. The scene was a bit young for him, if he was honest. But he'd been told he looked young for his age. There were some advantages to dyeing your hair, even if it was a ball ache when the roots started to show. He was stuck with the daily hair-straightening now as well. And the coloured contact lenses. It seemed a shame to obscure the natural radiance of his eyes, but he had to accept it was just too intense for some people to handle.

Anyhow, he wanted to go somewhere where no one knew him. It was a feeling he often got.

'Is this a gay place?' she asked, as they waited in line.

'No. They let anyone in.' It was a mixed crowd so he didn't know what had put that idea in her head. The name probably.

It was at that moment that he decided to kiss her. Maybe subconsciously he interpreted her question as a not so subtle way of asking if he was gay. He accepted, on one level, it might have been useful to encourage her in that misapprehension. Still, it pissed him off that she even thought it. He couldn't help it. He had to dispel the idea altogether.

It was a risk, he knew. Going in for a kiss so soon. But what's life if you don't take a few risks?

She was tonguey and tangy. And responsive.

When their lips parted, it was like they were coming up for air.

The line was moving slowly. Even if everything else was moving quickly.

'Hold our place,' he told her.

'Where are you going?'

He detected panic in her voice. At the idea of their separation? Of losing him? That made him smile.

He mouthed: *Pills.*

Her jaw dropped. She looked around to clock the bouncer,

making sure he hadn't seen. That made him laugh. She was so fucking cautious. He would have to cure her of that, he could see. Naive too. Didn't she know you could sometimes get gear off bouncers? You just had to know which ones to ask. These days, sure, they all came across as squeaky clean and über-professional. But that was just a front. Like everything in life.

He ran out into the road without looking. The night was ripped apart by the horn of the car that narrowly missed him. He felt the universe warp at its passing, a blast of air that almost knocked him off his feet. It felt good.

He looked back to see her horrified expression. He was conscious of the thought: *She is so easy to shock.* He couldn't help laughing as he cheerily waved to her.

He found the car parked outside a kebab shop on the main road. The lights were on, drawing attention, though there was no one standing outside. He could always rely on Sammy to park brazenly, defiantly. As if to say, *Yeah, so, what you gonna do about it?*

He'd MindMessaged his dealer earlier to let him know where he was going to be and what he wanted. He was a regular customer – more than that, they'd shared good times, had a laugh together – so Sammy naturally went out of his way to be there.

He knuckled the passenger window. It dropped an inch with a hushed mechanistic whir. A waft of marijuana smoke snaked out with a blast of dub. A deep, bollock-vibrating voice asked, 'What you want?'

'Fuck off, you big black cunt.'

There was wheezy laughter from inside. Followed by, 'My man.'

'You got the gear?'

'Have I ever let you down?'

'Well, come on, get on with it. Before the Old Bill sees us.'

'We just shooting the breeze.'

'I'll shoot your fucking breeze.'

'What does that even mean? That doesn't mean anything, man.'

'Just give me the fucking gear.'

Sammy handed through a sachet of pills pincered between two massive black fingers. 'Es, innit?'

'And the other stuff.'

'The other stuff is bad stuff, man.'

'What you saying? You ain't got it?'

'I got it. But, you know . . . I'm just saying. You never asked me for this shit before.'

'There's always a first time.'

'I don' like this shit. It's bad shit. I like you, my friend. I don't want you getting mixed up in any bad shit.'

'Who are you? My fucking social worker? My fucking priest? Are you my fucking mother?'

'I'm your fucking friend, mate.'

'You're my fucking dealer. Here's how our relationship works. I ask you for certain substances, you provide them. You didn't say when I MindMessaged you that you were gonna act like some fucking boy scout. You just said "sho". That was the entire content of your reply, if I remember correctly. "Sho." Correct me if I'm wrong, but doesn't that mean *yes* in street parlance?'

'It does.'

'So you got it?'

'I got it.'

'Can I have it, please.'

'I just wanna make sure I understood you right, man. You asked for R2, that right?'

'That's right.'

'You know what that is, man.'

'I know what it fucking is.'

'I'm just making sure.'

'What the fuck? Since when did you care?'

'I care about you, man! I don't want you getting into trouble!'

'You don't want it coming back to you, you mean.'

'You got me wrong, man. I care about you. I don't see you as no date-rape fucker.'

'It's not rape if she wants it. Really. Am I right?'

'I'm gonna give you the gear . . .'

'Of course you're gonna give me the fucking gear.'

'But I'm going to ask you . . . you know . . . be careful, man.' A pair of pills bubbled in a foil and plastic stub appeared through the gap in the window.

He snatched them eagerly. 'Don't worry, I'm not going to take them myself, you big wanker.' He slipped a couple of notes into Sammy's waiting hand. 'Let me give you some advice, my friend.

Spare the moralizing for someone who gives a shit. And another thing. You're a fucking drug dealer. You sell this shit. If you don't like it, get into some other line of business.'

'Maybe I will.' The window whirred up and the interior of the car was sealed.

By the time he got back, Sally was near the front of the line.

'I wondered what happened to you.'

'Don't worry, I wouldn't leave you.'

'It's not that. The way you ran in front of that car. Are you always like that?'

'Like what?'

'Reckless.'

He shrugged. 'It didn't hit me.'

'No, but it was close.'

'A miss is as good as a mile. That's a proverb.'

'I know.'

'It means . . .'

'I know what it means.'

'It means you've got to take some risks now and then.'

'I don't think it means that.'

'That's what I take it to mean. And then . . . well, what don't kill you makes you stronger. That's another one.' He flashed her a peek at the sachet of Es in his palm.

'Fuck's sake!' she hissed, her eyes boggling in alarm as she scanned around to make sure he hadn't been seen. 'Are you mad?'

'Relax.'

They got to the window. She wanted to pay her own way, but he got there quicker. Dropping notes like they were litter.

'You don't have to do that,' she said.

'You're my guest. I invited you here. When you invite me somewhere, you can pay.'

'It's a deal.'

He took her hand and led her inside. At the threshold to the first room, he turned to face her.

'Close your eyes and open your mouth.'

'Oh . . . I don't . . .'

'Don't be ridiculous.'

'I'd rather . . . it's not really my thing.'

'You've tried it?'

'Course! What is it?'

'Ecstasy.'

'I shouldn't even be here.'

'That's not very nice. How do you think that makes me feel?'

'Can we not just have a drink? I'll get them.'

'Close your eyes and open your mouth. I'm not going to do anything bad. I promise. Look.'

He popped two pills on to his tongue. And showed her them.

'Two?'

'One's for you.'

'How about a half?'

'Don't be a pussy.'

She gave him a pleading wince.

'Trust me. You've got to learn to trust me.'

She tilted her head back a little as she closed her eyes, her lips coming up receptively.

He locked mouths with her and allowed the softened pills to transfer to her mouth. Then broke away and put his hand over her mouth until he felt her swallow.

'You bastard!'

'I didn't want you wussing out.'

'You gave me them both.'

'Did I? Sorry. I didn't mean to.' Innocent face.

'You just can't do that to a person.'

'You'll be fine. Trust me.'

'The more you say that, the less I trust you.'

'Funny. That's funny. I'll have to remember that.'

'Well, if I'm taking two, you'd better take two.'

'That's more like it!' He popped two tablets of his own. Then grabbed her hand and led her to the dance floor.

RANDOM THOUGHT

What would be great, from a publicity point of view, is if someone actually died from playing the game.

I'm joking, obviously. But it does get to the crux of a little issue I have with all games, actually. They're not real. And I so want them to be real. I think all gamers do, deep down.

All I'm saying, really, I think, is that it should feel as real as it possibly can.

So if the player is hunted down by another psychopath and killed s/he should actually feel, if only for a moment, that s/he has died. Note for Technical: is there a way of achieving this? A hack in the software that modifies the headset? I mean what if we were able to generate a near-fatal electric shock at the moment the player's character loses a life? Obviously not really near-fatal. That would be insane. But I want it to feel as real as possible.

Everything goes black.

Some kind of impulse sent out that affects brainwave patterns. Closes down biorhythms. Slows the heart to near stopping. Induces a deathly chill. That sort of thing. CAN SOMEBODY LOOK INTO THIS PLEASE? I'M SERIOUS.

Hey, what would be really, really, really great would be if we could hack into the gamer's MindNet profile and download clips and shots from their lives, so that these are projected back to the player at the moment of the character's demise. You know what I'm getting at. The idea that just before we die we see the whole of our life flash before us.

Of course, logically, it should be the life of the character, not the player. Which would be easier to achieve, but less scary for the player. I mean, I know it's a logic cheat, but I really want to scare the shit out of people here.

I mean, that's what our fans want, right?

Development notes for PSYCHOTOPIA VR game.
Internal Alpha Games document. Not for release. For approved circulation only.

THIRTEEN

Not everyone was affected the way Annalise and Krystie were, with what Dr Arbus termed 'an arbitrary increase in libido'. Once or twice we did get psychos jerking off in the cells immediately after the test. Some of them liked it so much they asked for another go. The weird thing was, the ones that were turned on by it were spread equally across Ps and NPs. I asked Arbus if he could explain it and he told me to check out some paper he'd written. Like that was ever going to happen.

We got to be pretty good at judging who was going to come out P and who NP. It's true, we did pick up quite a few dickheads involved in gross acts of what you would have sworn was PGD only for them to come up as NP on the test. Typically, they were your classic bored, disaffected youth, with the added handicap of not being the brightest buttons in the button box. They literally did have shit for brains. I mean literally-literally.

Followers not leaders. Swept along in the prevailing mayhem.

Idiots rather than psychopaths.

The way you could tell them apart was, with the NP idiots, there was usually some kind of purpose behind what they were doing, however ill-conceived and half-baked it was. If you have nothing, if your life is shit and you see no hope of it ever being anything other than shit, it's maybe natural that you might want to smear some shit over other people's lives. It's almost a political statement. Vandalism, arson, assault, mugging, burglary, rape, even murder. Oh, and looting too. It was round about now that looting became a popular leisure activity. Something to do with the family on a pleasant summer evening.

You can make sense of it all when you see the kind of lives these people lead. You've heard the arguments. They don't have a stake in society, so why should they give a flying fuck for society? What did society ever do for them?

Plus, you can almost certainly add that pretty much all of them are off their heads on some kind of substance or another.

I'm not excusing them. They're all scum as far as I'm

concerned. We should lock them all up and throw away the key
if you ask me. But nobody does ask me, of course. I'm just trying
to explain the difference between the idiot and your genuine
psychopath.

To the untrained eye, the product of their behaviour might
appear the same: social disorder. But the processes that generated
it were very different. You could tell this because the ones that
tested P had nothing – or very little – to gain from what they
did. OK, I know what you're going to say, nobody has anything
to gain from smashing up a bus shelter. Except, in the case of
the disaffected youth I mentioned, it was some kind of expression
of genuine rage and frustration and despair. The Ps were not
even that angry. They laughed when they did shit like that. It
was all a massive joke to them. And if they joined in the looting,
they didn't take shit they needed, or shit they could sell on, they
just took shit. Random, worthless junk. Because, mostly, they
thought it was funny. A massive joke.

You can understand rioting and looting when it's driven by
something. But when it's just a joke? I mean a lot of these Ps
– not all, but a lot of them – came from good families.
Comparatively. They had money. They weren't stupid, I mean,
not in an IQ sense. You could talk to them. They knew stuff.
Actually they were quite entertaining to talk to. They told funny
stories. You might imagine yourself spending quite a pleasant
evening with them down the pub.

But it's just, I don't know, there was something missing there.
A reason.

Of course, as a cop, I didn't give a shit about the processes.
It was not my job to understand these people. Just to round them
up and take them out of action.

I guess I was spending too much time in Arbus's company. In
the beginning I was anyhow. Until he disappeared. He set up the
programme, trained the rest of my team, then that was it. We
didn't see him for a long time. Every now and then he would
send one of his research assistants to check up on us, make sure
we were fitting the ScanCap correctly and all that crap. But no
sign of the man himself. I guess he was busy.

Then one day I spied him in the station canteen. He had his
official visitor's lanyard around his neck and a harassed look on
his ashen face. I snuck in behind him in the queue, snaking

inexorably towards a choice of unappetizing lunch options. Nobody was trying any more. That was the trickle-down effect of all the madness in the world. Exhaustion, apathy, general fuck-thatery. Just doing enough not to get found out. That was very much the zeitgeist.

'Doc, how hangeth it?'

He grunted. 'Hmmm.' I think that was his way of saying how pleased he was to see me again. 'Inspector Parfett. How do you manage to be so relentlessly . . . cheerful?'

'I have a motto. What doesn't kill you . . . is funny?'

'You are very glib. Glibness is a key attribute of the psychopath. You should let me test you one day.'

'Over my dead body.'

'That wouldn't work.' I think that was his attempt at a joke. 'One day, you may have no choice, you know. Sooner than you think.'

'What are you talking about?'

'Compulsory Arbus-Lubany testing for police officers.'

'The Fed will never allow it.'

'They may have no choice. It will be positioned to them as a positive move. A way of building trust with the public.'

'That's bullshit.'

'Possibly, yes. But, in your case, wouldn't it be better to know in advance, so maybe you could leave the force discreetly before you are publicly forced out, with all the consequent disadvantages? You may find it hard to secure legitimate employment in the security field as a branded P.'

'You're gonna brand the fuckers?'

'I didn't mean literally. It will be on your employment record.'

'Ain't gonna happen.'

'Forewarned is forearmed. I'm just trying to help you.'

'I'll bear it in mind.'

We took our lunches – him that most English of dishes, chicken tikka masala, me steak and kidney pie – and found a table for two. Actually, I rather got the impression he was trying to shake me off. But I do a good line in not taking the hint.

'Seriously, though, Doc, how's it going – the pilot scheme, I mean? Are we doing good?'

'I'll make my report to the Home Secretary.'

'Yeah, yeah, I get that. You and the Home Secretary. You're

like this.' I showed him my two fingers tightly crossed. 'Ever since that Police Fed conference. Say, you didn't fuck her, did you?'

I think there must have been something wrong with the taste of his curry from the look he gave me.

'That reminds me, you ever see what's her name again? That journalist? Krystie Rothwell.'

He shook his head.

'Pity. She was . . .'

'Please, I won't tolerate any demeaning comments about women.'

'I was going to say she was an excellent journalist. What did you think I was going to say?'

'It doesn't matter.'

'I seem to remember, when you gave your presentation to conference, you had big plans for this machine of yours. It was going to be in every school in the country, wasn't that the idea?'

He gave the tersest of nods.

'I guess it all depends on how well we do here in our little pilot scheme?'

'It doesn't just rely on you.'

'Oh?'

'I *have* been visiting schools in the area too.'

'So that's why you look so knackered?'

'It's been a busy time.'

'But it's what you want, right? It's your plan? The government's getting behind your plan?'

He nodded wearily.

'So why the long face?'

He shrugged. 'There's a lot to do. And, as always, never enough time to do it.'

'You love it.'

I got him there. He couldn't keep the little smirk of triumph off his face. 'We're very close to rolling it out nationally. Very close.'

'How close?'

'The Home Secretary just needs to make sure the political will is there. Across the board. She needs to nip any opposition in the bud before it takes hold.'

'And how does she plan on doing that?'

'How are these things ever done?'

'Well, I guess a major outbreak of PGD kicking off on an unprecedented scale might tip the political pendulum in her favour?'

Arbus looked at me for a long time without speaking. I had the feeling he was fascinated by me, like he had once been fascinated by that girl psycho Annalise Carpenter. He left my question hanging.

I didn't care. It wasn't a question anyhow.

Arbus and his political masters got the main event they were waiting for soon enough. It turned out perfectly for them. So perfectly, you might even have thought they'd planned it. But that would be crazy, hey? I mean, a government that deliberately seeds civil disorder? That would have to make you question who the real psychopaths were here.

And you know, actually, that kind of conspiracy theory shit, it's not really necessary. Because something like this was going to happen anyway, sooner or later. All they had to do was wait.

You know what I'm talking about of course. The Black Friday riots.

I have always hated Black Friday. My instinct is always to punch in the face anyone who ever mentions it as a thing. It is not a thing. Not a natural thing. It is a monstrosity. An aberration. I always said it should be banned.

Course they banned it now, after the riots. Should have banned it before, that would have been the clever thing to do.

Seventeen town centres across the country completely trashed in the course of one day and night. Shop fronts smashed in. Cars and buses turned over. Police stations torched. Not just police stations. Shops, pubs, restaurants, hotels, hairdressers, and yes, certain places of worship. Friday night, you see. What you might call a captive audience in the mosques and synagogues. The buildings hit even included a nursing home and a sports centre, where a wheelchair tennis tournament was in play.

Even some private residences got stormed. Stormed, gutted and stripped. Not just fancy-schmancy high-end mansions either.

In Manchester, a night club collapsed. Maybe that was unrelated. Or maybe it just panicked. I mean, how could rioters make a building collapse? Unless they went there armed with the sledge hammers and masonry chisels which the Manc police found abandoned at the scene.

All told there were 362 people dead, including fourteen police officers, 121 devout of the Jewish and Muslim faiths, thirty-six confused old people, seventeen teenagers, four Team GB disabled tennis athletes, and twenty-two children including one sleeping baby. I forget how many thousands of injured.

To be honest, you had to think it was a miracle it wasn't more when you saw the images of the marauding crowds on NewsNet.

It was eerie to watch the CCTV footage of the cities affected in the hours before it kicked off. You gradually noticed the change in the people on the streets. First you saw one or two wearing masks. It was impossible to say where they came from. They just appeared. Slowly you noticed that the number of masked individuals was increasing, along with the total number of people there. Then suddenly you realized that the streets were packed with crowds and every single fucker was wearing a mask. And not just any mask. They all had on those weird negative black pierrot masks. Like it was some kind of flash mob of depressed mime artists. The CCTV being silent added to that impression. But I heard from cops who were there in some of the towns where it happened that they were all pretty much silent. In the run-up anyhow. When it kicked off you couldn't hear yourself think for the din.

No one spoke. No one looked at their phones. They just seemed to know what was happening and where and when. There was no trace of any coordinated planning on MindNet either. Even though it appeared to be closely synchronized across all seventeen cities.

The creepiest thing of all was when they all looked up and stared into the nearest CCTV camera behind their masks. It happened at exactly the same moment – 12.21 p.m. – in every single city. They held the stare for ten seconds, then nodded once in complete synchrony, and let rip.

The silent crowd found voice. Their roar was not recorded on CCTV. You can hear the audio of it on some of the clips that were uploaded to MindNet. But unless you were actually there in one of the cities where it happened, you can only guess what it felt like to hear it in person. Or be part of it. How frightening to hear. How fucking awesome to make.

I think I read somewhere that the last time a sound like that was heard on earth was in some medieval battlefield.

And of course, the really crazy thing was the only place where nothing went down was the Thames Valley police area.

Like I say, they couldn't have managed it better if they'd planned it.

GENERAL GAMEPLAY NOTES, III

S till thinking aloud here. Well, not really, but you know what I mean.

There should be some kind of supreme über-psycho (ÜPsy?) among all the other psychos. You have the Randoms. The mayhem causing but not necessarily homicidal crapwits. They represent the bottom of the psycho food chain. At the top is the ÜPsy. (Which is not necessarily the player's character, but could be?) The aim of the game is to become the ÜPsy. The cock of Psychotopia. This is achieved by killing the existing ÜPsy and absorbing all their life force.

So how does the player know which is the ÜPsy? Not easy – and complicated by the fact that the ÜPsy engages in face theft (as does the protagonist) so their identity is constantly shifting.

However, one thing that fixes the ÜPsy is a tattoo. The ÜPsy has WHAT YOU KILL MAKES YOU STRONGER tattooed on their . . .????? Back? Neck? Arm? Thigh? Face????

I think face. But you never see it because it is always covered by a stolen face. So how do you know it's there?

Well, there are two things that we could do here.

One is you do get a kind of shadow of the tattoo showing through. A mere literal palimpsest. Not enough to read the words (which are maybe written in a non-Roman script, e.g., Arabic, or Hebrew, or Cyrillic, or Sinograms, or even ancient Egyptian hieroglyphics?).

Two is – of course – the player does not know that this is the clue they are looking for. They have to subconsciously register the telltale palimpsest and repeatedly clock it on the various manifestations of ÜPsy (without getting bumped off by ÜPsy), then work out that this is significant and that this marks the individual out as a target.

If ever they succeed in killing ÜPsy (which is not a given), the tattoo then transfers to them. Which necessitates that they engage in face theft – if they have not been doing so already. (It is by no means certain that they have, by the way. Guidance in this game is minimal. They just gotta work this shit out!)

If they succeed in becoming ÜPsy but do not engage in face theft they will be easily identified by other players, or game-generated psychos, and therefore targeted.

Development notes for PSYCHOTOPIA VR game.
Internal Alpha Games document. Not for release. For approved circulation only.

FOURTEEN

Postnatal depression. That was what they put it down to – the health workers, the GP, Callum, Edie, Mum and Dad. Callum, of course, was the most understanding of them all. 'You're ill,' he said. 'You'll get better. One day, when you least expect it, it will lift. You'll look at her and see how beautiful she is and realize how much you love her.'

His words were meant to make her feel better. But they provoked her deepest, most protracted, most utterly inconsolable fit of weeping yet. Proper snot-running-out-of-nose-body-quaking-uncontrollably convulsions.

Callum had to hold her for a long time for it to pass.

Aimée didn't deny the baby was beautiful. Physically perfect. It was just that it was a perfection she recognized only too well.

Every time she looked at her, she saw *him*. The one who could not be named. She might as well call him Voldemort and have done with it. No, not Voldemort. That gave him too much power over her. Voldejerk, she'd call him instead.

She had her moments of bitter humour. When she would glory in reviling him and abasing herself. For however bad he was – and she liked to frame him now as simply a pathetic loser – she had to conclude that she herself was far worse. She was the fool who had fallen for his ridiculous act in the first place. And the even bigger fool for still allowing him to dominate her thoughts.

She wouldn't allow herself to be the victim in this. She was just a vain, self-centred bitch on heat who had got her comeuppance.

So, yes, in her mind she mocked him and belittled him and abused him. But it was hard to laugh. Because her laughter would always, eventually, turn to tears.

'It'll be fine, you'll see,' insisted Callum.

But Aimée couldn't see how it could ever be fine. Not when she couldn't bring herself to look at her beautiful, perfect baby.

They hired a childminder when the baby was just a few months old, so Aimée could retake her final year of professional training as soon as possible. Maybe it was too soon. The feelings were unresolved. It was too much like running away. But it was the only way she could cope. The work was a blessed distraction. While she was working on some tiny detail of a massive landmark project – bespoke door handle designs for a new hotel in Dubai – she could almost believe she didn't have a baby. It was only when the time approached to go home at the end of each long day that she felt it: the cold heavy stone settling in the pit of her stomach.

It wasn't fair on Callum, of course. Let alone the baby. But it was Callum she worried about. He was doing all the parental heavy lifting. As well as holding down a demanding job of his own.

He was the one who dressed the baby in the morning. Aimée had tried. But each time Callum found her paralysed by fear, babygrow hanging limply in her hands. She was invariably staring at an illustration of a cow that they had hung on the nursery wall. Looking for meaning in a nursery rhyme. But the expression on the cow's face appalled her. It seemed gleeful, gloating, heartless. *Here am I jumping over the moon, and there are you stuck with a baby you cannot love.*

More and more, she left everything to Callum.

It was Callum who got the baby to the childminder's in the morning. Callum who ran out of meetings to pick her up at the end of the day.

Callum who woke up in the middle of the night to go to her when she was crying. Callum who dealt with her night-time feeds, sterilizing the bottle and preparing the formula milk. Doing it all with one hand because he was carrying and comforting the baby in his other arm.

It was Callum who changed her nappies. Who bathed her. Who put her down for sleeps. He was the one who dealt with her croup and her colic. He was the one who mushed up the avocado when she moved to solids. Who spent hours online browsing baby fashions and chatting on MumsMind.

She told herself it was what he wanted. That she was taking a back seat to let him be an involved father. Hadn't the nine months before the birth been totally down to her? And hadn't he looked jealously on as she formed the new life inside her? Now it was his turn to be the nurturing parent.

That's what she told herself. And sometimes she nearly believed it. But she knew it was an excuse. And she knew there was a danger, if she wasn't careful, that she could lose him.

So she tried. She knew she could never love her daughter. But she could at least try to mask her true feelings. Which was not so much hate as supreme distaste. There was an unhealthy mixture of shame and fear in there too. Shame for how the child had been conceived. But also for her part in concealing the paternity from Callum. And the fear was of what would happen if Callum found out the truth.

Perhaps she was a more calculating bitch than she had ever reckoned. Was she subconsciously letting Callum do all the work so that he would bond with the baby all the more? So that if it ever did come out that he was not the father, it would be too late. Emotionally, he would already *be* her father – certainly more of a father than Voldejerk ever was.

The name was Callum's choice. It had chilled Aimée to realize that it was a matter of supreme indifference to her what her baby was called. And it seemed to mean everything to Callum. So she let him have his way. Siobhan. His grandmother's name. It was a beautiful name, she had to agree.

Some days, she almost persuaded herself that she was wrong. What if Callum was the father after all? It wasn't impossible. She'd made sure of that. Calculating bitch that she was. But no, she only had to look at that child to know. Which was why she preferred, if at all possible, not to look at her. For as long as she didn't look at her daughter, she could believe that Callum was the father.

And every time Aimée managed to bring herself to glance in her daughter's direction, it shocked her to see how much the baby had developed. She was thriving like a cuckoo chick. It ought to have delighted her. To see how big her daughter had grown while she had not been looking. How dextrously now her fingers grasped and pointed. She could sit up on her own now, support her head and hold her gaze on whatever caught her attention. More often than not, the focus of her gaze was her mother. Of course! There was nothing sinister about it at all. It was perfectly natural. But Aimée persuaded herself otherwise. There was something about both the fixity and emptiness of that gaze that unnerved her. If Siobhan had done the old trick of pointing two fingers at her own eyes and then switching them to point at Aimée, it wouldn't have surprised her.

There was something about the look that suggested the child was biding her time. It wouldn't be long before she was standing up. And then walking. And that look seemed to say, *I'll be coming after you.*

She was gurgling bubbles and testing the feel of syllables shaping on her lips. Tentatively moving to speech. And Aimée dreaded to think what her first words would be.

She was being ridiculous, she knew. But she couldn't prevent the dark, unwelcome thoughts from popping into the loop of her internal monologue. And once the words 'Devil Child' had been thought, she couldn't unthink them.

Fortunately for them all, Callum had the kind of job he could do anywhere, and more or less at any time. So when the child-minder said she couldn't look after Siobhan any longer (couldn't or *wouldn't*? Aimée wondered), Callum managed to arrange things so that he could have her at home full-time for a while, just until they found someone else.

But he made it a condition that Aimée agree to seek help for her depression. 'It's more common than you think, you know. I've being talking to some of the mums on MumsMind. One in ten mothers suffer from it.'

'You've been talking to other women about me?'

'I . . . I pretended it was me . . . they think I'm a mum.'

She let out a half-sob, half-laugh.

'What you have, it's an illness. If you had a broken arm or a pain in your belly, you wouldn't hesitate.'

But it wasn't his reasoned arguments that persuaded her. It was the fact that he felt it necessary to make the ultimatum in the first place. She could no longer kid herself that he was happy with the situation as it was. And seeing the brimming panic in his eyes, she had her first inkling of how lost she must have seemed to him.

Her GP prescribed beta-blockers and referred her to a psychiatrist.

The psychiatrist was a woman, Dr Ruth Sherman-Lowe. She was about ten years older than Aimée. Slim and beautiful and stylish, she struck Aimée as the wisest, calmest, most unshockable person she had ever met.

She confided everything to her within the first five minutes of meeting her.

And felt immediately the confessional unburdening of her soul. The Catholic in her, that would be.

Together, over the course of a year, they worked through Aimée's fears and guilts and anxieties. And what you might call her 'unresolved issues'.

Most of the sessions involved hypnosis. She was taken back to relive her long weekend with Voldejerk. She scaled again the heights of ecstasy and pleasure. And experienced again the plummeting shame of his betrayal.

Only this time – unlike all the other times she had flashbacked to this – she was permitted to say to Charlie (she was no longer unable to say his name – Dr Sherman-Lowe would not let her get away with that, or Voldejerk), all the things that she had never been able to.

She told him that she was still in love with him. And that was the most freeing thing of all.

Whatever Dr Sherman-Lowe did, it worked. It took time, but it worked.

She no longer feared or hated her daughter, or even felt the slightest shudder of revulsion when holding her. She was able to dress her, feed her, change her, read to her and even cuddle her.

She loved her. Because she allowed a part of herself to love him, Charlie.

Part of the therapy was that she was required to be honest with Callum.

That was tough. Something came down in his eyes when she talked about the feelings she still had for Charlie. She felt that she had got back her daughter but was in danger of losing her partner. And so she held back. She didn't tell him everything.

Even when Callum said: 'But I don't see what all of this has got to do with Siobhan?'

That was her opportunity. If she was ever going to say it – *because he's her father* – it was then. But she let the opportunity slip.

The years went by. And with them came and went a succession of childminders and nannies. Somehow they could never manage to hold on to one for long.

But now at least there were two parents engaged in bringing up their child. Juggling deadlines and meetings, each of them learning to compromise on their dreams.

After she qualified, Aimée chose to take a job in a slightly less prestigious partnership in Islington, because she thought it would give her more flexibility over working hours. More time to spend with Siobhan, in other words.

She was no longer seeing Dr Sherman-Lowe. Now it seemed inconceivable that she had ever not loved her beautiful, perfect daughter.

True, there were some tense moments at parent and toddler groups. Siobhan could be quite determined and self-willed. If she wanted something, she would generally just take it. But weren't all children like that at her age?

Aimée began to notice that there were some mothers who would habitually steer their child away from Siobhan. She even heard one mother mutter the words 'Devil Child' as she carried her howling son away from whatever interaction had just taken place between him and Siobhan. She felt her cheeks flush with rage and a burning sense of injustice on her daughter's behalf. Though her reaction was somewhat complicated by the fact that the very same thought had once occurred to her.

But she had few anxieties now about her own relationship with her daughter. She knew Siobhan wasn't exactly the perfect angel her doting grandparents thought her to be. She was just an ordinary little girl, testing barriers, learning how to socialize, making mistakes and learning from them (she hoped). Growing and developing into the person she would one day be.

They had their ups and downs. A definite up would be her extravagant joy at getting a pet rabbit, at the age of four, after months of pestering them. She called him Mr Fluffy and demanded that she be allowed to cuddle him. For some reason she could not articulate, Aimée was relieved to see Siobhan's obvious affection for her pet. Unfortunately, the poor, petrified animal leapt out of Siobhan's hands as soon as he was placed in them, despite Siobhan grabbing a little too roughly at one of his hind legs. No coaxing could persuade Mr Fluffy to allow himself to be cuddled by the little girl. She was inconsolable.

And yet, when Mr Fluffy was found dead in his hutch a few days later (one of the downs), she seemed strangely unaffected.

It was almost as if he were a toy she'd grown out of and put aside.

Perhaps she didn't understand that he was dead, or what death is. Aimée had to prefer that explanation to any other.

That she just didn't care, for example.

It was her relationship with Callum that concerned Aimée now. They just didn't seem to have any time for each other any more. Since her partial confession, she had felt a shutter come down between them. He was no longer quick to take her in his arms – in fact, he was scrupulous in his avoidance of any unnecessary physical contact.

He was always tired. They both were. They still had sex, infrequently, and usually at her instigation. He never denied her. But she had the sense that he was going through the motions. No doubt he appreciated the physical release it allowed, but sometimes it felt like there was nothing more to it than that.

She felt him slipping away from her. And began to feel scared and more alone than she ever had.

Then, somehow, she managed to fall pregnant. She couldn't work out whether this was the best or the worst thing that could possibly happen. She hoped it would bring them together again. Because at least, this time, there was no doubt. He was the father.

The new baby would heal them.

Siobhan was six.

PROGRESSING FROM
LEVEL THREE, I

Level Three is defined as the immediate locality around the high-rise secure unit from which the player's character has escaped. There are two ways out of it. One via a move backwards. The other via a move forwards.

First the backwards move:

There is always the possibility that the player may be caught by the police and either (a) returned to the secure psychiatric unit (or possibly a different psychiatric unit? – look into budget implications of developing multiple secure units), or (b) incarcerated in an ordinary prison/correctional facility. If the latter, the player's aim in this stage of the game is to persuade the authorities of their judicial insanity. They must feign psychosis. This will then produce effectively the same result as (a) – return to a secure psychiatric unit. This represents failure in Level Three of the game and essentially return to Level One. Progress from Level One to Level Two can be achieved more rapidly than before because the player has learned the various strategies required. NB, the character should be wearing a stolen face (e.g. from a murdered tramp), which will mean that they are not recognized upon return to the unit and can begin life there with a clean sheet.

Now the forwards move:

We have to create some obstacle or barrier which prevents the player from simply walking their character out of the Level Three area. This could be a physical barrier or a psychological barrier. Just riffing here, but let's say that in the Level Three stage of the game, the further the player moves from the secure unit the faster their powers drain. And consequently, therefore, the more frequently they need to kill to top up their power levels. The more frequently they kill, the more likely they are to get caught. But there are dangers in staying too close to the secure unit as well. They may get seen and identified by staff going in and out. The need to move on from Level Three is driven by a two-fold pressure: 1. The depletion of prey – at some point they're going to run out of victims. 2. The danger of getting caught. So, progression needs to occur at some point. There will be a perfect moment for this. The player should recognize it when it comes along, though will not be forewarned.

I imagine it to be a car pulling up, the passenger door opening, and the unsolicited offer of a ride from a character hitherto not encountered in the game. I'm calling him Mephistopholo for now. We can go with that until someone comes up with anything better.

Development notes for PSYCHOTOPIA VR game.
Internal Alpha Games document. Not for release. For approved circulation only.

FIFTEEN

So after the Black Friday riots, the government had little trouble persuading people to accept the national roll-out of Arbus's machines. They didn't even pretend it wasn't about psychopathy any more. There was public uproar. The more tabloid elements of NewsNet were clamouring for something to be done. All the government had to offer were the machines. So there was no more of this 'demographic survey' bollocks. We were weeding out the psychopaths and everybody knew it.

Initially, it was just to be in police stations. And solely on individuals who had been caught engaged in what seemed to be PGD-related activities. But then the old horse-stable-door objection was raised. So it was broadened out to include anyone who was being investigated for any offence whatsoever – a little like routine DNA swabbing. The thinking being if you could tag these people on the database, whenever there was any trouble in the future you'd know who to pull in first.

That's fine so long as the Ps are relatively few in number. But when the number of Ps in society starts to approach the number of NPs, then the distinction becomes less useful, if not totally meaningless. I mean, it's like, what's the point of a sex offenders' register if every fucker in the country is on it?

It was concerns like this that led some outrider law and order pundits to go on the screens saying that police station testing of offenders/suspects was not enough. What you had to do was identify the psychopaths before they had had a chance to do anything psychopathic. They brought out Arbus's old proposals for testing infant school children. They were pretty close to calling for universal Arbus-Lubany testing.

It was fairly obvious to me that the government was putting them up to it. They were just testing the public mood, to see if people were ready for something so out-there yet. And these pundits were far from the drooling right-wing nut jobs you might imagine. They were presentable, plausible and persuasive. My old fuck buddy Krystie Rothwell was cropping up everywhere interviewing them. She had gained a certain amount of celebrity due to her early-adopter-style testing on the machine at the Fed conference. She was the go-to journo for anything Arbus-Lubany related.

Whenever I saw her on a screen I couldn't help remembering our time together. She never did call me. She was a busy girl, all right. And I certainly had enough on my plate. Still, I couldn't deny it would have been nice to have a rematch at least once, even twice. Maybe I was flattering myself, but I kind of got the impression she'd had a good time too.

What the fuck did I care though? It was up to her. I definitely wasn't going to go chasing her.' Way to get an exclusion order. And it wasn't as if I wasn't getting any elsewhere. Even if I had to use my badge to get it from time to time.

All this time, as you can imagine, Arbus was a man much in demand. He was flying all over the world talking to foreign governments who were trying to deal with similar issues in their own countries. You can bet they didn't have anything like the same qualms about universal testing as there were over here. Of course, it helped the authorities here if our friends and allies overseas were ahead of the curve. They could see how things panned out in these other countries, then bring in their own proposals accordingly. Plus they were very happy to be exporting homegrown expertise and technology.

For me personally, the aftermath of the Black Friday riots meant a transfer to the Met, working out of a dedicated PGD unit based in New New Scotland Yard. I was brought in to help implement P testing across the force, training their officers in the operation of the Arbus-Lubany machines. That was fine by me. I was ready for a change and it was either London or Manchester – and there was no way you'd get me going up north. Psychopaths I can handle. Mancs, you've got to be joking.

It was the end of the road for me and the Terrorist.

'Keep in touch,' said Rashid.

'Why?' was my question.

He came back with, 'Don't be a cunt all your life.'

As you can see, it was emotional.

So far the government here was of the view that the majority of the population was in favour of suppressing and controlling PGD. At one time, that would have been such an obvious statement that it didn't need making. But you don't need me to tell you how things turned out.

It was about this time, after the Black Friday riots and the roll-out of the Arbus-Lubany machines, that the libertarian backlash started. The pro-psy marches. You'll have seen the banners: PSAY NO TO PSYCHO TESTING.

This was the start of the movement – they called themselves human rights activists – that grew into the P party.

I caught Krystie interviewing their leader, the civil rights lawyer Bartholomew Bartholomew, on NewsNet. A weird-looking guy, I think we can all agree. First there was that undertaker-chic dress sense that he seemed to go in for. And then his head – what was that all about? Completely shaven, but with an ink-black tattoo covering his scalp. His sunken cheeks gave his face a somewhat cadaverous look. I could mention the blank, staring eyes, but they all had those.

For all that, he was weirdly engaging, funny, persuasive – likeable, even. And also a complete psychopath. You didn't need an Arbus-Lubany machine to tell you that.

The argument, as put forward by Bartholomew (that double name of his really pissed me off, by the way – I mean, his parents must have been psychopaths too, to call him that) was as follows:

'The great danger here, Krystie, is of criminalizing people who have done nothing wrong. It's a data protection issue too. Let's say you have a P result, and that information is placed on your file. Who has access to that information? Can prospective employers, for example, check to see whether someone is P or NP?'

'Wouldn't that be a good thing?'

'No! It's a fundamental violation of an individual's human rights.'

'But you saw the destruction that was wreaked in the riots. The government has to do something to stop that happening again, doesn't it?'

'Arrest those guilty of criminal acts.'

'Well, that's easier said than done. Most people took steps to conceal their identities.'

'That does not give the authorities the right to brand great swathes of our populace as criminals.'

'*Potential* criminals, I think they would say.'

'What happens if one of these machines malfunctions? If someone has a false positive result. Technology is fallible. Human beings are fallible. Can we trust the police officers operating these machines? Is there any right of appeal against a test result? Can the result be fixed?'

'So you have no faith in the testing procedure whatsoever?'

'That's not what I'm saying. What I'm saying is that if there is even the possibility of a single error occurring then we should ban the use of these machines.'

'But doesn't it go deeper than that, Mr Bartholomew? Aren't you in fact defending the right for people to behave in destructive, dangerous and antisocial ways? Aren't you fundamentally arguing for the right to be a psychopath?'

'Well, there are two separate things there, Krystie. No one has the right to engage in destructive, dangerous and antisocial acts. That's absolute. So of course the government has the right to arrest and subject to the judicial process those individuals it can prove have been involved in such activities. However, an individual indisputably has the right to be a psychopath. Because it is not something they choose to be, rather it is something they simply are. You can no more outlaw psychopathy than you can outlaw certain skin tones. Imagine the outcry if a government tried to do that! By the way, we prefer the term "psychopote". The pote is for *potential*. We believe this particular condition is not a disorder or a handicap or even an illness, but is rather a super-enhancement of the human organism. Humanity is a work in progress. Psychopotes are a step along the way to something more perfect, more powerful, more evolved. Yes, there are issues at the moment, with regard to problematic socializing. I see them as teething troubles. I would urge people not to panic. We should wait and see where this takes us and I think it will be to quite an extraordinary place. People should not be afraid of Ps but should embrace them.'

'Hug them? Hug a P – is that your slogan?'

'Well, you're trivializing my words now, to try and make me look ridiculous. But if you like, yes, I have no objection to being hugged by you, certainly.'

'So you are a P?'

'I have never been tested, Krystie. And the issue is not whether I am a P or an NP. It is a broader issue of human rights. Ps are still human beings, you know. We should not forget that. I think what frightens people about psychopotes is that they are completely free. Freedom is a scary thing for most people, but not for psychopotes. This freedom from conventional mores—'

'Rules, you mean? The laws that the rest of us have to abide by?'

'I'm talking more about the intellectual constraints that are placed on us by society. The whole burden of received, unchallenged, conditioned thinking – if you can even call it thinking. It's more like programming. Psychopotes don't recognize that as something they should be bound by. That is a level of freedom that many people find disturbing. And also, if I'm honest, I think there is a degree of envy mixed into people's reactions.'

'Envy? Are you serious?'

'Yes, they envy the psychopote's courage.'

'Is it courage to beat a nine-month-old baby to death with a softball bat?'

'Isolated incidents. We can all pull out isolated incidents to prove our point one way or another.' It was Bartholomew's next sentence that really gave the game away. 'But yes, even that, on some deep, unacknowledged level, even that. Not that I condone such acts.'

'Will you condemn them?'

'I think what you have to consider here, Krystie, is that what such acts show – if you look at them objectively, rationally, and without unnecessary sentiment – is the psychopote's ability to do whatever the hell he wants. And to have no concern whatsoever about the consequences. Who wouldn't envy that, Krystie?'

The camera cut away to Krystie. She looked so pale she was almost green. I think she was shaking, or there was some problem with my screen. I reckon they must have cut just as she vomited.

PROGRESSING FROM
LEVEL THREE, II

So Mephistopholo. (Or maybe we should spell it Mefistofolo?) We need to think some more about him. (He is definitely a he, by the way.)

The name is devilish. Supernatural. Character design should reflect this. Is he the über-psycho we postulated above? I prefer to think of him as above all the psychos, even the über-psycho. He is a god. The god of the psychos. Essentially the devil. I think that's what my subconscious was thinking when it gave me the name.

I'd like to consider some kind of link between Mefistofolo and the spider that helped the protag escape from their cell in the secure unit. They are one and the same being. The spider is a manifestation – or form – of Mefistofolo. So there should be some spidery aspect to his appearance. A spider tattoo?

First thing, Mefistofolo is pissed off with the protag for the way they pulled off his legs when he was a spider. He trusses the protag up in some kind of silky web substance. The twist is the protag must not fight this, but has to go along with it. For it is when they are caught in Mefistofolo's web, bitten by Mefistofolo and paralysed by his poison, and then, in fact, eaten by Mefistofolo – it is only then that transition to Level Four is achieved. Mefistofolo's car is not the method of transition. Though first, of course, the player experiences a stonkingly thrilling ride in said car. (At one point Mefistofolo takes his hands off the wheel, leaving it for the player to wrest control of the car. Must avoid crashing! That would be bad. That would result in hospitalization, which would delay progress in the game, or even death of character, which would mean end of game for this play.)

Memo to experiential engineers: once again consider auto-hack-modification of VR headset/suit so that the player actually feels they are being consumed by Mefistofolo.

Development notes for PSYCHOTOPIA VR game.
Internal Alpha Games document. Not for release. For approved circulation only.

SIXTEEN

E die stood beneath a cloudless sky, allowing the unmitigated sun to gently, insidiously burn her face. It was not quite hot enough to be painful. But she was aware that there was danger as well as pleasure in the sun's rays.

Her eyes were half-closed, in the same way she half-closed them when she was watching horror movies. But actually, she felt calm. Almost happy.

It felt like a moment from her childhood. She could imagine the whole of a long summer vacation stretching ahead of her. She thought of family holidays in Devon with Mum and Dad and Aims. Messing about on a little dinghy that Dad had hired. Life jackets on, trailing lead-weighted fishing lines from the stern. They never caught anything. There was that time when . . . had she drifted off, or had some spirit of perversity entered her? Was it a lapse in concentration, or a moment of devilry born out of boredom? At any rate, she had let go of her line. Maybe it was just to find out what would happen.

What happened was it disappeared – the weight, the bait, the line, the little wooden frame it was wound on, everything – beneath the surface of the water in Salcombe Bay. With a sudden, irretrievable, heart-lurching plop.

She had been inconsolable. So big sister Aimée did the big-sister thing and handed over her own line for Edie to hold.

It was surely devilry when she let go of that one too. Daddy had been so proud of Aims for being so grown up. And even now, Edie knew that part of her had wanted to get back at her sister for that. To hurt her. For the way she had come selflessly to her aid.

Children. Little monsters. Little . . . psychopaths.

Thank God she turned out all right. Well, not too bad, all things considered.

And all her life she had been looking for an opportunity to make amends to Aimée. To come to her rescue when she needed it.

Maybe that was why, when that nonsense happened with the arsehole, when all their stuff had been stolen, she couldn't get too upset about her own losses. Not like Aryan had, the wanker. She was more concerned about Aimée.

She hadn't thought about it like that at the time – as making amends. It was more natural than that. Her sister was hurting and she just had to do everything she could to ease her hurt. It was as simple as that.

Edie opened her eyes and scanned the unspoilt sky, searching for fault lines. A network of vapour trails was etched across it. As if a large petulant child had scribbled over the sky's perfection.

She was convinced things weren't as bad as everybody made out. There was a general air of despondency and catastrophe about. But she preferred not to give into it. The thing was if you spent too long plugged into the MindNet, you could end up believing the world was going to end tomorrow. For as long as she could remember there had always been this sense. And it hadn't ended yet.

You had to take the fight to them, the fuckwits and the trolls and the fascists and the haters. You had to take them on. Not let them get away with any of their shit.

And though you might not be perfect yourself – you had your fair share of mistakes and flaws to contend with, your heavy baggage of regrets to trail around – still you were better than all of them put together.

Part of the thing you had to do was fight against the spirit of dissolution and decay. Of the world just letting itself go. Of no one giving a shit any more. Of things falling apart.

And that wasn't easy. You had to work hard at it.

It was easier to say there was nothing you could do about it. You were just one person. How could you hold everything together on your own?

That was the point. You couldn't. Not on your own. So your first task was pulling the good people towards you and holding them tight.

It was as simple as that.

This was what she told herself.

It may have been simple, but it wasn't easy. Sometimes good people didn't want you to pull them to you. Sometimes they gave

into the despair and defeat. And you had to shake them out of
it. Or not shake them out of it, no, that wasn't right. Love them
out of it.

Sometimes what it took was staying absolutely still till they
came to you.

Like Aims after Siobhan was born.

But they'd got through that. They were in a better place now.
All of them were. Which just went to show. The world hadn't
turned to shit yet.

And if they could get through that, then people, she thought,
could get through pretty much anything.

Her present mission was a case in point. She'd tracked down
Sal, who she hadn't seen for literally years (the problem had
been Aryan, but Sal wasn't with Aryan any more) and pretty
much railroaded her into meeting up for lunch. Wouldn't take
no for an answer.

Sal had just landed a new job, was mega-busy, didn't know
when she could get out. But Edie was having none of that.

And so here she was, standing in the little plaza beneath a
mirror-fronted office building close to Old Street roundabout,
waiting for her old friend to come out.

She'd already MindMessaged Sal to let her know that she was
here. And she'd rather wait outside feeling the sun on her face
than step inside that building. The impenetrability of its facade
repelled her. And the glimpses she had caught of the reception
in the opening and closing of the doors were not enticing. She
had no desire to sit in some wanker's idea of 'a cool space'
(which actually to her eye looked like nothing so much as an
oversized adolescent boy's bedroom) being bombarded by over-
excited action sequences from the company's games projected
on wall-high VirScreens.

She'd take fresh air and sunshine over simulated explosions
and virtual violence any day.

At last, Sal came out. Her friend looked pale and thin, her
eyes masked by heavy black sunglasses. Sal waved shyly as she
approached. They hugged. And Edie held on to her friend as if
she never wanted to let her go again.

Then she looked her over with unhurried solicitude. 'You look
tired.'

'I feel like shit. I was out last night.'

'Really? Where?'

'I went out with my boss.'

'Oh? Is that wise?'

'No.'

'So he's cute, this boss of yours. I presume.'

'I suppose so. I don't know. To be honest, I think he's a bit of a psychopath.'

'Isn't everyone these days? I hear it's very much the thing.'

'I've got the hangover from hell today. A hangover like I've never had before.'

'Where did you go?'

'I don't remember. I don't remember anything.'

'Fucking hell, Sal. That's not good. That's very very not good.'

'Oh, it's all right. I took something. Es, I think. I'm just not used to it.'

'You don't know what you took?'

'Es. It was Es. I've never taken them before so I didn't know they were going to affect me like that.'

'Like what?'

'I don't know. I got tired. I guess I passed out.'

'I don't think Es do that to you.'

'Can we get something to eat, please? I need to eat something. Something stodgy.'

'OK. Where's good for stodge around here?'

Edie's arm shot out protectively around her friend's shoulder as she scanned the plaza shops and restaurants for somewhere suitable.

They settled for an Italian chain. Pasta smothered in a cheesy sauce seemed to do the trick for Sal.

She must have picked up on the concerned scrutiny coming from Edie.

'I drank too much. It was my own fault. It wasn't really anything to do with the . . . you know. And besides, he took them too. I think he was trying to, you know, be generous . . . for him that's kind of a treat. He was trying to get me to loosen up. I think he thinks I'm too uptight. But you know, nothing bad happened. I promise you.'

'You can't remember what happened.'

'I'm sure nothing bad happened. I would know about it if

it had. He was a gentleman. He called a taxi and took me home. I woke up in my own bed. Alone. Fully clothed. And you know, I have a tamperproof seal on my underwear, and that was intact, so I know nothing happened.'

'I'm glad you can joke about it.'

'He was not going to do anything. He's my boss.'

'Uh, hello? What the fuck's that got to do with it? You said yourself he's a psychopath.'

'Not that kind of psychopath. Just a messing-with-your-head kind of psychopath. He plays these games. It's fine. He's the same with everyone. Worse with some people.'

'It's not healthy! It's not good. It shouldn't be allowed.'

'He's a genius, though? He can get away with it.'

'I don't care! Christ! You're only making computer games here.'

'VR games,' Sal corrected. At Edie's blank look, Sal explained. 'You know, VR. Virtual Reality. We also do AR, Augmented Reality.'

'Whatever. It's not like you're, you know, saving humanity or anything.'

'Funnily enough, that was kind of my job description.'

'What?'

'Oh, nothing. It doesn't matter. Listen, I'd better get back. It's been lovely seeing you. And . . . that . . . was . . . beautiful stodge. We should get the bill.'

'It's my treat.'

'Edie! Why?'

'So you are obliged to get the next one.'

'OK. I'll allow that.'

They walked back across the little plaza without speaking. It was even hotter now. Or maybe that was just the effect of coming out of an air-conditioned restaurant. As they approached the entrance to Alpha Games, Edie sensed Sal tense up.

'Shit. It's him. Don't say anything. And don't look.'

But it was too late for the last prohibition. Edie had already caught the direction of her friend's sly, evasive glance. And followed it. And saw him. Only for a fleeting second, as he pushed the high glass door to be swallowed by the building.

'Fuck. You know who that is, don't you?'

'What do you mean? Who?'

'It's *him*. It's that fucker Aims picked up at Rick and Dave's party that time. The one who said he was a DJ or something. Studying psychology. But he was just a fucking psycho.'

'No. It can't be. It can't be him. Didn't he have blond hair?'

'You can dye your hair, Sal.'

'And what was he called? He wasn't called Oscar. My boss is called Oscar.'

'He called himself Charlie. Who knows what his real name was.'

'I don't . . . no . . . I just don't see it. It can't be him.'

'I'm telling you. It's him. I saw him close up. He fucking tried it on with me. I will never forget his face.'

'I don't see how it can be, Edie.'

'What's he call himself now?'

'Oscar Winslett.'

'Oscar Winslett. And what does he do here?'

'He's Head of Game Development.'

'Is he now? He's done all right for himself, then, hasn't he?'

The door had sealed him in now. He was invulnerable and beyond her reach. All she could do was look at the flawless sky reflected in the sheer glass facade.

PROGRESSING FROM
LEVEL THREE, III

So we left the protagonist suspended in some kind of weblike prison, wrapped in a shroud of sticky devil-silk, paralysed, helpless, being eaten alive by a kind of spider devil who just happens to be the patron saint/god of psychopaths. Not just watching this as a spectator but *experiencing* it. The point being this must feel like the nadir. The low point in the game. Like all is lost. But actually, it isn't. It is the beginning of a new phase, progression to a new level.

The key thing here is that the player has to realize, at some point in the process of being consumed, that, hey, actually, this is a good thing. They have to surrender, emotionally, to being eaten. Not just surrender but embrace it. Love it. (Some way of picking up emotional/sensory responses built into the technology? Must be a way of making this happen. We're pushing the boundaries here, folks, but that's what's going to make this game great.)

I mean for a psychopath, what could be better than being eaten by the god of psychopaths?

Also, the protagonist stays alive throughout the eating. They are able to experience the gradual loss of first their extremities, then entire limbs, gonads, internal organs. Their head, and some kind of consciousness of what is happening to them, remains to the end – the last possible moment.

Then there is darkness. More than darkness. Nothingness.

Then there is a sense of something emerging within the nothingness. A fragile pulsing. The tiny, tenuous, urgent hammering of new life.

Mefistofolo, who, now that I think about it, is somehow both male and female, has – in his spider aspect – laid a nest of spider eggs. Let's say one hundred spider eggs. (That number may have to be revised, downwards most likely, as we explore the playability of Level Four.) These eggs will hatch to form one hundred 'Spiderpaths'. Beings who are able to switch between human and arachnoid form. The player has control of the Spiderpaths (so maybe 100 is too many?) – not simultaneously, but by switching from one POV/consciousness to another. While he is not within the consciousness of a particular Spiderpath, he has no control over its actions.

So Level Four is not a different place, after all? It is just a transition to a different way of playing?

Or perhaps the Spiderpaths are distributed to many different places? In the way that exotic spiders from Brazil (or wherever) sometimes find themselves over here in a case of bananas?

Development notes for PSYCHOTOPIA VR game.
Internal Alpha Games document. Not for release. For approved circulation only.

SEVENTEEN

Neither the Prime Minister, Gleb Jackson, nor his Home Secretary, Jessica Thorndike, would consent to debate with Bartholomew Bartholomew. Naturally. It was beneath their dignity to do so. Not just because he didn't represent an official political party (yet), but also because he was, well, not to put too fine a point on it, obviously a psychopath. (By the way, if you ask me, it was that 'obviously' that they really objected to. If only he hadn't flaunted his psychopathy so much, maybe they could have found a way to work with him.)

They did allow some of their outrider pundits to sit across the studio table from him and air a broadly government position. Bartholomew chewed them up and spat them out. He reminded me of nothing so much as a spider in its web. Patient, waiting, predatory. You had to admire him. I mean, one of the defining characteristics of a psychopath is that they are only in it for themselves. The idea of them organizing and working together for some higher group purpose is anathema. As individuals, they have no purpose, other than to fulfil their predatory instincts, whether they be sexually, financially, or violently directed. Remember, I know of what I speak.

But Bartholomew Bartholomew was different. Bartholomew Bartholomew had a vision. He realized that if he could unite all the psychopaths under his P is for PHREEDOM banner, he could create a powerful force for – well, for Bartholomew Bartholomew, I guess. For change, at any rate. And there's always a huge constituency willing to sign up for change of any kind. For some reason, they automatically assume that any change is going to benefit them and make the people they hate suffer.

He promised freedom, or *phreedom* as he lamely insisted on spelling it, which the way I interpreted it meant the freedom to indulge every conceivable psychopathic whim or appetite, with impunity. It was an interesting manifesto. Of course, he didn't write an actual manifesto. And anything he did write didn't openly reveal his aims at all. The guy was a psychopath, remember. Deception and misdirection are the psychopath's stock-in-trade.

So whenever there was some egregious outburst of PGD, he was very careful not to condone it. And equally careful never to condemn it. Sometimes I worried for him. Those words are so close. I was afraid he was going to get them mixed up. That's just the kind of thing a psychopath does – and thinks is hilarious. But I guess he was more buttoned-down than that.

It was about this time that I was surprised – correction, utterly fucking gobsmacked – to get a MindMessage from Krystie Rothwell. You know the kind of thing, or maybe you don't.

Hi. Long time no C. B gd to catch up? MindMessage me.

That kind of thing.

I didn't flatter myself. I knew there had to be something she wanted. And I'm not talking about picking up where we left off in her hotel room in Bournemouth however many years ago it was now. She may have tested NP but that didn't mean she wasn't a cold-hearted, manipulative, self-centred bitch. That was kind of why I liked her, I suppose. I had a soft spot for clear-sighted, hard-as-nails women, women who knew what they wanted and were prepared to do whatever it took to get it.

You knew where you stood with them.

So I MindMessaged her back.

Happy to. Where?

We arranged to meet at NewsNet's London studios. So that was it. She wanted to get me on the screens.

It wasn't much to look at from the outside. A nondescript three-storey building on a bleak, semi-industrial wasteland in Haggerston. There were a number of company names on the sign outside. All of them I guessed were other media and tech companies, probably all owned by the same holding company, which was of course MindNet.

Not very sexy, but functional. A pain in the arse for interviewees to get to. But I guess that was testament to NewsNet's clout. There was never any shortage of volunteers willing to haul themselves out to East London for a face-to-face grilling by Krystie, who was rapidly turning out to be everyone's favourite inquisitor. Of course, there was no real need for interviewer and interviewee to be in the same room any more. But it did undoubtedly add to the on-screen chemistry. There was always a certain frisson, which was lacking in screen-to-screen interviews. Most of those who made the journey saw it as a staging post on their career. It was ambition that brought them here, in other words.

Me, I had other motives. I just wanted to have another look at Krystie. I guess in the back of my mind I was half-hoping I would get a fuck out of it. Though I did remember her strange aversion to storeroom sex.

The sky was holding itself in. The weight of an impending downpour was starting to give me a headache. Hey, what can I say? I'm sensitive like that.

Anyhow, it was a relief to get inside. One thing I will say for MindNet, they may not pay their taxes but at least they have functioning air conditioning in their buildings. It's a pay-off, I guess.

I'm not an easy man to surprise. But I'll admit I hadn't expected to bump into Dr Arbus there in the reception.

'Doc, my man.'

'Inspector.'

'You here to see Krystie?'

'Ms Rothwell? That's right.'

'Me too.' I had to admit, I was a teeny bit disappointed. And felt a teeny bit less special. 'What about, do you know?'

'I'm not sure it's any business of yours?'

'I'm just trying to be friendly. For fuck's sake. I'm here to see her too.'

'And why are you here?'

'I think she wants to suck my dick.'

I don't know why, but he didn't seem to find that funny. I've heard it said these academic types can be a bit on the spectrum, if you know what I mean. No sense of humour.

'Other than that, I got nothing.'

The conversation, such as it was, kind of dried up after that.

Though both of us sat up when Bartholomew Bartholomew came through the front door and checked in at the desk.

'So that's it,' said Arbus.

'What?'

'She asked me if I'd be prepared to debate the ethics of testing with a notable opponent. Precisely who that would be was not confirmed.'

'If she'd told you it was going to be him, would you have declined?'

'Of course not. I'm prepared to discuss the issues with anyone. But I might have prepared differently, had I known.'

'I think Krystie likes to keep us all on our toes. That makes for better NewsNet. More chance of creating something that will go truly viral.'

Bartholomew Bartholomew glanced briefly over in Arbus's direction. He might even have allowed himself a tiny smirk. It could just have been an involuntary spasm signalling nothing. Or maybe it was meant to be a gracious acknowledgement of a worthy adversary. Or maybe it was an anticipatory relishing of the pleasure to come: the pleasure of taking the co-inventor of the Arbus-Lubany machine apart, live, in front of an audience of billions.

Just as I was wondering how this was going to play out, a young female production assistant in combat trousers and an olive-green T-shirt called for me by name.

We media-lovie kissed. That is to say, on the cheeks, but so lightly there was barely contact. And with a loud, pointless *mwa!* from her each time.

Let me tell you, it was a far fucking cry from our last physical brush with one another.

To be fair to her, Krystie gave every impression of being pleased to see me. But, if I'm honest, not pleased enough for my liking. It was a surface pleased, if you know what I mean. And the surface was weirdly, perplexingly, unruffled. You would have said, from watching her performance, that there had been nothing between us. Or, if like me you knew that there had been *something*, you would be forced to conclude that either (a) she had forgotten about it, or (b) it meant nothing to her. Or both (a) and (b), of course. Because (a) kind of implied (b) after all.

Look, don't get me wrong. It's not that I gave a shit. But I have my pride. When I fuck someone, I like to think they remember it. I like to think they feel it in their core. That it is not something that leaves their surface unruffled.

Of course, I knew that she did remember it. How could she not? It's just that this was professional Krystie now. And when professional Krystie was in the house, there was no room for dirty, slutty, give-it-to-me-now, give-it-to-me-hard Krystie.

Course, I couldn't get that Krystie out of my mind, even when I was dealing with professional Krystie.

'So, Inspector . . .' Her big lipsticked mouth spread into a lopsided smile, cranked high on the left side of her face. This was the closest I was going to get to an acknowledgement of our *thang* in Bournemouth.

'Please, call me Glen. Or had you forgotten my name?'

She gave a little sympathetic pout. 'Ooh? What's that? Hurt feelings? I didn't know people like you had hurt feelings.'

'People like me? What does that mean?'

'Big tough policemen.'

'For a moment I thought you meant something else.'

'You could always have got in touch with me, you know.'

'I don't think so. That would make me some kind of weird celebrity stalker. It was better I left the initiative with you.'

'That's very gallant of you. Or maybe it just shows . . . you weren't that interested.'

'I was interested.'

'Well, here we are.'

'Yes.'

'Again.'

'Yes.'

And for a moment I thought we were going to rip each other's clothes off again. But this was professional Krystie. 'Of course, it's wonderful just to see you again.' She must have caught the sarcastic angling of my left eyebrow. I always use the left for sarcasm. 'No, really, it is, Glen. I mean that. And afterwards, if you have time, if you don't have to rush off back to Reading, or wherever it is you've come from . . .'

'I'm stationed in London now.'

'Well, that's just great. So there you are. We could . . . after . . . it would be nice to catch up over a drink?'

'After what? That's what I'm wondering.'

'OK, yes. I have a little proposition to put to you, Glen. A business proposition. Which means of course that you will be financially compensated. I've lined up a live debate between Dr Arbus and Bartholomew Bartholomew.'

'And where do I fit in?'

'Well, what we thought would be great is if we had someone Arbus-Lubany tested live in the middle of the debate.' She gave me a coy little look like she had just asked me if I minded being handcuffed to the bed.

'No fucking way. Why are you even asking me? You know I wouldn't do it.'

'I knew you wouldn't do it at the conference that time.'

'So why should I do it now?'

'Because, as I say, we are prepared to compensate you.'

'It would have to be some fucking compensation. I mean, if the test went the wrong way, I might never be able to work as a cop again.'

'You'd still be employable. In some ways, your market value might increase. There are certain individuals and organizations who are always on the look-out for someone like you. A P result wouldn't deter them. In fact, it might make you more attractive.'

'I don't want to leave the force.'

'Well, there is no law – currently – that says you would have to.'

'Currently. I wouldn't put it past this lot to bring it in as soon as they have proof of their first serving P cop. Why me, anyhow?'

'It has to be someone who has a lot to lose.'

'You can say that again!'

'So . . . let's talk about a figure.'

'There isn't a figure.'

'How does four million sound?'

'Four million what?'

'MindCoins, silly.'

I have to say, that was a figure that made me think.

'Just let me get this straight. I get that either way? Whatever the result is? I mean, I know you're hoping for a P, but what if it's an NP?'

'You get it either way.'

'You think I'm a P?'

'It doesn't matter what I think.'

'It's a gamble.'

'It's a gamble in which you win, whatever happens.' She gave
me that big lopsided grin again.

I had to admit, four million MindCoins was a lot of money.

A lot of money to walk away from.

A hell of a smile to walk away from too.

LEVEL FOUR

I don't want to say 'this is where things get really interesting', because to be honest they sure as hell should be interesting already.

At every level, every stage, the interest has to be cranked up. To be damn straight with you, we should be well past merely 'interesting' by now. We should be at total life-consuming, job-losing, relationship-threatening, baby-neglecting addiction by now. If we don't get at least one child taken into care as a result of this game, we've failed. (Joking! Lighten up, Legal.)

But imagine. The player is basically in control of an army of psychopaths (who have the ability to transform into spiders at will) who are running rampage in a multiplicity of richly imagined settings. It's going to take a lot of work to make this work, people, but believe me it is going to be worth it. It will be so much fun, I cannot tell you.

The danger we need to watch out for is that it gets too complicated for the player to have fun. The game must still work on the simple role-playing killer rampage level. At any given time the player is given a singular POV. That of whichever Spiderpath they have taken control of at that moment. The player must learn not to attack other members of the Spiderpath brood, because each dead Spiderpath, while not fatal to the player, does diminish the overall power of the group. There should be a fatality watermark, below which the number of Spiderpaths cannot pass. Or let us say, once they drop down below this number, their individual life/energy forces begin to diminish uncontrollably. The surviving Spiderpaths must kill ever more prolifically to maintain a survivable level of life force.

For argument's sake, assuming we start with 100 Spiderpaths, let's say the fatality watermark is 25. Once the number of Spiderpaths drops below that, their rate of attrition significantly accelerates.

The multiple Spiderpaths are, of course, clones of the one original character, designed by the player. Clones? Or aspects of? Would appreciate some brainstorming to work this through. We need to get the character detailing right. My personal hunch is that each Spiderpath should exhibit broadly similar traits, but that there should be some subtle differences – individual traits – worked in. Maybe not into them all, but into one or two or ten. The loss of these subtly differentiated Spiderpaths is more damaging to the group.

Of course, the player doesn't know this. They must defend the integrity of each Spiderpath equally.

The one thing they must not allow is for the Spiderpaths to turn on each other.

So naturally, we will build that into the gameplay, because, let's face it, it would be fun!

Development notes for PSYCHOTOPIA VR game.
Internal Alpha Games document. Not for release. For approved circulation only.

EIGHTEEN

I t was Callum who interviewed her. Birgitte. From Denmark, via the agency. Of course, Aimée was reconciled to the fact that all the nannies were inevitably younger and – so she believed – prettier than her. She felt it especially now, as her due date loomed. There was no neat, torpedo bump this time. Just an all-over spread of maternal gigantism.

They were no longer living in the two-bedroom flat in Hoxton but had moved out to a house in Enfield Town. They had swapped a cool postcode and no space for a suburban family home in the virtual sticks. It had turned out to be a far easier trade-off to make than she had ever imagined.

Looking back, she realized that she could spot a subconscious bias in the nannies she'd hired – rather closer to the overweight and plain end of the attractiveness scale compared to Callum's appointments. It got to be a bit of a joke between them. They got through so many nannies and au pairs that there really was a reasonable statistical base to draw some extrapolations. He liked them pretty. She less so.

But Birgitte. Birgitte exceeded the pretty. Birgitte was completely off the attractiveness scale. She broke the gauge.

A wry 'Seriously?' was the extent of her laconic reaction when she finally got to see the girl, as she worked a trial babysit. She was dark, contrary to the Scandinavian stereotype in that respect at least. In all other respects – well, she was young, she had an unfeasibly perfect body, slim, lithe and almost breathtakingly proportioned, with breasts the generous rotundity of which she noticed Callum slyly taking in.

'What?' protested Callum, slightly overdoing the innocent face. 'She's perfect.'

'Yeah, right.' But she had to admit Birgitte came with gushing references. And looking at her playing Uno with their daughter in the playroom, it did seem as though she had already managed to build up some kind of rapport with Siobhan. Which was extraordinary.

She studied Birgitte's CV. 'She doesn't stay long at any one place, does she? I mean, if all these people think she's so great, why didn't it ever work out?'

'She's young. That's what young people do. They move around.'

'You never did.'

'I was different.' Callum's voice struck her as suddenly defeated. There was a lost, empty look in his eyes, as if he was reconciled to disappointment. It shocked as well as saddened her. There seemed to be an edge of recrimination to his look too.

Let him have his pretty nanny, she thought. 'OK. But you'd better not get any ideas, matey.'

The joke fell flat.

'Come off it. As if she'd ever look twice at a bloke like me.'

It was not quite the reply she'd been hoping for.

There was something about Birgitte, though, other than her outstanding physical attractiveness, that unsettled Aimée. And if she was honest, as disloyal as it was to admit it, it was the bond that seemed to form almost immediately between the new nanny and her charge. Perhaps it was jealousy on her part. But no, it was a darker emotion even than that. It was a kind of suspicion – fear, almost. She knew, deep down, that Siobhan was a difficult child to like. That was why they'd had such trouble hanging on to nannies and au pairs in the past. Nothing you could put your finger on. It just seemed that somehow, eventually, Siobhan repelled anyone who spent any time looking after her.

No one ever said why. Although she did once overhear one girl on the phone to a friend, just before handing in her notice. The girl, a Kiwi, was speaking very quietly, almost mumbling. She seemed depressed. Aimée recognized the signs. She strained to listen, almost fearing the worst. She was sure she heard the girl say, 'The little freak creeps me out.' She had no doubt she was talking about Siobhan.

And that was the thing about Birgitte. She creeped Aimée out.

She seemed not quite human, in some way.

It was irrational. And no doubt mistaken. But she couldn't shake it off. It was visceral. She didn't trust her.

The girl was perfectly polite. But was there – maybe, just – some edge of superiority in her attitude to Aimée? A complacent knowledge of her own surpassing excellence. A kind of super-cilious disdain. Was it pity, almost, that she detected in the girl's glance?

No doubt she was imagining it. Being unfair to the girl, who was, after all, very young and in a foreign country, far from home, trying her best to communicate in a language that wasn't her own. Maybe the attitude Aimée detected in her wasn't attitude at all, but just shyness, loneliness even. The awkwardness of youth, compounded by the difficulty of communication.

And Birgitte could hardly be blamed for her beauty.

The fact was she did seem to be able to handle Siobhan. And Siobhan even seemed to like her. Aimée couldn't deny her daughter was more manageable, calmer, since Birgitte had arrived. Why should that be a cause for concern? She ought to be happy.

And so Aimée decided to let it go. She had other things on her mind. She hadn't finished work yet, was keeping going until the last possible moment. She was invariably exhausted when she got home. She had to admit it was great to come home to a tidy, calm house, with Siobhan already bathed and in her pyjamas. Callum seemed less stressed too. For which she was grateful, though it did provoke some pangs of guilt because it made her realize how much of the burden of Siobhan he had borne over the years.

On balance, she had to admit, Birgitte was a good thing.

It certainly made life a lot easier when she went into the NLMega to have the new baby.

She had no enthusiasm to go back there, was dreading it in fact. But given the Health Corp plan they had – the only one they could afford – they simply had no choice.

She just wanted to be in and out of there as quickly as possible.

But at least now there was someone to look after Siobhan. That was one less thing to worry about.

Everyone had told her that the second time would be easier. The baby would just pop out. But that wasn't the case. He got tangled up in the umbilical cord on the way out. There was some talk of possible oxygen-deprivation to the brain. On top of that, she lost a lot of blood. Needed a transfusion, which was late in coming. Some problem that was never explained. She went in and out of consciousness.

Afterwards, she awoke to find Callum clasping her hand.

'I thought I lost you,' he said. And then he started crying.

'The baby?'

'Fine.'

'Really?'

'Yes, really, absolutely. Everything is good. Considering . . .'

'Considering what?'

'Considering it was a difficult birth.'

'There are problems?'

'They're keeping him in intensive care for now.'

'Intensive care?'

'Don't worry. It's just a precaution. It's the best place for him to be. They can look after him there. That's what we want to happen.'

'Is he . . .?'

'It's going to be fine. *He's* going to be fine. Whatever happens, it'll be fine. OK? We'll get through this. You and me. Together.'

He gave her hand another squeeze. She felt her whole body relax as she surrendered herself to a future she could not control. At that moment, she was not afraid, or even anxious. Maybe she was just too exhausted. Or maybe she was calmed by the thought that, whatever else happened, she had got Callum back.

She certainly could have no complaints about the care that was given to little Liam. That was the weird thing about the NLMega. It was so dire and dysfunctional in some respects that it made you want to throw your hands up in despair, or even bang your head against the nearest blood-smeared wall. But then some member of the staff would surprise you by going so far out of their way to help you that you worried for them. That seemed to be how it was going in society in general, as far as she could tell. The world was dividing, and it was not along class, race or religious lines.

It was between those people who still gave a fuck and those who didn't.

After observing him closely and subjecting him to a bank of tests, they decided that he was a perfectly healthy neonatal boy and returned him to his mother. He was tiny. A tiny mite. But he was full of strength and the determination to live. He latched on to her nipple and began suckling straight away. And she felt a wave of deep, unconditional love transfer into him along with her milk.

Only two days later than scheduled, they were allowed to take him back to Enfield.

As she carried a sleeping Liam across the threshold in the baby seat, she gave a gentle call-out: 'Hello! We're home!'

There was no reply. But then she had deliberately kept her voice down so as not to wake the baby. Callum went looking for Siobhan and Birgitte. He came back a moment later to report that the house was empty.

Aimée gave a quizzical frown. 'I thought you MindMessaged Birgitte to let her know we were on our way?'

'I did.'

'Oh. That's odd. I mean. They've gone out? Would you not have thought . . .?'

'Yes, well, you know what Siobhan's like.'

'Yes.'

The old stone of dread that she had not felt for so long settled again in her stomach.

Callum sent Birgitte a MindMessage to let her know that they were home.

He got back the rather cryptic and not entirely satisfying: *We r havin fun.*

To which he replied: *Tell S new baby brother wants to meet her.*

To which came the reply: *O yeh sure.*

They turned up half an hour later. Birgitte nonchalantly explained that Siobhan had wanted to go to the park. It seemed reasonable, but then again, strange.

Aimée had placed the car seat with Liam still asleep in it on the sofa. Siobhan walked straight past it and went into her play-room, where she busied herself with her dolls.

'Siobhan?' Callum called gently. 'Don't you want to come and see your brother?'

She looked up, angled her head thoughtfully, before coming to a decision. She laid down the dolls and dutifully got up to come back into the living room. She walked over to the car seat, made a show of looking at Liam, nodded once emphatically, and then went back to the playroom without saying a word.

Aimée and Callum exchanged a look of wry bewilderment, all four eyebrows hiked up as far as they could go.

'It's fine . . . she's . . . you know . . . it's a lot for her to . . . she'll come round. Don't worry.'

All Aimée could do was let out a deep sigh.

Edie came round to admire her new nephew.

'He's beautiful.'

'He is. Yes.'

'And how are you?'

'I'm fine.'

'You look . . .'

'What exactly?'

'A little bit tired, maybe?'

'Well, yes. You should try this giving birth business. It *is* tiring. But at least we have Birgitte to take Siobhan off my hands for a while.'

'Yes. Siobhan. How is she? How is she taking it? The new sibling.'

'Oh, you know Siobhan.' But it was a curiously meaningless thing to say. No one ever had the sense that they really knew what was going on inside Siobhan's mind. 'She's dealing with it in her own way. Which is more or less by completely ignoring him.'

'Ignoring this cutie? How could anyone ignore a face like that! She'll come round, I'm sure.'

'It's quite a big age gap. So . . . I'm not so sure, actually. I think she resents him and she'll just grow to resent him even more.'

'Did you resent me?'

'It's not such an age gap.'

'That's not really an answer, is it?'

Aimée chuckled silently, enjoying the easy, relaxed intimacy with her sister. They were just joshing each other. The playfulness came from a place of trust and love.

'Where is she anyhow? I have a present for her.'

'You're a good auntie.'

'The best.'

Aimée looked down at her sleeping son. They were going to be all right. Everything was going to be all right.

And then she heard a new note enter her sister's voice. A strange, hesitant, grim seriousness. 'Hey, listen, you know . . . I saw . . . *him.*'

She knew immediately who Edie was talking about.

It was him. Edie was sure of it. She had entered the name Sal had given her – Oscar Winslett – into MindNet and had come up with several images and videos from over the years. He'd changed his appearance superficially, but there was something about his mannerisms that he couldn't hide. Then, when she'd entered a photo of Winslett into a facial recognition MindNet search, it had thrown up multiple other identities. One of whom was called Charlie Turner. This Charlie Turner had the same curly blond hair and startling blue eyes of the man Aimée had known all those years ago. And the face of Oscar Winslett. MindNet confirmed it.

She was about to show her sister the searches she'd made on her phone but Aimée refused to look.

'But it's *him*! It is him.'

'So?'

'What do you mean, so?'

'I mean, so what? So what if it is him?'

'Well, we can go to the police. Get him arrested.'

'What for?'

'What for? He robbed us. Or have you forgotten?'

'But we can't be absolutely *sure* it is him. I mean, maybe they're twins? Or doppelgängers.'

'It's the same person. MindNet does not lie about these things.'

'No. I don't want to do anything about it. It was all so long ago. And . . . I don't want to drag it up again.'

'You're going to let him get away with it?'

'It isn't a question of that. I'm over it. Over all that. It sounds like he's straightened himself out now as well. Got a job. Maybe he just had a bad patch?'

'No! I don't believe this! You've got to go after him. What about Sal?'

'What about her?'

'He . . . he's after her. I think he may even have drugged her and for all I know raped her.'

'For all we know he may have done a lot of things. But if we can't prove it, the police won't want to know. They've got enough on their plate these days.'

'They can do that test on him.'

'And? What good will that do?'

'It will prove he's a psychopath.'

'I'm not going to do anything about it, Edith. And I don't want you to either. And whatever you do, please, don't say anything to Callum.'

Edie shook her head in disbelief. She gave a sharp snort of frustration and incomprehension.

'Promise me.'

'I'm going to find Siobhan. I've got this present for her.'

Liam woke abruptly with a hungry, demanding cry. Aimée lifted him and pulled him to her urgently.

It was soon after this that the marks started to appear.

LEVEL FOUR, CONTINUED

I don't want the Spiderpaths to be sub-Spiderman-type creatures. They are either spiders or humans. Not humans with spider powers.

There are some advantages to being in spider form. Evasion of capture, for example. They shrink to tiny size, making them effectively invisible to adversaries.

Also, speed of movement. (Is a spider faster than a human? Someone check this out for me please.)

Disadvantages: relative weakness and vulnerability. It is easier to kill a spider than it is to kill a human. Easier to pull their legs off too. (There could be an interesting loop here: a Spiderpath becomes the spider that facilitates the release of the original protagonist in Level One play? Or in a multiple player version of the game, the player experiences the sensation of having their spider legs ripped off by another player as they escape from the secure unit? I'm just throwing out balls here – it's for other people to catch them and run with them.)

Something else to consider: when in spider form, the Spiderpaths receive nourishment from eating the insects that they are able to catch. (Is there a way to hack the VR device so that the player actually tastes insect when the Spiderpath they are controlling is feeding?) So the Spiderpath in spider form must catch and kill insects. OK . . . There must be a penalty for remaining in spider form for too long? Spiders have shorter life spans than humans. (Someone check this out for me, please.) What I suppose I'm saying is that the Spiderpath has to use their spider form carefully. They may run out of spideriness and switch back to human form at an inconvenient moment. We could consider some kind of virtual gauge which tells them how much more spider time they have. They are able to renew or recharge spider time when in human form by performing certain tasks. (When in spider form, eating insects obviously recharges their spider time.)

I suppose what I'm saying here is that we need to put some

texture and detail into the Spiderpaths. Character Designers, I'm looking at you. But it's not just about how these creatures look. It's about how it feels to be inside them. Let's set up a brainstorm.

Development notes for PSYCHOTOPIA VR game.
Internal Alpha Games document. Not for release. For approved circulation only.

NINETEEN

I caught the debate live on my way back to New New Scotland Yard. It was a pretty dull affair, to be honest. The usual predictable ding-dong. I mean, it's always the same, isn't it, when you line up two people who basically can't agree what's black and what's white. Neither of them is going to shift their position. And you've heard them each state their case many times before. So unless you can add some new dimension to the proceedings, you're just left rehashing the same old stale arguments. I guess that's why Krystie was so keen on having me take a live Arbus-Lubany test. She did make some brief passing reference to my refusal and tried to turn it into some kind of story in its own right. 'What does it say when the police are not prepared to undergo the test themselves?' But the only real answer you can give to that question is that it says the police aren't stupid.

Of course, Bartholomew Bartholomew wouldn't consent to be tested. Arbus would. But that would hardly make viralizable screentime. You can bet he'd already tested himself privately and knew what the result would be. Either that, or he knew how to fix the output. He denied that was possible, of course. Apparently there was some secret code built into it that not even he knew because it was randomly generated by a central server at unknown irregular intervals. Yeah, right. If anyone could do it, your money would be on him.

Then when Krystie let slip how much they'd offered me, you can bet they got a lot of incoming with other cops volunteering to take the test on screen themselves. And not just cops – all kinds of people. Some of them I'm sure were Ps. Had to be. Krystie had to turn them all down. 'I had my reasons for wanting that particular officer to be the one.' She gave the camera a certain stare that seemed to be meant only for me. Or maybe I was kidding myself? Either way, I couldn't for the life of me tell you what she meant by it. What did it matter anyhow? We were through for good now.

So yeah, the debate. If you ask me it completely failed to deliver the promised sparks. They just seemed to be going through the motions. Even the participants seemed bored. Bartholomew Bartholomew did his best to needle Arbus and draw him out from his measured scientific stance with his own brand of ill-informed cock-swagger. But Arbus seemed to take the view that it was beneath his dignity to even argue with the man. Whenever BB called into question the legitimacy of the testing, or the reliability of the machines, or Arbus's qualifications to be in charge of the programme, Arbus's stock response was along the lines of: 'If you'd read my paper to the *Such and Such Journal of Whatever*, you'd know that blah blah blah.' It was his standard method for closing down any lay criticism, as I knew from my own experience.

I kind of wished I hadn't turned down Krystie's offer when I saw the show. For one thing, it would have livened things up. She wasn't wrong there.

For another, she looked even more fuckable now I knew it was never going to happen again. That's a special kind of regret. I dare say the French have a word for it. If they don't, they should have.

For a third thing, it was something Arbus said, his comment on Krystie's account of a police officer refusing the opportunity to take the test live. (Remember, he must have known the officer in question was me, given our little tête à tête in the studio's reception.) He said: 'What that officer has to bear in mind is that his reluctance to take the test is almost certain proof that he is an NP.'

Still, that 'almost certain proof' wasn't quite good enough for me. And I still didn't put it past Arbus not to fix the result, whatever assurances he was in the habit of giving. I mean if MindNet was prepared to pay me four million MindCoins to take the test, God knows what they would be willing to offer him to fix it.

Everybody has a price. Even scruffy psycho-anthropologist types.

I MindMessaged Arbus later.
That tru wot u sed?
Wot?

Me NP?
Ps luv risk. If u P you'd gamble.
Wot if i don't trust u?
U can trust me.
2 late now.

His reply didn't come immediately. So I thought that was the end of the communing. Maybe there was a snafu on MindNet. Or maybe he was in two minds. But in the end the reply came:

Single malt? My round.

Then he MindMessaged me the location of his hotel.

First I had a witness to interview. One Edith Walsh. She was a funny little creature. Birdlike and intense. Something fierce inside her that gave her this weirdly sharp expression. Something had certainly got her goat.

It was a strange one, this. She was all worked up about some guy called Charlie who she claimed had pulled some kind of con on her sister and her and some other people. It was all far too complicated for me. I had a real job keeping up. But it seems this Charlie fella had cleaned out her sister's bank account and stolen possessions from the house they were all living in. But the thing was it had all happened seven or so years ago.

'Why didn't you come forward at the time?' was my quite reasonable question.

'Because we didn't know who he was. He just disappeared. But I've seen him now. His name is Oscar Winslett.'

'I thought you said he was called Charlie?'

'That wasn't his real name. Or who knows? Maybe Oscar isn't his real name. Anyhow, he works at this company called Alpha Games now.'

'Alpha Games? I know them. Isn't *Random Rage* one of theirs? That's a cool game, that is.'

'I don't know! I don't play VR games. Is that important?'

Like I said, she had something fierce inside her.

I shrugged. How the hell did I know what was important? 'I don't know what you want me to do.'

'Arrest him!'

'But it's going to be difficult to prove anything after all this time. He can simply deny it was him.'

'You do that test on him that you do. The P test. That'll prove it.'

'That might prove something, but it won't prove he was the guy who fucked over your sister all those years ago.'

'Is that it then? That all you've got to say?'

'I've got the streets crawling with active, rampant, florid psychopaths. Smashing up buildings, abducting minors, raping old ladies. That's happening now. Right now, as I'm sitting here talking to you about some minor felony from ancient history, where as far as I can tell nobody got hurt, except your sister maybe got her pride a little dented? I'm guessing.'

She gave an impatient sigh. As if that was completely beside the point. And maybe it was. 'You can't let him get away with it.'

'What's his name again?'

She spelled it out for me and I entered it into PolNet. 'Clean. Nothing. No criminal record. No record of any connection with PGD. A model citizen. Not even traffic offences and everybody has those. Look, I'm afraid I just don't have sufficient grounds for bringing Mr Winslett in.'

'He raped somebody.'

'I beg your pardon?'

'OK, I can't prove it. But he gave her drugs. And she passed out. He must have done something.'

'Who? What? I . . . look . . . even as you're saying that, you must realize, I can't do anything with it. Who is the victim? Why isn't she here making the complaint? When did it happen? I mean, I'd like to help, but I honestly can't.'

'What? You have to wait until you catch him doing something really bad?' She seemed outraged at this notion.

'Well, yes. That's generally how it works.'

'I thought those machines were supposed to stop people doing bad stuff.'

'Yeah, they do . . . but . . . you know, there are rules. To protect people. Listen, what I can do is I'll talk to the girl you allege he raped, I'll get a statement from her, and if it seems possible that we can do something with it, we'll take it forward.'

'She won't talk to you. She says he didn't do it. She's in denial. He's her boss.'

So that was it. Maybe I shouldn't have laughed. But, Christ, what did she expect me to do?

She gave me a fierce little look on the way out.

SOME THOUGHTS ON
GAME LEVELS

What we may have stumbled upon here with the introduction of the Spiderpaths is a completely innovative approach to game levels. That is to say, the whole structure of the game's level system changes from hereon in. Until now, the game has proceeded with the progression of one central player-operated protagonist from level to level. At the extinction of that protagonist, the player goes back to the beginning of the game, at Level One (with a new protagonist character or with the existing protagonist reborn?).

With the splintering of the protagonist into multiple Spiderpath characters, progression is no longer conventionally horizontal, or even linear. The Spiderpaths are distributed throughout all available levels. (All? Consider the possibility of creating superfluous hidden levels that can only be accessed through cheats leaked through GameMind, etc.) This means the player is capable of operating in different levels, and of switching between levels at will, as they switch to and from different Spiderpath POVs.

We need to think through the impact on the gaming experience of this novel structure. If you remove the traditional opportunity to progress through levels, do you remove some fundamental and psychologically rewarding element of gameplay? In other words, is there a risk that it will make the game less satisfying? Or might we actually be moving VR gaming to a whole new level, so to speak?

I have an open mind on this. Maybe we need to research it. For what it's worth, my instinct is that the Spiderpath part of the game narrative could be an interlude, relatively short-lived. The Spiderpaths are doomed to burn out. They give the player a glimpse of the various game levels ahead. But they do not affect true progression.

I think it might be helpful to proceed on this basis for now. Though I am open to alternative suggestions.

Development notes for PSYCHOTOPIA VR game.
Internal Alpha Games document. Not for release. For approved
circulation only.

TWENTY

S he tensed at the feel of his hands on her shoulders. She was sitting at her desk, engrossed in reviewing the preliminary designs for the secret project he had her working on. He had sneaked up behind her and started to give her an unsolicited massage.

'You seem tense.'

She rippled her shoulders to shake him off. 'Please stop.'

'Not until I feel all the tension go from you. I am a trained masseur, you know. I have certificates and everything.'

'It's making me uncomfortable.'

'That's because you're not allowing yourself to open up. I detect some level of distrust here, Sally. You have to trust me, Sally. Otherwise, this just isn't going to work.'

'What do you mean by that?'

'Hmm?'

'When you said *this* isn't going to work? What were you referring to?'

'This. The massage. Of course. What did you think I meant?'

'I don't know. It seemed like . . . like you were threatening me?'

At last he broke off his unwelcome attentions. 'Threatening you?'

'Yes. Like you'd have me fired if I didn't do what you wanted?'

'Please, Sally, what kind of a monster do you take me for?'

'When we went out the other night, what were those tablets you gave me?'

'You want to talk about that now? Here?'

'Just tell me what they were.'

'I already told you. Es.'

'Why did I pass out? Why can't I remember anything that happened?'

'I don't know! Different people react differently, I guess.'

'Shouldn't you have called an ambulance? I mean, that kind

of a reaction to Es is dangerous, isn't it? Why weren't you more freaked out?'

'Because, OK, they weren't Es.'

'I knew it!'

'They weren't anything. They were harmless sugar pills. Placebos.'

'What?'

'You didn't pass out. You just fell asleep. Because you were tired. And I guess you'd drunk a lot. But those tablets had nothing to do with it.'

'I don't believe you. Why would you give me placebos?'

'Because freedom, release, empowerment – these things don't come from pills. They come from within. They come from you. A placebo is just a way of tricking the mind into allowing itself to be free.'

He took out a bottle of pills from his pocket and tipped out some of the contents into one palm. 'Look, see. This is what I gave you. Recognize them?'

'I didn't see them. Except on your tongue.'

'They looked like this though, right?'

'I guess so.'

He threw the handful of pills into his mouth and noisily crunched on them until he was able to swallow them. It took several swallows to get them all down. Then he did the same thing again until the whole bottle was empty. He then stood for a moment before suddenly allowing his legs to buckle at the knees. But this was just his little joke. He grinned and stood up straight again.

'But you went to buy drugs?'

'Playacting. To make you believe. So the placebo would work.' But he had to see her face to know if his words were having any effect. 'Look at me, for fuck's sake!' He managed to hit just the right note of outraged innocence.

She turned round. Her face registered something between fear and uncertainty. Perfect. As far as he was concerned.

He was in full-on shouty mode now. Sally closed her eyes, wincing out his words, and blocking the inquisitive glances of her colleagues in the open-plan office. 'What are you accusing me of here? What do you think I gave you? R2? Is that it? You're saying I dosed you up with R2 and then raped you? For fuck's

sake, look at me! You can at least look at me if you're accusing
me of that.'

She was crying now. Her face flushed with emotion. Maybe
he'd gone too far. But he had to make it convincing. Besides,
not all of his outrage was feigned.

He leaned in, lowering his voice to a gentle murmur. 'Look,
I'm sorry. I didn't mean to upset you. I guess I was upset? I
mean I hate that shit. Guys who do that are scum. I would never,
never, never do that.'

She knuckled away a tear and sniffed noisily. But was still
not looking at him.

He risked a guiding finger on her chin, tilting her face up
towards his. 'You believe me, don't you?'

Of course she did. How could she not?

He wasn't even lying. Because, essentially, as far as he was
concerned, there was no such thing as lying. The truth was what
you wanted to believe. What you needed to believe. What you
were able to make someone else believe. Which pretty much
amounted to saying the truth was anything you wanted it to be.
There were no lies.

It was true that he'd given her R2. But he hadn't laid a hand
on her. That was the whole fucking point. The point was knowing
that he could have. That was where the power resided. Even in
declining to take a step, you proclaim your ability to do so.

In placing her in a state of supreme vulnerability and danger,
and not taking advantage of it, he had proven his magnanimity.
He had proven that she could trust him. If only he could have
explained it all to her.

The thing was, he wanted her to give herself to him willingly.
It didn't mean anything if she didn't. He achieved nothing by
raping her. Except a cheap, tawdry, passing sense of power. He
wanted more than that. He wanted real power over her. The
power to destroy her utterly and leave her blaming herself for
everything.

He had realized all this as he sat next to her in the taxi, her
head slumped on to his shoulder.

Besides, he hadn't liked the looks the driver had given him.
If there had been any fallout, he could be sure the fucker would
have shopped him. So, all in all, he had decided to bide his time.
His stroke of genius was to offer the driver a massive tip to help

get her upstairs safely. He had him wait outside her flat with the door ajar but made sure he could see – and hear – him while he had walked her to her bedroom. He hadn't even risked a sly grope, though God knows no one could have blamed him if he had.

And now, this, actually, this could play to his advantage.

No one could doubt that his outrage was genuine. If he'd been guilty of what she was suggesting, would he have gone off on one like that in front of everybody? Wasn't it more likely that he would have tried to close her down, talk to her in private, subtly threaten her with repercussions? But just to lose it like that. There was only one possible interpretation: he was innocent.

She'd see that now. And start to feel guilty about wrongly accusing him. Pretty soon she'd be looking for a way to make it up to him.

TO RECAP

Maybe now is a good time to take a step back and see just what this game is shaping up to be. And to think about where we can take it next?

To weigh up the things we like. The things that get our juices running.

And any possible pitfalls we can see.

You know the way this works, people. Play it in your head and see how it feels.

Where are the gaps?

Where are the opportunities?

What's fun?

What's not?

Don't hold back. You're not helping anyone if you pull your punches.

But try to back up your comments with reasons why. (Don't just say 'I think this section is a bit shit' – tell me why you think it's shit.)

I will start the ball rolling.

What I like.

The premise. A game about psychopaths. What's not to like?

The uncertainty. The player is never quite in control. Even of the character they control. Also, they do not know who they can trust. Correction: they cannot trust anyone. Even the doctors treating them at the beginning may be other psychopaths.

The face thefts. They are cool, no?

Multiple player potential. I think this game will come alive when played with multiple players across the GameMind.

Killing tramps. There is no downside that I can see. Good old-fashioned fun for all the family. Ish.

Spiderpaths. I think they need more thought/development. But my gut feeling is they could be very fucking cool indeed. And massively fun.

The possibility of making the player actually feel/experience what their character is feeling/experiencing. The obvious problem here is current technological limitations. Who do we need to speak to to make this happen? I don't fucking care if it's NASA or even MindNet or even that guy who is doing all that P testing. Someone must know how to make this happen!

Controversy. This game promises to be our most controversial yet. It will piss the moral majority off even more than *Random Rage* did. This is what we are aiming for. We mustn't lose our nerve. The climate is right for this game. It is very much of the zeitgeist. Trust me.

What I don't like so much.

I worry about the pace. I think it might be a bit slow to pick up in the beginning. The secure unit section. Maybe the protagonist is too constrained at the beginning? Not enough opportunity for ACTION! We may have to revisit the game starting point. The secure unit is like some kind of negative aspect – punishment – it kicks in when the player fucks up overly. Consider possibility of starting it in an act of outrageous, wonderful, uninhibited psychopathy. Some kind of deep, dark, joyous naughtiness? Any ideas on this very welcome. We should make it as dark and dangerous as we can get away with.

Complexity. The game needs a certain level of complexity. But does the gameplay as it is so far imagined get bogged down in places? E.g. the Spiderpaths. I'm convinced there's something great in them, but we need to get the number right so that it stays manageable and playable.

So far I have no clear idea of what the game universe looks like. Other than drab urban decay. I think it needs to be beautiful. Not depressing. People have to be seduced into the world of psychopathy. Before they realize it, before they have a chance to put their moral barriers up, we have to make them love being a psychopath.

Phoniness. We have to get the psychology and the motivations right. Otherwise it will not chime with the player's inner psychopath. It's that inner psycho who is our audience here. So we need to get in touch with our own inner psychos. I might suggest some psycho-bonding activities. Maybe a weekend away killing homeless people? (Joke. Obvs. Though now that I think about it . . .)

Development notes for PSYCHOTOPIA VR game.
Internal Alpha Games document. Not for release. For approved circulation only.

TWENTY-ONE

Arbus was staying at this new boutique hotel on St Martin's Lane. Just a handful of ridiculously overpriced rooms, the decor so über-designed it came out the other side: it looked like a ragbag of haphazard items thrown together by someone who had trouble holding a single thought in their head for longer than a second. No doubt they had some kind of theme going on, but it escaped me.

The bar area was like the contents of several very different domestic living rooms had been sucked up and spewed out higgledy-piggledy into a commercial warehouse. I swear there was even an armchair overturned and lying on its side. I'm not sure whether that was part of the 'concept' or whether it was just the aftermath of a recent fight. Anything was possible these days.

There was a grand piano in the corner. The pianist looked about twelve. He was playing a string of jazz classics with impressive proficiency for one so young. I have to say, he looked a little panicky though. Out of his depth, you might say, almost as if he wasn't supposed to be there. Maybe he was covering for his dad who was off scoring drugs or prostitutes or something. That was the little narrative I created anyhow. OK, maybe he was closer to twenty than twelve, but I had to occupy myself somehow while I was waiting for Arbus to turn up.

There was something bogus about the place. People like Arbus – or his employers, which I presume was the government – might have been happy to pay over the odds for the privilege of staying here, but it made me feel uncomfortable. I think because it was trying so hard to do the opposite. The lo-energy lighting, the soothing music, the home-from-home styling – it put me on edge. Give me the good old soulless monotony of the Nightjar chain any day – or night. At least they never tried to be something they weren't. They never pretended to be your home. Which is almost as bad as someone pretending to be your friend.

I was just about to MindMessage Arbus – had *where the fuk*

r u? all lined up ready to send – when I felt a hand on my shoulder.

I glanced down at that hand with a calibrated look, which I then swivelled up to Arbus's face just to make sure he got the message. He removed it pretty sharpish. He looked a little deflated all of a sudden, like I'd just kicked his puppy. Or he *was* the puppy.

'You can put it back if you want,' I said. 'I just didn't realize we were shoulder-touching buddies.'

'I'm not gay, if that's what you're worried about.'

'I don't give a shit what you are.'

'I do admit to having a little trouble with personal interactions. I tend to be rather remote as a rule. And consequently, from time to time, I try to overcompensate. I can make mistakes. Misjudge the nuances. I apologize if . . .'

'Forget it.'

'It does make it hard to . . . I don't have many friends.'

'Asperger's?'

'Yes.'

'Well, at least you're not a psychopath.'

'And neither are you.'

'So you say.'

'Seriously, one of the strongest indicators of NP is the fear of being P. I could test you privately if you want. Or you could do the test on yourself, secretly. Just to set your mind at rest.'

'What makes you think it would set my mind at rest?'

'Wouldn't you prefer to know, if you're not?'

'It's too late for me to claim my four million.'

'I admire you, you know. For turning that down. It would rather have demeaned what we're trying to do here.'

'But you would have gone along with it?'

'Well, yes, I suppose I would. I was being offered a comparable sum, which of course would have gone towards funding further research.'

'Of course. So . . . you mentioned something about buying me a drink?'

'Oh, yes. Sorry. That's another example, I suppose. Of my lack of social functioning.' He did the honours, though he didn't bother to check with me what I wanted. Just got in two double Glenfiddichs on the rocks. I guess it was hard for him to imagine someone not wanting the same as him. Empathy was not his strong point, obviously.

We clinked glasses.

'So, what did you make of Bartholomew Bartholomew, now that you've had a chance to see him up close?'

'He's dangerous.'

'To the advancement of your project, yes.'

'Therefore to society as a whole.'

'But he does have a point. I mean, the government does seem to be on the way to criminalizing a mental health condition. Effectively. I mean, how would you like it if they did the same thing for people with Asperger's Syndrome?'

'But they wouldn't. Because that condition does not pose a mortal threat to public safety.'

'Yeah, but psychopaths don't choose to be psychopaths. There's nothing they can do about it. By all means, if they break the law, catch them, arrest them, lock them up if you can. Take them off the streets, out of action. But tagging individuals as psychopaths before they've done anything, that's just an intrusion of privacy, isn't it?'

'This isn't just about tagging for the sake of it. It's about prevention of future disorder.'

'What? You seriously think these people will be constrained by the knowledge that they are registered Ps? That that will be enough to keep them in line?'

'No. Obviously not.'

'So . . . I don't get it. There's something I'm missing here.'

'Yes.'

'Would you care to tell me what that is?'

Arbus looked at me without answering and held the silent stare for a few beats longer than most people would have felt comfortable doing. He was weighing something up. It almost looked like he was about to say, *If you promise to be my friend.* Fortunately, his filters caught that one in time.

'Testing is only the first phase,' was what he did say.

'I see.' I nodded for him to go on.

'My colleague, and co-inventor of the Arbus-Lubany machine Mark One, Adam Lubany, is currently working on the development of a Mark Two Arbus-Lubany machine.'

'So what's the difference between Mark One and Mark Two?'

'Mark One merely identifies an individual as either P or NP. The Mark Two will be able to . . . well, I won't say *cure*, but shall we say *modify* the aberrant cerebral structures of the P subjects so that they are more conformant to NP-type behaviour.'

'Say that again in words I can actually understand?'

'If we accept psychopathy to be a disorder of the amygdala, effectively the Arbus-Lubany machine Mark Two will be able to, as it were, rewire the amygdala so that it functions more correctly. This will happen automatically as the test is administered.'

'Is that even possible?'

'We are testing a prototype right now.'

'Testing? On who?'

'Volunteers. Drawn from the prison population. Where there is of course a high proportion of Ps.'

'Dare I ask, how is it going?'

'We have managed to achieve some modification of behaviour. But so far not entirely the desired modification.'

'What have you done?'

'We have so far succeeded only in converting NP subjects to P subjects, rather than the other way round.'

'That is very fucking far from the desired modification.'

'It shows, however, that changes can be affected. Which is encouraging.'

'You are manufacturing more psychopaths.'

'The numbers of these individuals are very small.'

'Well, that's all right then.'

'We have to do something, Inspector. You yourself said that simply tagging is not enough.'

'Yeah, but from *we have to do something* to what you're actually doing is a big leap, my friend.'

It was kind of pathetic to see the big broad grin he cracked at my use of that word. He didn't seem to realize that I meant nothing by it – less than nothing. Evidently he was as weak on irony as he was on empathy.

NOTES FOR GAME DESIGNERS AND EXPERIENTIAL ARCHITECTS

Designers – this game has to look like nothing else out there. Go to your dreams for reference.

Experiential architects – this game has to feel like nothing else out there. Bring your nightmares to life.

Development notes for PSYCHOTOPIA VR game.
Internal Alpha Games document. Not for release. For approved circulation only.

TWENTY-TWO

To see his tiny body, blemished.

After he had survived so much: the trauma of strangulation at the very moment that he came into the world.

He had kicked and clenched and screamed against the assault of his own tangled birth. Until that first fragile hold on life had grown into something unassailable. Into strength.

He was a fighter all right. He had proven them all wrong. The doctors who whispered their fears that he wouldn't make it, or would be brain-damaged, or have cerebral palsy, or worse. The midwives who shook their heads over him despairingly.

It was uncanny how much he looked like Callum. The same snub nose and small mouth that seemed to form itself naturally into a quizzical dot. Dubious rather than doubtful, it hinted at healthy scepticism, rather than uncertainty. There could be no question over *his* paternity. And if his father was anything to go by, he might grow up to be a man of few words, but quiet goodness.

An outrage, it was, to see the two purple petals appear on his Celtic-pale skin. A dark bud of fearful portent, made up of two small symmetrical semi-circles facing one another.

That he had survived so much, only to have this fresh injury inflicted on him.

She noticed it when she was changing him.

'Cal. Have you seen this? On Liam's chest.'

Callum's irritated distraction evaporated as soon as he saw. 'That's . . . odd?'

'What could have caused that?'

'It looks like . . .' Callum's words trailed off. He made a pincer action with his thumb and forefinger in the air. That was exactly what it looked like. Someone had pinched him. And by the depth and intensity of the discolouration, with some viciousness.

They both looked, without conferring, towards the playroom where Siobhan was engrossed in some tremendously delightful la-la-la little girl business. Her play was solitary – there were never any play dates any more – though Birgitte watched her at a distance.

Aimée shocked herself, not just because she had silently accused her daughter. It was the speed and readiness with which she had done it that was unnerving. And the fact that Cal had had precisely the same thought, at the same time.

She tried to draw back from the horror that her look implied. 'No. It's not possible. I don't know . . . it must have been an accident. Maybe something fell on him?'

'What, though? What would leave a mark like that? And why didn't we hear it?'

'Now that I think of it, I did hear him cry out this morning. I came to check on him, but he was fast asleep again by the time I got to him. I thought it had been a bad dream or something. Or wind.'

'Did you see anything that might have fallen down?'

'No.'

'And was . . .?'

'No. There was no one there.'

Callum's eyes remained fixed on Siobhan, framed in the doorway of the playroom, his mouth forming the small questioning dot of wondering that Aimée recognized in her son. 'We should probably talk to her. Let her know this isn't OK.'

She followed his gaze and watched her daughter lost in what seemed to be the most innocent game any little girl had ever played.

'OK. Yes. You're right. We have to talk to her.'

'Nip it in the bud,' said Callum. 'So to speak.'

They went into the playroom together. Birgitte looked up from her seat and treated them to that curious smile that was her speciality. It should have been beautiful. But the lack of any emotional content from her expression made it somehow chilling.

Callum took the initiative. 'Hi, Birgitte, could you just let us have a few moments with Siobhan?'

'Sure.' But she made no move to leave.

'Alone. Please.'

It seemed odd to be asking a stranger – for she was still a stranger to them – whether they could be alone with their child.

Birgitte raised her eyebrows extravagantly, as if this was the weirdest request any parent had ever made of her. But, hey, it wasn't her place to say anything, so she went along with it.

Aimée struggled not to slap the girl as she brushed past her with her superb bemusement all over her unfeasibly beautiful face.

'Siobhan, look at Daddy, please.'

'I've got to finish this.'

'You can just break off from the puzzle for a moment.'

'I can't, Daddy. You told me I have to finish things.'

'Yes, but that was your homework.'

Siobhan's laughter sounded empty and artificial. A child's laughter should not sound like that, Aimée couldn't help thinking.

'Silly Daddy!'

'Just for a moment, please.'

The little girl gave a momentous sigh. And finally looked up at her father with big, blinking eyes the colour of innocence.

'Siobhan, did you do something to Baby Liam?'

'Do something? What do you mean?'

'Did you . . . hurt him? It's all right. Maybe you lost your temper with him. Or it was an accident? Don't be afraid. Just tell us the truth.'

'No.'

'He's got marks on him, you see. Two little bruises. You didn't pinch him, did you?'

'Pinch him?'

'Yes. That really hurts, you know, when you pinch someone.'

'No, it doesn't.'

'It does. I mean, if I pinched you now, you wouldn't like it, would you?'

'It doesn't hurt *you* when *you* pinch someone.'

'No, but it hurts the person you pinch.'

Siobhan gave a frown of the profoundest perplexity. She really was struggling to understand the concept Callum had just explained to her. In the end, she conceded defeat with an *if-you-say-so* shrug.

'You mustn't pinch Liam. Or hurt him in any way. He's so little, you have to be very very careful with him. You mustn't pinch anyone. Pinching is naughty. You know that, don't you?'

'I know that, Daddy.'

'So promise me, no more pinching Baby Liam?'

'I promise, Daddy.'

'And just so you know, what you should do, if Baby Liam
ever makes you cross, or you have bad feelings, and you feel
like you might want to pinch him, what you should do is come
and talk to me or Mummy. And we'll give you a big hug till you
feel better and make sure Baby Liam is safe. Because we know
you love Baby Liam and you don't want anything bad to happen
to him. Isn't that so, Siobhan?'

She nodded stiffly. 'It wasn't me, anyhow.'

Aimée couldn't let that go. 'What do you mean?'

'Birgitte doesn't like Baby Liam.'

A swinging weight of forged steel set Aimée's heart pounding.
She shot Callum a look that transmitted the brunt of her shock.

His expression absorbed her anger, acknowledged it, and
somehow also counselled caution.

In the following days, she charted the slow mutations of his
bruise. The spread of yellow behind the lurid core. First the
darkening then the fading of the purple bloom. It reminded her
of the bruise that had blossomed around the needle-prick of
her transfusion. So she knew that the scale of the marks did not
necessarily relate to the size of the original wound. But it wasn't
so much the severity of the wounds that had been inflicted on
her son, as the deliberate, malicious purpose behind them.

Callum persuaded her that they could not confront Birgitte
openly. They only had Siobhan's word to go on. And even if
they could trust her, what she had said was by no means conclu-
sive proof. As Callum said, she had been known to lie before.

'But she likes Birgitte,' Aimée protested. 'I don't think she'd
get her into trouble if it wasn't true.'

His mouth contracted into its dot of scepticism. 'I'm not sure
Siobhan actually likes anyone, you know.'

It was an observation that had wormed itself silently into her
own thoughts many times. But it was shocking to hear Callum
say it. She somehow had always assumed Callum was on
Siobhan's side. He had spent more time than anyone looking
after her when she was a baby. It was almost devastating to think
that that had counted for nothing.

She did not allow herself the hypocrisy of correcting him.

'Well, what do you think we should do?'

Callum didn't answer. But he tilted his head slightly and nodded in that distracted way he had when an idea was forming.

In the meantime, the two vicious little bruises faded.

Months passed. No new marks appeared on Liam. It was almost as if they had imagined them.

Maybe Callum's words had hit home. Siobhan had learned her lesson – if it was Siobhan who had done it. Or if it was Birgitte, then the message must have got through to her somehow.

At any rate, their vigilance seemed to be paying off.

It's true that there were occasions when she put Liam down for a nap and she'd settle down to do some work or see what was happening on MindNet. She might even drift off herself. Then suddenly the peace of the house would be shattered by Liam's screams. It wasn't normal baby crying. It was something urgent and appalled. The blind instinctive reaction of the organism to an outrage committed upon it.

That was how it sounded to Aimée anyhow.

She'd leap up and run to the nursery, but there was never any sign of an attacker by the time she got there. Liam's crying would have abated to something more like the routine inconsolable misery of a pre-language infant. She'd pick him up and hold him until the howls became sobs and the sobs became distracted shudders and the distracted shudders softened into the settling motion of sleep.

She'd lay him gently back in his cot and carefully pop open his babygrow, checking for marks.

But there was never anything.

It was only after she had comforted and settled Liam that she would go looking to see where Siobhan and Birgitte were.

When she found the ring of red spots around his wrist, there had been no crying. No warning at all.

It could have been – perhaps – a rash, or a cluster of insect bites. Except for the regularity of the arrangement: a thin line of more or less evenly spaced dots as if his hand was being marked out for amputation.

It spoke of intent. Someone had done this to him. Callum was away at the time, on an overnight business conference. Was her isolation part of the intent? Had they waited for her to be alone to do this?

She thought at first the marks had been made with a red pen. But when she ran her finger over them, she felt the minuscule bumps in his skin. And Liam gave a whinging cry, nothing major, but enough to suggest that he felt some mild sensation of discomfort there.

That night she had Liam sleep in the bed with her. It was one way of compensating for Callum's absence. But more than that, she wanted her baby close to her, so she could protect him.

In the morning she left him sleeping while she took a shower.

As soon as she killed the shower, she heard the high, ragged looping of his screams, like some kind of living siren. She ran naked and dripping back into the bedroom.

He was still lying on the bed, his face knotted and red with pain, rage and fear. On the side of his neck she saw a single droplet of blood standing out. It slowly burgeoned until it had gathered enough mass to run down his neck on to the pillow.

Aimée dabbed at the wound with a tissue, revealing a tiny V-shaped nick. As if someone had snipped at his skin with the tip of a pair of scissors.

She showed the marks to Callum when he came home.

'Oh, for God's sake!' His cheeks were rouged with fury.

'I think we should just . . . tell her we don't need her any more. Let her go.'

'Siobhan?'

Of course, he was joking. But the joke revealed a bleakness at the centre of their lives that laughter couldn't touch, let alone redeem.

'I'm talking about Birgitte.'

'We don't actually have any proof that it's her.'

'It's a fifty-fifty chance. If we take her out of the equation, and this stuff carries on happening . . . Then we'll know . . .'

'We'll know we fired an innocent person.'

'Why are you defending her? Oh, don't tell me. Could there be . . . mm, I don't know, two reasons why, maybe? Her fucking tits, maybe?'

'Do you really think I'm so . . . crass? Is that what you think of me?' His anger was all directed against her now. It scared her. Whoever was doing this was tearing them apart.

'OK, I'm sorry. It's just I don't think we should take any

chances. Not when it comes to the safety of our child. I mean, I think that takes priority over everything else. Like our nanny's employment rights, for instance.'

'We need proof, Aims.'

'Isn't this proof enough? What more do you need?'

Callum put a finger to his lips and crossed to the living-room door. He opened it sharply, peering out to check that there was no one about on the other side. When he was satisfied, he closed the door softly and turned to Aimée. 'Listen,' he said. 'This is what we're going to do.'

Once again, there was now a pause in the appearance of odd little stigmata on Liam's body. As if whoever was doing it – whether it was their nanny or their daughter – had suddenly stepped back from the brink, horrified by the senselessness of her own actions.

Even so, Callum and Aimée couldn't ever quite relax. They were held in an anxious limbo. Perhaps that was part of the torture. The pauses were every bit as sadistic as the abuse. Only they were designed to torment Callum and Aimée rather than Liam.

Aimée took to monitoring her son obsessively for new marks, as well as checking to see how the existing ones were healing. Once, she had the impression that far from fading, the dots around his wrist were angrier than they had been, as if they had been gone over afresh. If that was true, then surely it suggested Birgitte was the perpetrator, because their daughter would have lacked the dexterity necessary to prick the same points again so precisely.

But she had to admit Siobhan was very neat and careful with her colouring-in. She was proud of the way she never went over the lines now.

Then one night she was wrenched from her dreams by her growing awareness of something incomprehensible having found its voice. Incomprehensible, because such sounds could only belong in a nightmare. And yet they clearly originated outside her dreaming mind. It was almost as if her subconscious was rejecting the sounds as being too horrific, too outlandish, too incredible even by its standards.

'Liam!'

The baby's raw howls of pain and outrage had stopped now. There was just a relentless, sickening *thump-thump-thump*. And then that stopped too.

The front of his cot was open. Liam was on the floor beside it. He was silent, ominously silent, and eerily motionless.

His tiny fragile head was covered in blood. And already misshapen.

She rushed to pick him up. The warmth went out of his body as she hugged him to her.

It was then she saw the smears of blood on the wall, obscuring the cheerful dinosaurs in the wallpaper.

The room dipped and swam. It was filled with a high piercing howl of suffering. She had no sense of herself as the source of this sound. She had no sense of anything other than the deep chill that was taking her over, spreading through the marrow of her bones, turning her internal organs to ice.

She was still walking him around when the ambulance got there. Gently shushing him, almost but not quite kissing the top of his damp head, as if she feared the touch of her lips – however so lightly, tenderly applied – might do him even more damage.

But he was beyond further hurt now.

They had to prise him away from her. A stranger pulled her clinging arms away from the tiny bundle of her son. That was the greatest outrage of all. That she would not even be allowed to hold on to him, to comfort him in his loneliness. No one so young, so small, should have to suffer such desolate loneliness.

Callum whispered to her to let him go. And his gentle words struck her as a betrayal. *You too?*

When Birgitte came out of her room, drawn by the countless different commotions, Aimée let loose a savage elemental shriek of accusation. It was enough to send the girl running for cover back into her own room.

Callum shook his head. While she had been desperately trying to mother her son back to life, he had reviewed the hidden camera footage, ready for the police. He refused to show it to her. All he would say was: 'It wasn't Birgitte.'

But she wouldn't believe him, *couldn't* believe him. How could their daughter have done this? Apart from anything else, how could a seven-year-old girl have the strength?

So when the police turned up and Callum played them the footage, he let her watch it too.

Perhaps that was cruel of him. But she did not want to be

spared. Why should she be spared? In the same way, she refused the tranquillizers that the paramedics offered her. She had to feel the full pain and suffering of her grief. She would not allow any of it to be dulled or blunted. After all that her poor little darling boy had suffered, why should any mercy be shown to her? Hadn't she allowed this to happen, after all?

Worse than that, she was responsible. She had given birth to the monster that had done this.

For after watching the brisk, purposeful way her daughter strode into her brother's bedroom and went about her bloody business, wresting him from his sleep and swinging him by the ankles so that his head was bashed repeatedly against the wall, before carelessly throwing him to the floor like a discarded toy . . . after seeing all that, Aimée could only think of the creature responsible as a monster.

All Callum could offer her were unanswerable questions. 'How could she do this? How could a child do this? How could any child do this? How could *our* child do this?'

She hadn't meant to tell him, not now, not like this – not ever, in fact. But somehow it just slipped out. Maybe she was trying to console him, to let him off the hook. Letting him know that he had no part in this.

'She's not your child,' she said.

Or maybe she meant to hurt him, so that he could feel some of the hurt she was suffering. As if she believed he wasn't suffering enough. As if there could never be enough suffering in the world to counterbalance this.

Or maybe she was in some way getting him back for the sequence of images he had just inflicted on her. In some way, it was all his fault. After all, it was his idea to install the hidden camera. Somehow, in some primitive, irrational part of her mind, she half-believed that the presence of the camera had brought forth the terrible action it had captured.

It was almost as if she believed Siobhan had been putting on a show for them.

EXPERIENTIAL ENHANCEMENTS

We have already discussed the possibility of hacking consoles/headsets/controllers so that the player may experience for real some of the emotions, not to mention sensations, of the game. Be great if it can be done. I realize it is pushing the boundaries of what's possible, but hey, that's what Alpha Games is all about, no?

On a similar note, I would like to see if we can incorporate real-time, real-life events, experiences, people into the game. May have mentioned this in passing, but I think it's worth pulling it out as an idea and exploring. Link into the player's MindNet profile to bring in MindNet buddies and family members. Possibility for player to work out deep issues, for instance by killing parents? Might be interesting to introduce reality alerts to those people who have been incorporated into the game, so they can be told the player has killed them?

So far, so fun. Could we also bring in live reality events that are taking off on NewsNet and incorporate them into the game? E.g. if there is a riot going on outside, there is a riot going on in the game?

The basic idea is to blur the boundaries between reality-reality and virtual-game reality.

So maybe if there has been some major NewsNet occurrence trending – e.g. the little girl who smashed in her brother – that can crop up in the game. Wouldn't it be fun to have her suddenly as a character in the game?

Are there any legal implications of this and who do we have to lobby (!) to get the law changed in our favour?

This could be massive so lobbying (!) budget shouldn't be a problem.

What would be super cool is if we set up some kind of feedback loop through the game – i.e. the game is influenced by reality and in turn the game starts to influence reality.

Imagine how massive that could be!

Development notes for PSYCHOTOPIA VR game.
Internal Alpha Games document. Not for release. For approved
circulation only.

TWENTY-THREE

B ut it was after the Siobhan Ardagh case that everything
went really crazy. Especially once the hidden cam clip got
out.

Because of my job as a police officer on the Met P unit, I got
to see the footage sooner than most. I have to admit, it was
mesmerizing. Addictive. Even I'd never seen anything like it
before. I don't think most people could have imagined something
like that was even possible.

It was as if what you thought the world was, what people
were, was suddenly changed by what that camera had recorded.
And you were changed by watching it. It made you into something steelier, colder. Emptier. If you weren't empty already.

That's the price you pay for staring down into the abyss.

Each time you watched it you were shocked by it afresh. And
you kept watching it, unable to believe that it would always turn
out the way it had the last time. It was almost like you were
willing something else to happen. Something not so fucked up.

Maybe this time she'd turn around and go back out before she
got to the cot. Or just look down at her sleeping brother. Or
maybe she'd open up his cot as usual. But only to take him out
and give him a cuddle.

This time, for sure, the parents would get there first, and take
the baby from her before she had a chance to slam his head
against the wall.

But every time it turned out the same.

Every time she gave the same straight-to-camera look just
before she yanked him out of his cot. I think that was what freaked
people out the most. You would have sworn she even smirked.
She seemed to know the camera was there. And that one day
virtually the whole world would be watching her do this thing.

Because, yes, the clip went viral on MindNet. In the beginning, for every ninety horrified below-the-line comments there
were, say, ten cheering her on. You had people saying shit like:
Yo! Girl! You showed that baby who da boss!

She bangin!
Look at she go!
Baby shut the fuck up now.
Hahahahaha! I love this fucked up shit.
Oops, mummy. I think I broke the baby! LMFAO!!!
That girl iz made of awesum.
I hate fuckin babiz. All they do is shit and scream and shit.
I could go on. But you get the idea.

I have to say, I thought I was a cynical bastard. But some of those commenters made even me look good.

Over time, those people who monitor these things, people like Arbus, started to notice that the ratio of Siobhan-cheerleaders to Siobhan-haters was shifting. It got to the point where there were as many comments approving what she had done as there were appalled by it. But when the lovers outnumbered the haters, we knew we were in a new place.

It was almost as if something had been unleashed. As if little Liam had been sacrificed to some wild and savage god who was now on the rampage.

In the immediate aftermath, there was a spate of fresh rioting. What was different from the Black Friday riots was that now the crowds wore masks with Siobhan Ardagh's face on. She had become the official poster girl of the P movement.

Bartholomew Bartholomew was everywhere again. He went further than before in voicing his 'understanding' of the rioters, while neither condemning nor condoning them. Apparently, they were sending some kind of message to the authorities. As far as I could tell, all the message amounted to was 'Fuck you!'

The government's reaction to the Siobhan Ardagh case was to rush through the introduction of compulsory Arbus-Lubany testing at age five. Some say the riots were a response to this. But I think they would have happened anyway.

The world was split into those people who were out on the streets reaping the whirlwind and those who were cowering in their panic rooms and bunkers. Official advice was to stay in your own home with the doors locked.

But you know when you tell people to stay inside and it doesn't make any difference because the madness knows where they live and comes to their door and kicks in their door and smashes all their windows and finds them hiding in their cellar?

That.

Our Prime Minister, Gleb Jackson, tried to take the sting out of the protests by agreeing to be Arbus-Lubany tested himself live on NewsNet. Not only that, he wheeled out his children, Carla, age six, and Jack, age eight, to have them tested. My old fuck-buddy Krystie was presiding over the circus. Dr Arbus was doing the honours with the machine.

The result was NP, of course.

I MindMessaged Arbus.

How did you fix that?

He didn't reply. Which was how I knew he had fixed it. After all, hadn't he once told me that Jackson was undoubtedly a psychopath?

And this was years – at least a decade – before Shiri Patel came out as the first openly P cabinet minister. Most politicians still subscribed to the notion that it was in their interests to represent the NP majority. It was weird to see how they switched once the NPs were in the minority. Some of them even managed to revise their Arbus-Lubany readings. Which kind of devalued the whole basis of testing. I half-expected them to abandon testing. I mean, once nobody gave a shit any more, what was the point? Unless it was to stigmatize the NPs as some kind of inferior subspecies, which was pretty much what we began to see happening.

But I'm getting ahead of myself.

As for Siobhan Ardagh herself, nobody really knew what to do with her. Up until now, this kind of crime, perpetrated by a minor, was so rare that there were no real structures in place to deal with it. It wasn't really a child protection issue, because she was the child and, let's face it, it was other people who needed protecting from her. She was below the age of criminal responsibility, so there was no question of arresting her or charging her with murder.

They gave her the Arbus-Lubany test, of course. Dr Arbus himself was parachuted in to personally oversee it. That was some kind of honour for her, I guess.

The result was P. No surprises there then.

I got the impression Arbus was acting a little frosty towards me, though it was hard to tell given his social skills deficit. Maybe he had taken offence at my impugning his integrity vis-à-vis the Prime Minister's test result. More likely, he was somewhat over-awed to find himself in the presence of this murderous child prodigy. He wasn't the only one who was finding it hard to know how to exist in Siobhan's wake.

She was acting for all the world like nothing especially bad had happened. Talk about butter wouldn't melt. She crayoned over all the sheets of paper we found for her. Filled them with pretty pictures of flowers and princesses and unicorns and, for some reason, bunny rabbits. She never scribbled over the line once.

She even drew a picture of her family. She included baby Liam. Everyone was smiling.

She was pushing it, though, when she ran up to her mother excitedly with that picture. Was she trying to make amends? Or did she know exactly what she was doing? Another twist of the knife in her mother's wound.

We'll never know the answers. Certainly, Arbus's machine couldn't tell us. Probably Siobhan herself didn't know why she did it.

'So what happens now?' I asked Arbus when we had the result.

'Have you not been notified? She is to be released into my . . . care.'

At least he had the decency to stumble over the word.

'You're going to cure her?'

'She will be given all the therapy that she needs.'

'And you'll rewire her brain?'

'It will be a unique opportunity to study the effects of the Mark Two Arbus-Lubany on a juvenile psychopath. If it can be shown to work on her, then there is hope indeed.'

I looked over to where Callum and Aimée Ardagh were sitting. The mother's eyes were red raw, not so much as if she had been crying for a long time, as someone had sanded away the sclera of her eyes with emery paper. She had that vacant, wasted junkie look, though I heard she had turned down every drug that had been offered to her. She was off her head on grief. The dad just held his head in his hands the whole time. If you got close to him, you could hear him keeping up this low, murmuring mono-logue. As if he was trying to reason with someone or talk some-thing through. Every now and then, he would cry out. Something

like, 'No!' or 'Why?' or 'What?' Something bleak, bald and
unanswerable. What struck you most was how they were cut off
from one another. Each of them was stranded in their own separate
suffering.

'What about them?' I asked Arbus.

He frowned as if the question was an irrelevance. 'I don't
think they will object. I rather get the impression they will be
glad to see the back of her.'

He'd kind of missed the point of my question, I guess.

You can imagine my surprise when I saw Edith Walsh with them.
You remember, that strange and intense little creature who had
come to me with those vague complaints about some guy from
Alpha Games. It only stuck in my mind because I'm such a big
fan of one of their games, *Random Rage*. It turned out that she was
Siobhan's mother's sister. Not only that, but this was the sister she
had been telling me about, the one who'd been done over by the
Alpha Games guy before he was the Alpha Games guy.

She gave me a weird recriminatory look, as if all this was
somehow my fault. I had her down as a classic man-hater, until
I saw her locked in a huddle with her brother-in-law. She seemed
to be the only one who could get through to him. I said before
that there was something fierce in her. As I watched, I saw it
pass from her to him.

In the event, the parents put up no objections to Arbus's
proposal. Nobody seemed to have any better ideas, so that was
it. It wasn't for me to say, but I myself didn't see him as the
natural foster-father type, and as far as I knew there was no Mrs
Arbus on the scene to provide a mother's touch. I guessed he
would just hire that help in. The government was behind this, so
money was no object.

The parents were left to get on with their lives. Which kind
of has a hollow ring to it, you have to admit. I think they were
offered all the usual counselling. But who on God's earth is
qualified to counsel parents in their situation? And if ever 'all
the usual' wasn't going to be enough, it was now.

MindNet and NewsNet were fascinated by them for a while.
There were the usual headline recriminations. Why wasn't
anything done? Why weren't the warning signs picked up? Where
were the social services? The police? Someone had to be to
blame. Someone other than that sweet-looking little girl.

Pointless rumours started to spread. Some said the father wasn't really Siobhan's father. Some said he wasn't Liam's father either. There were even rumours he'd killed Liam and faked the video footage to frame Siobhan. According to this theory he'd been having an affair with the nanny and wanted to get his whole family out of the way.

There were plenty of people ready to blame them both for what their daughter had done. Which struck me as kind of like rubbing salt in their wounds. I mean, as if they weren't blaming themselves enough already.

ONE FINAL THOUGHT

Could we incorporate into the game an augmented reality aspect as well as a virtual reality aspect? That is to say, the game is played in real settings in real time. The players are out there in the world, headsets on and wearing control gloves. So in some levels of the game they are moving through real town centres, among real people, into which we insert game characters. It is an extra level of challenge – the player has to work out which are game characters and which are real people. Character design must be über-realistic. It will in fact be so good that the real people will seem less real than the game characters. Which will lead to the interesting result of players attempting to murder and face-steal from actual live people.

Call me a mad fucking bastard but that sounds like fun to me.

Development notes for PSYCHOTOPIA VR game.
Internal Alpha Games document. Not for release. For approved circulation only.

TWENTY-FOUR

S ometimes it was a long game, a long con, building a woman's trust.

It didn't happen overnight. Not always, anyhow.

Sometimes he could gain it in a glance, or with a word, the right word. Sometimes all it took was a certain gesture. The sympathetic smile. The wry shrug, perfectly timed. The hand on the shoulder, weighted with concern rather than desire.

You just have to show them that you understood. And that the last thing on your mind was, well, the thing you actually have in mind.

He was, or had proven himself to be, the master of all those techniques. There had been times when he had amazed himself at how quickly he could do it. But these days, he had learned to be more patient. Some instinct had kicked in.

It was not that he had grown more risk averse. Just more focused. Smarter.

In the old days, for instance, he never counted the times it didn't work. Hardly noticed those. It was part of the game. Moving on. Not looking back. Like a shark. But maybe somehow, over the years, he had acquired a sense of the ones that got away. So much wasted energy. Maybe, subconsciously, he had shifted to a different technique. The waiting game. The war of attrition.

Build them up. Then rip them apart.

Metaphorically, of course. He was not a complete psychopath.

But it was true, his favourite animal was the shark. He found them incredibly satisfying to look at. Some lunchtimes he even took a U-car to the London Aquarium. They had some sand tiger sharks there, along with a few other species.

He loved the look those sand tigers had going on. They were fantastically mean-looking, with those vicious, long narrow snouts of theirs. But his favourite shark of all was the great white. Unfortunately, they didn't have any great whites at the aquarium. They probably would have eaten all the other fish.

He never dreamed. It was just not something that his psyche

was equipped for. And so the idea of dreaming fascinated him. Sometimes he wondered if it was his inability to dream that had led him into the games industry. Creating game worlds was a vicarious way of dreaming.

He certainly had a vivid fantasy life. Waking daydreams of extraordinary complexity and surreality. Unlike ordinary dreams (or what he had been told about them), these daydreams were consciously created and controlled. He could summon them up at will, sometimes returning to the same daydream as if to a place of comfort and familiarity. You could say these daydreams expressed the truest essence of his identity. For he chose them and immersed himself in them willingly.

The one he returned to more often than any other, the one that gave him the deepest pleasure, was the fantasy of swimming with great white sharks. Not just swimming with them but becoming one of them. Hunting with them. And feeding with them.

He imagined a girl swimming naked. He and the other sharks circled her, gradually reducing the circumference of the circle of attack.

He imagined her first of all blissfully unaware of their approach.

And then her panic as she caught sight of the telltale fins out of the corner of her eye. Her limbs thrashing, churning up the water, in a futile attempt to escape. For there could be no escape. There was nowhere to escape to. Unless she somehow found a way to sprout wings and take flight. But this was his dream, not hers. And he wasn't about to allow that to happen.

And then the attack itself. The release of tension that was almost sexual. Sudden, explosive, precise. An orgasm of savagery.

And then after, sated, righteous, invincible. The sense of an animal fulfilling its nature, gloriously, proudly, perfectly. Swimming heedlessly, blindly through thick incarnadine clouds, taking in her blood through his open, hungry gills.

Of all these phases of the daydream, the one he most enjoyed, he had to admit, was the first. The pre-lapsarian innocence of the girl. The moment before she was aware of her impending doom. Sometimes he varied the details of their approach. Instead of circling, they would come at her like missiles fired towards her from all the points of the compass. Or he would attack her on his own, a solitary predator, the tip of his snout honing in on her from below.

Sometimes, he liked to look at pictures of shark attack victims. He found them on MindNet easily enough. (You can generally find whatever you're looking for somewhere on MindNet.) He found it almost therapeutic looking at them. Not that he wanked over them or anything. They had the opposite effect on him, in fact. Calming him down when he was stressed out. (Once or twice he had to catch himself as he was about to recommend it as a relaxation technique to colleagues.)

But it was interesting to see how cleanly a human leg could be taken off by one bite of those massive jaws. And he liked the patterns that the shark's teeth make in human flesh. No doubt it helped him with the daydreams. He liked to imagine what it must be like to have that many teeth. What it must be like to have such powerful jaws. It was, he realized, the power of the animals that appealed to him most of all. The pure remorseless power.

One thing that impressed him about sharks is how the fear they generated was way out of proportion to the actual harm they did. Their reputation preceded them. Just by looking mean and constantly moving, and every now and then biting a hapless surf dude in half, they had managed to become the embodiment of primordial danger for human beings.

Of course, they hadn't manufactured this amount of fear all on their own. Humans had helped them, producing movies that had portrayed them as relentless death machines, existing only to kill.

It's what they're programmed to do. If there is one in the water with you, you are as good as dead. If you survive, it's not through any talent or virtue on your part, but through pure dumb luck. This is a lottery where if you don't get the winning ticket, you die.

That first phase of the daydream expressed this essential vulnerability. It showed him that there is nothing protecting us from the ultimate danger, from death. Nothing *can* protect us, whether we give death the shape of a great white shark or a mask-clad P rioter. It will get us in the end.

The only way to transcend the fear was to become the shark. That was why this particular daydream was so appealing to him.

It was also the inspiration for a game, *Shark Bait*. The player gets to control the shark picking off the swimmers at a New England beach resort. It was one of Alpha Games' biggest sellers to date. It turned out he wasn't the only one fascinated with other people's wounds.

Sally Mann was like the naked girl swimming in the still water. She hadn't started thrashing her arms about yet. So this ought to have been the bit he liked. But something was wrong. Something was spoiling his enjoyment. He had the sense that she had some inkling of what was to come. Still, it wouldn't save her. The naked girl never outswam the shark.

It must have been that bitch he'd seen her talking to in the plaza. Her face had set a faint bell ringing in his head. Maybe she was one of the ones who got away? But he got that feeling about a lot of women these days. The ones that looked at him in a certain way.

Sally had even started looking at him like that.

He was going to have to make his move soon, or it would be too late.

Suddenly he regretted wasting the R2 on her. He couldn't even remember what point he'd been trying to prove now. That he didn't need the amnesia pills? That he still had the magic touch? That he could still make a woman want him, without cheating?

He had to be honest, it was looking less and less likely that she was going to crack. She was starting to close herself off from him. Her look was becoming guarded and wary. Where was the trust? Jeez, it made him mad that she wouldn't trust him.

Maybe he was getting lazy, but there were times when he wished he still had the pills on him. True, he could always get some more, but he'd have to find a different dealer.

But no. He still believed it didn't really count unless she gave in willingly. Getting her to consent to her own undoing was all part of the game.

There was nothing to match the feeling of truly touching another person at the deepest level. And then completely fucking them over.

He had to give her something. That was for sure.

She'd stopped bringing up that crazy idea about changing the world through game design. He could hardly believe he'd had the front to spin her something so out there. Let alone that she'd fallen for it. But what was that old saying? If you're going to lie, lie big? Something like that. The guy who came up with that one certainly knew what he was talking about.

But of course, as far as Oscar was concerned, it wasn't lying. Not if people wanted to believe what you're telling them. If they needed to believe it. You weren't lying to them. You were simply reflecting their desires back to them. Maybe that was why he found it so easy to get people to like him. He was a bit like Jesus, in a way. Everyone worshipped Jesus because he promised them salvation, life after death and God knows what other shit. Obviously lies. But no one called *him* out for being a liar.

Thing was he could tell that she had stopped believing in the whole changing-the-world thing. Which meant she'd stopped believing in him.

He had her working on Psychotopia, the new game that would actually make them some money. Her face had adopted an expression of wounded misery, like one of those bombed-out refugee orphans you see on NewsNet. He couldn't stop looking at her. Part of him was tempted to keep piling on the disappointment and disillusion, so that he could watch her suffering increase. How shit would he have to make her life, he wondered, before she finally snapped?

The danger was that he would push her so far that he would lose her for good – and before he'd had the chance to open her up.

It was time to start building her up again. He called her into his office and even had Mario go out to get them coffees.

'You remember when you first came into my office?'

She frowned a little, uncertain where he was headed with this. That was good. Confusion is good. It meant she was wrong-footed.

She didn't say anything. Waiting to see what he had for her.

Oscar continued: 'I took one look at you, and I knew . . .'

'Knew what?'

'I knew you were the future. The future of gaming. You, Sally, you have the potential to go all the way. You have the potential to be one of the true stars – one of the global stars – not just of Alpha Games, but of the whole gaming industry. I've never met anyone with your vision, your ideas, your talent. But what makes you really special in this industry is your idealism. That makes you unique.'

She gave a little twitchy shrug, which seemed to come out of her despite herself. It was the first sign of the battle going on inside her: between her desire to believe what he was telling her and her scepticism.

'I'll tell you what pissed me off about you, though?' He gave his voice an angry, questioning hike.

She sat up at that. Half-outraged, half-afraid.

'You didn't believe in yourself! It made me really angry, you know? I knew that you were capable of doing great work. The kind of stuff that makes people sit up and take notice. But the one thing that was stopping you was . . .' He tapped the side of his head firmly twice with the tips of his fingers. 'Inside your head. Do you know what I'm talking about?'

She gave a brave little nod.

'You don't like working on Psychotopia, do you?'

'No. I don't.'

'Why not?'

'It's not what I came here to do?'

'Yes, it is.'

'What?'

'I thought you wanted to change the world, through games?'

'Yes. But I don't want to change it into a world of psychopaths!'

'Psychotopia is going to be massive, you know that, don't you?'

'I guess?'

'You guess? It's going to be our lead release this year. We're putting everything behind it. Pulling out all the stops. There are things being done in that game – technically, and creatively – that simply have not been done before. And you're walking around with a face like a smacked arse?'

'But it's just so . . . nasty?'

'It will make us more money than any game has ever done.'

'It's all about money then?'

'No! It's all about doing something that has never been done before! You are getting the chance to work on a ground-breaking game. What you learn doing Psychotopia, you can apply to whatever project you turn to next. And if we are to do what we talked about when you came into this office that day, we have to be a viable functioning business. We have to be in

profit. We have to be *more* than in profit. We have to be the
big swinging dicks of the game world. We have to believe that
we can do whatever we set our minds to. We can turn the world
into a community of psychopaths. And we can reset the
world, turn the dial the other way, and recreate the next generation in your image, Sally Mann.'

'But I still don't see why Psychotopia is necessary? Couldn't
we make a game that does well, but is just a little bit less . . .
horrible?'

'No, here's the thing, Sally Mann. After Psychotopia, I will
be retiring from Alpha Games. My role will be split in two. There
will be a new Head of Game Development and a separate Head
of Virtual Architecturing.'

'Why? Why are you doing that?'

'Because the time is right.'

'So who will they be, the new heads?'

'Well, I haven't decided on the Head of Game Development
yet. But the future Head of Virtual Architecturing is sitting right
opposite me.'

'What? No! That's ridiculous.'

'There you go again with that lack of self-belief.'

'I'm just being realistic. I don't have the experience?'

'You know, every President of America, when elected to office
for the first time, has no experience at being President of America.'

'I don't know what to say. It's . . . What will you do?'

'I will see the error of my ways.'

'What does that mean?'

'It means I'll enter a fucking Tibetan monastery or something.
The company will go in a completely different direction under
your leadership. It is essential for the success of your grand
project that I am no longer associated with Alpha Games. I will
come to represent evil Alpha Games. You will be the beautiful
face of good Alpha Games.'

'Are you serious?'

'Yes.'

'And what do the board think about this?'

'The board will do whatever I tell them to do.'

'You haven't talked to them about it yet?'

'It's a formality.'

'When will it happen?'

'After Psychotopia is released. That will be the catalyst. We all know it will be a highly controversial game. We've designed it that way. Deliberately. We will ride the storm of the controversy and emerge completely transformed. I have drawn up a document. It's kind of like a living will, I suppose, but strictly to do with the business. What I'm proposing is that you come over to my place tonight, we have dinner, we go through it . . . And whatever you want in there, if it's not in there already, we'll put it in. We can work on it together.'

'Oh.'

'What does that mean? That "Oh", like that?'

'Nothing.'

'You think I'm doing all this just to . . . what?' He shook his head incredulously. He couldn't bring himself to form the words. But he trusted the wounded look he threw her was eloquent enough.

'I don't know why you're doing it?'

'I'm doing it because it's the right thing to do.' From somewhere he summoned up the fire of righteous anger.

She was biting away at the lining of her mouth. He took it as another encouraging sign. She was chewing over what he had said. On the way to relenting. To trusting him again.

Maybe it was time to lighten the mood, hit her with a gag, show her that he didn't bear a grudge, that they were cool again. 'Hey, aren't you even a little bit interested to see where I live? You do know I have a tank in the basement filled with sharks? I have my dwarf henchmen throw my enemies into it. You telling me you don't want to see that?'

'Only if you promise not to throw me into it?'

'You're not my enemy, Sally. You're my hope.'

That gave her something to think about. And maybe, just maybe, he'd done enough.

Hope, you see, is more powerful than R2.

He spent the rest of the day drafting the non-existent document that he'd made up on the spur of the moment. He had to have something to show her when she came round. He didn't worry about what he would do when she realized that he had no intention of delivering on anything in the document. That day was a long way off. And he trusted he'd always find some way of averting it.

All that mattered now was that she believed in him again. For one more night. So he drew up a catalogue of her ideals and dreams and hopes to present back to her as a done deal. Who could say no to that?

And of course, it wasn't lying if it was something she wanted to believe, something she needed to believe. The document itself would be true – it truly existed, didn't it? – at the moment she was reading it.

Besides, it was a work of genius, even if he did say so himself.

He left the office early to do a little shopping on the way home. He remembered that she was a vegetarian – and that he was supposed to be one too. There was some steak in the fridge. He'd have to move it to the back of the drawer in the bottom of the fridge, out of sight in case she went nosing about inside. He certainly wasn't going to throw it away.

He called in at a wholefood store near his building. Filled the trolley with all kinds of healthy superfoods. The kind of rabbit food girls go mad for. Some organic wines too, to oil the wheels and seal the deal. And Fairtrade chocolates. Got to be Fairtrade. To show he's one of the good guys.

Naturally, he slipped a couple of items straight into his pockets, just for the hell of it. Added a little spice to an otherwise boring shopping trip. And he liked to keep his hand in, so to speak.

He told her to come round for eight o'clock. There was no cooking to do as he'd bought a range of pre-prepared dishes. It was just a question of making them look nice on the table. He chose some intriguingly idiosyncratic world music to have droning away in the background – personally he couldn't stand all that warbling jingly-jangly bollocks, but he had a feeling it was the kind of shit Sally went for.

The EntryCam sounded at seven fifty-seven. She was keen. A good sign. Though her face in the screen seemed somehow tense. It was back, he thought ominously. The suspicion. The lack of trust. He saw it in her eyes. She was starting to piss him off. Maybe the evening wouldn't go so smoothly after all. He may not have an actual tank of sharks in the basement, but he did have a way of dealing with bitches who pissed him off.

Still. She was here. That had to mean something.

He buzzed her in. And went for the heedless blithe act. 'Hi, honey. Come straight up. Sixth floor. I'll pick you up at the lift.'

He checked his smile in the mirror on the way to the door. If that didn't melt her little heart and win her over, he didn't know what would.

He lived in a semi-vacant high-rise. He liked the fact that so many of the apartments were unoccupied and owned by wealthy absentee foreigners. Most of them were furnished. And he had somehow contrived to come into possession to the entry codes for most of them. A little bit of bribery here, some blackmail there, and occasionally some good old-fashioned deception. Sometimes it was convenient to pretend that you lived somewhere other than where you actually did. Some of the entertaining he did got a bit messy, and he didn't see why he should be the one to clean up after. And sometimes it was just for the hell of it, as with the shoplifting. It made life more interesting to fuck a whore in a stranger's bed.

You might have thought he'd get lonely surrounded by so many empty residences. Far from it. He found the sense of richly furnished desolation suited his temperament perfectly.

The high-speed lift decelerated with a whispered shush. The doors opened. And some random guy he'd never seen before in his life was squaring up to him.

'It *is* you,' the guy said.

Had they met before? He had no memory of the guy's face. But then he wasn't good on faces. He didn't look at them to remember them. He looked at them to discover weaknesses. But there was something about the guy's tone he didn't like. He didn't like the way he couldn't see his right hand either. He kept it in his coat pocket. Like he was ashamed of it. Maybe it was a misshapen claw or something. Or there was some kind of unsightly rash all over it. Pustules. Yes, that had to be it. Pustules. He looked like the kind of guy who would have boils and pustules all over his body.

'I'm me. That's true. The question is, who the fuck are you?'

'Do you remember a girl called Aimée?'

'What? You used to be a chick? Did I fuck you when you were a chick? I don't think so.'

'Aimée is my wife.'

'I'm very happy for you. Now if you don't mind, I have a hot date.' He made a show of looking behind the guy, though he knew there was no one else in the lift with him. 'She must be coming up in the other lift.'

'Sal's not coming up. I sent her home.'

'You know Sally?'

The guy gave a grim little nod.

'What the fuck is going on here?'

'This is what's going on here.'

And now he realized why he didn't like the way the guy was keeping his hand out of sight. It wasn't misshapen or plague-ridden or anything like that. It was holding a gun.

He couldn't help it. He had to laugh. It was so fucking funny to have this guy he didn't know waving a gun in his face. What else are you going to do but laugh?

It was only the deafening explosion of the gun that silenced his laughter.

FOR IMMEDIATE RELEASE

Welcome to Psychotopia!

Alpha Games announces the launch of its most innovative, most controversial, most exciting, most insane, most challenging, bravest, bloodiest, most bad-assed game ever: PSYCHOTOPIA.

Mixing both VR and AR elements, PSYCHOTOPIA is the brainchild of the games genius Oscar Winslett, whose early death at the hands of a jealous husband could have come straight from the gameplay of one of Oscar's own thrilling creations.

They say he died laughing. We can believe it. This is a game created by the kind of man who dies laughing.

PSYCHOTOPIA gives players the opportunity to enter into the mind and get beneath the skin of a deliriously cold-blooded psychopathic killer. And to walk in their shoes as they go on a glorious – or should that be *gory*-ous? – killing spree. There will be blood. There will be bones. There will be brain spatter. And as you play this uniquely immersive game, you will live and feel every moment of the murderous mayhem. You will never feel more alive than when you're hunting down and mercilessly killing your victims.

Featuring stunning game architecture and hyper-realistic character design, this is the closest you can get to killing without actually killing. In fact, we have it on good authority that it's *'more fun than killing'*. We can't tell you who said that, but take it from us, he knows what he's talking about.

Unpredictable, death-affirming, terrifying, relentless and unashamedly gross, PSYCHOTOPIA is . . .

The game for the times we live – and die – in.

The game you have played in your sickest nightmares.

The game the world has been waiting for.

In a final twist added after the death of the game's creator, Oscar Winslett himself appears in the role of Mefistofolo.

As everyone at Alpha Games agrees, it's what he would have wanted.

- Single-player and multi-player modes
- Real-time gameplay
- Includes hidden features
- Psychotropic interaction may result in modified personality
- Game played at player's own risk

For more information, MindMessage Clarice(M)@alphagames
SUITABLE FOR ALL AGES

TWENTY-FIVE

I still don't get it. Why he did it. It's not as if he was a P. We tested him. Naturally. We tested everyone who we pulled in, especially the ones who have blown some random stranger's brains out with a gun they bought on the DarkMind.

I really don't like it when civilians mess with the DarkMind. Don't they know it's not for them? They should leave it to the paedos and the psychos and the terrorists. And the paedo-psycho-terrorists. We do get those, believe me.

He tested NP, of course. He was shaking so much and weeping so much you didn't need an Arbus-Lubany machine to know what the result would be. I think he might even have pissed himself, he was that upset.

Maybe it would have made more sense if he had been a P. Though sometimes I wondered if labelling people P was a way of avoiding making sense of things. A way of not understanding what was going on. Of taking refuge in an easy answer, when the truth is just too hard to get your head around.

Whatever his reasons, I have no doubt that the seed of the deed was planted in that fierce little huddle I witnessed between him and his sister-in-law. She gave him some kind of purpose then. I could see it, though at the time I had no idea what that purpose was.

Maybe I should have tested the sister-in-law.

He didn't try to get away with it. Handed himself in at the nearest functioning police station. We all know there aren't many of those left.

I took an interest in the case because of the family connection. They let me sit in on a few of the interrogations. The most we ever got out of him was 'No comment'. His privilege.

We talked to his wife. She had no idea he was going to do it. And was pretty much in a state of catatonic shock. As you'd expect. She'd lost her whole family now. In a way that might have been thought bizarre once, but it just seemed to be of a piece with the times.

I got the impression that Callum Ardagh somehow blamed this guy Winslett for everything that had happened. So maybe he believed Winslett was Siobhan's father, or something.

We took a DNA sample from Ardagh. Standard procedure. The idea is to see if it matches any DNA we have on unsolved cases. Drew a blank there, of course. But you have to do things by the book. That gave me an idea, though. I MindMessaged Dr Arbus to see if he fancied DNA testing his ward. Given his theories about heredity, I thought it might be of some interest to him.

When I told Ardagh the results we got, he looked like I'd just murdered his baby all over again.

'No, it's not possible . . .'

I handed him the printouts so he could see for himself. 'It's all there in black and white. You're Siobhan's father. No doubt about it.'

I guess it was time for Dr Arbus to get himself a new theory.

As for the man himself, after the attempt was made on his life by a P Party thug, Arbus went into hiding, taking Siobhan Ardagh with him. Not strictly legal, or ethical. But I guess he had his reasons. I think he saw her as some kind of talisman and didn't want to let her out of his sight.

The last time I heard from him was a garbled MindMessage. This must have been about the time that Bartholomew Bartholomew swept into power on a landslide.

Mark 2 machine now in operation. Save yourself.

It's all very well telling someone to save themself, but what's the use unless you also tell them how? Or what they're supposed to be saving themselves from?

Left to work it out for myself, I guessed he and his partner never did find a way to resolve that glitch he told me about. Which meant the new government was allowing the use of machines that converted NPs into Ps. We really had reached the tipping point.

If that was true, I could see only one way forward. It wasn't like I had a choice. Rumours were flying about that compulsory testing for police officers was finally just around the corner. Only now, the purpose of testing had been revised, if not reversed.

I reckoned there would always be some stigma about the wrong result, even if they didn't use it as an excuse to weed you out.

Instead of a distinction between NPs and Ps it would be all about
natural versus induced, or some such bullshit. The pure-born Ps
would rule the roost, whatever roost you cared to talk about.

You could just about tell the difference between the Mark
Twos and the the Mark Ones. They'd made some subtle modifications to the design. The Mark Two was a tad slimmer and
lighter than the Mark One, with a shallower curve at the edges.
The on/off button was in a different position. And the Arbus-
Lubany logo was engraved into the frame rather than simply
printed on it. Pointless changes there only to justify some product
designer's job.

I signed a machine out on the pretext that I wanted to test a
suspect. Took it to the toilet and locked myself in a cubicle.

It felt strange fitting the frame and ScanCap on my own head
after I'd tested so many suspects. The whole experience was, as
you can imagine, somewhat surreal. A bit like going into a photo
booth but the photo you were taking was of your soul, not your
face.

The device felt heavier than I expected once it was in place.
Also I found it trickier than I'd imagined to operate the controls
while wearing it. I was kind of blinded by the machine, so I had
to just grope at the remote and guess with my fingers. But soon
enough I heard the tone that let you know the main feature was
about to play.

Imagine you've been put inside a glass missile and fired naked
through Hell. I guess whether you find that an enticing or a
terrifying prospect is a pretty good indicator of what result you're
going to get.

I don't know for sure what I saw. I think there were human
faces in there. I had the impression that they bore the marks of
what I can only describe as a savage cruelty. Though whether
they were the faces of the victims of that cruelty or its perpetra-
tors, I couldn't say. Everything was disconnected from everything
else. But it hurtled into me – or me into it – at such speed that
it was all blended together into one big mess of impossible ugli-
ness. Like a mash-up of all the ugly things in the world, and a
few from some place else. Things that should not have been put
together suddenly were. Limbs, internal organs, bones were ripped
out of any bodily context and pieced together as if in some insane
three-dimensional jigsaw puzzle. A great depression came over

me. It was the feeling you might have if you saw a burned-out wasteland strewn with the corpses of dead children, like so much litter. I can't say for sure that's what I saw. But it's what it felt like.

Then the depression lifted and was replaced with an equally great elation. I could not call it happiness. Because I knew that its cause was the same as the cause of the depression. The thing that felt like a field of dead children.

The whole thing lasted for only a matter of seconds. And it was weird how one moment you hated it; it sickened you to your core. And then you reached a point where suddenly you didn't want it to ever end.

The bleep came to signal it was over. I unclipped the machine from the frame and swiped the screen to show the result. NP.

As I looked at it, the N flickered and disappeared.

I can't remember how things felt before I did the test.

But everything feels good now. Everything feels very good.

ACKNOWLEDGEMENTS

Writing a book is always a risk. Especially when the book is something of a departure for the writer, as this is for me.

I'd like to thank all those who have supported and encouraged me in my recklessness, and even shared the risk.

First, the team at Severn House, in particular Kate Lyall Grant for saying yes to something that's a little different for both of us; Sara Porter, whose restless attention to detail has helped make this book the best it could be; and Claire Ritchie, for her meticulous copyediting.

My agent, Christopher Sinclair-Stevenson, for his calm and consistent optimism.

And my wife, Rachel Yarham. All I can say is it's good to have someone who is never wrong on your side.